Sarah's Garden

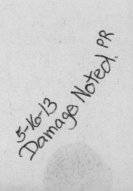

Sarah's Garden

KELLY LONG

Love Inspired

Recycling programs
for this product may
not exist in your area.

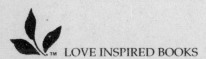 LOVE INSPIRED BOOKS

ISBN-13: 978-0-373-78710-4

SARAH'S GARDEN

First published by Thomas Nelson, Inc. 2010

This edition published by arrangement with Love Inspired Books.

® and TM are trademarks of Love Inspired Books, used under license.
Trademarks indicated with ® are registered in the United States Patent
and Trademark Office, the Canadian Trade Marks Office and in other
countries.

www.LoveInspiredBooks.com

Printed in U.S.A.

For Brenda, who would not let me quit.

Glossary of Pennsylvania Dutch Words and Phrases

ach: oh

aldi: girlfriend

Alli mudder muss sariye fer ihre famiyle: Every mother has to take care of her family.

Ausbund: hymnal

Bass uff, as du net fallscht!: Take care you don't fall!

boppli: baby

bruder: brother

danki: thanks

Der Herr: the Lord

Der Herr sie gedankt: Thank the Lord

doddy: guest house next to the main house

Dummel dich net: Take your time; don't hurry.

Englisch: non-Amish people and their ways

Es fenschder muss mer nass mache fer es sauwer mache: One has to wet the window in order to clean it.

frau: wife, Mrs.

geh: go

gern gschehne: you're welcome

grossmudder: grandmother

guder mariye: good morning

gut: good

Hallich gebottsdaag: Happy Birthday

Ich kam sell neh geh!: I cannot tolerate that!

jah: yes

juddekaershe: husk cherries

kapp: prayer cap

kinner: children

kumme: come

Lob: traditional second hymn

Mamm: mom

narrish: crazy

nee: no

Ordnung: unspoken rules that govern the community

rumspringa: running-around time

schweschder: sister

sei so gut: please

vrolijk: frolic

Wann er schnarit, halt er much waker: When he snores, he keeps me awake.

Was in der welt?: What in all the world?

Wie geht's?: How are you?

windel: diaper

wunderbaar: wonderful

Author's Note

In researching this novel I discovered the fact that Amish communities differ from one to another from both simple to larger-life activities. For example, there are dialectal differences in the spelling of such words as "dawdi" house, which may also be spelled "doddy" or "daudi," depending on the region in question. In addition, praying aloud at the dinner table may also, at times, be a voiced prayer when there is a particular praise offered.

The Amish man who was my main source of information, the truly forthright and dry-humored Dan Miller, told me that it would be difficult to find two Amish communities exactly alike. While all may share basic beliefs in the Lord, family, and work ethics, diversity still exists.

It is a lesson to me as an *Englischer,* that though the Amish may appear to live "the simple life," their differences provide a rich culture for both fact and fiction, and it is my honor to represent some small threads of their ways of life.

—Kelly Long

Prologue

The King Farm
Pine Creek, Pennsylvania

Letty King chopped zucchini on a wooden board and scraped the skins to one side to be fried as a side dish for dinner. She grated the dense centers into neat piles and glanced out the small kitchen window. Her husband, Ephraim, was spending a rare few minutes with their toddler, Sarah, staking up tomatoes in the kitchen garden. When Letty finished her task, she covered the vegetables with a damp tea towel, praised the carrots her five-year-old daughter, Chelsea, was busy scraping, and ventured outside for a stray moment of pleasure in her husband's company.

Ephraim's brown eyes greeted her with warmth, and then he glanced down to where two-year-old Sarah touched the tomato vine.

"*Ach*, Letty, *kumme* and see; our Sarah loves the plants like I've told you."

Letty smiled ruefully and moved to pat her younger daughter's crop of fine, blonde curls. "Ephraim, you haven't shown any of the other *kinner* this kind of notice. You will turn Sarah's head for sure."

Ephraim laughed aloud. "*Nee*, Letty. It is not me; *Der Herr* has given her a gift. The Lord, Letty. Even now, she knows how to touch a plant, to nourish it."

"Perhaps, but Ephraim, is it seemly to draw attention to the child?"

"It is not Sarah I draw attention to, Letty. It is *Der Herr* whom I honor through the child. It is the Lord working through her whom I praise."

Letty sighed. "That's true, but now I must change her *windel* before the others return from school." She scooped up the baby and patted her damp cloth diaper as the toddler's lip puckered and she stretched over her mother's shoulder for the vine.

Ephraim made a soothing sound in his throat as Letty carried the baby away.

When Letty reached the house, she sneaked a brief glance back to find her husband still studying the plants. She sighed to herself and went inside, closing the blue door firmly.

Chapter One

The King Farm
Pine Creek, Pennsylvania
Eighteen years later

Sarah King passed the mounded dish of mashed potatoes to her older sister, Chelsea, then caught up the bowls of boiled turnips and fried apples to bring to the table. It was nice to have Chelsea visiting. It was her first long visit home since her wedding to John Kemp five months earlier, and having her there certainly helped when it came to feeding her three brothers. Twenty-year-old Sarah felt that being the youngest of five was not always easy, especially when spring planting came around and the boys were ravenous from working the fields from sunup until dark.

Sarah caught her mother's approving eye at the food-laden table and slipped into her own place on the long bench at her father's left hand. She folded her hands into the lap of her apron and bowed her head.

The general rumble of male voices ceased as her father began to pray.

"*Der Herr sei gedankt* for this food and for those who have labored over it, from the fields to the table. Amen."

There was a chorus of amens, and the boys dove for the food.

"*Ach*, I nearly forgot…" Father held up his hand, and the boys froze in their scoops with the ladles and spoons. They dropped them with a low groan when Father bowed his head once more.

"And *Der Herr sei gedankt* for Chelsea and for the *boppli* she carries for John Kemp."

Sarah smiled. A baby! She should have known, since Chelsea had been closeted with *Mamm* and Father for a hurried conference in the pantry just before serving time. Her brothers patted John on the back and made good-natured jokes while Chelsea glowed and met Sarah's eyes. Sarah knew that many in her Old Order Amish community did not speak of pregnancies openly, but Father and *Mamm* encouraged conversation of all sorts in the privacy of their home in an effort to keep the family together in spirit and prayer.

Sarah was so excited at the prospect of being an aunt that she forgot to eat. Father jokingly nudged her arm and set the whole table laughing at her untouched plate. Sarah joined in the laughter, though she would not have laughed as outrightly had she been anywhere but home with her family. She gazed down the table to the tanned faces of her older brothers and the always-moving gentle hands of *Mamm* and thought how blessed she was.

"And," Father pronounced, startling her, "I think that Sarah might make the baby quilt for my first grandchild. What do you say, Sarah?"

Sarah ducked her head at her father's words. She knew he only made an innocent suggestion; it was her own insecurity about extending her creativity beyond her garden that shook her. She had only attempted one quilt, when she was thirteen, and her *Grossmudder* King had so criticized her handiwork that she'd never picked up a needle again. But the table was waiting for a reply, and she nodded.

"*Jah*, I will try."

Chelsea rose and came around the table to kiss and hug her sister. "*Wunderbar*," she exclaimed and returned laughing to her seat.

Sarah smiled and adjusted her hair covering, tucking back the stray light brown strands that tended to escape at her temples.

Her brother Luke stopped eating and opened his eyes wide in a comedic manner, which grabbed everyone's attention.

"*Was in der welt*, Luke?" *Mamm* asked in mock exasperation.

"I just thought of something, *Mamm*!" Luke exclaimed. "Now that Chelsea is married and working on the Kemp farm, she won't be able to run the roadside stand. And it's supposed to open again next week! Who will take care of the stand this year?"

The table rumbled in perplexity, and Sarah bit her lip in thought. The King family roadside stand was no mere plank of wood on sawhorses. Indeed, Father and the boys had built a full-length, open-fronted shed, well shingled against the weather and able to house many tables of produce, baked goods, and canned items in the spring and summer as well as baskets of walnuts, beechnuts, scented pinecones, and bundles of firewood in the autumn. It was a source of income for the family and was the most successful of all the roadside stands in the local Amish and English communities. To spare a boy from the fields would be unthinkable, and Chelsea was busy on the Kemp farm. *Mamm* had all of the housework…

"Your mother and I have thought of this, eh, Mama?"

Mamm cleared her throat and folded her cloth napkin before replying. "*Jah*," she announced. "Sarah will take over the running of the stand when it opens again next week."

The sudden silence around the crowded table did nothing to ease Sarah's swimming head as she stared at her mother in confusion. Father took up the conversation and reached to pat Sarah's cold hand in reassurance. "*Jah*, Sarah will do it."

Luke laughed aloud—a brief chortle cut short by a glare from his mother—and then looked apologetically at his younger sister.

"Forgive me, please, Sarah. It's just that you're always with your plants… I just thought…" His words trailed off and Sarah felt a quick wash of pity at his floundering.

"It doesn't matter, Luke. It's strange for me to think of it also," Sarah admitted.

Chelsea spoke up. "Sarah can do it," she proclaimed stoutly, so that her father nodded in agreement and a murmur of ascent went around the table.

"Yes, Sarah, you can." Father went on, "It is your nature to hide among the garden plants you love, *jah*? But there are others to minister to, a world to understand so you can be sure that you do not conform to its ways and people. Sarah, there are people to meet and to serve."

Sarah nodded, but her heart was thumping and she felt sick to her stomach.

"*Jah*, Sarah, perhaps you'll meet your husband at the stand this year, unless you marry your old friend Jacob Wyse," Luke suggested, then ducked when John Kemp gave him a cuff on the shoulder.

"What?" Luke asked. "She might."

Chelsea smiled down the table at her brother. "Maybe it's you, Luke King, who should visit the stand… *You* might find a wife!"

Luke flushed as his brothers laughed. It was a common joke among the family that none of the boys had yet to marry, with James, the eldest, being nearly twenty-eight. The simple truth was that there was barely time for courting when they all worked a farm as large as the one the Lord had provided for the King family.

Despite the laughter around her and her brother's sincere apology, Sarah had no time to worry about a husband when faced with the prospect of dealing with the responsibilities of the stand and all the strangers who would stop as customers. It was one thing when the King family hosted church meeting and she could stay in the background, or at picnics or berry picking when she busied herself with the younger children. But to deal with a parade of strangers on her own… and *Englisch* strangers at that. She swallowed hard at the staggering thought and questioned her fears. She couldn't recall any reason for her reticence; she'd only ever known kindness from those in her community. Yet she was afraid.

She realized that conversation had resumed around the table and the world was spinning for the others of her family. Her brother Samuel was speaking.

"There's been more work done today at the Fisher farm, Father. I noticed when I was plowing the south end. Soon we'll have new neighbors."

"Yes, we will, and they will be *Englisch* neighbors."

There was brief silence around the table, though Sarah couldn't quite pick up the threads of conversation from her own miserable musings.

"It's a strange thing to think of *Englischers* working an Amish farm," Luke commented and Father raised an admonishing hand.

"It was an Amish farm, but all of the earth belongs

to *Der Herr*. And I must say that the *Englisch* may care for the place much better than the Fishers ever did. As our neighbors, we must extend goodwill and, further, good expectations. You all know this."

Luke nodded in agreement as Father continued.

"It is good to remind ourselves on occasion—kindness, fairness, goodwill. All as *Der Herr* would do Himself and as the *Ordnung* instructs."

"I will make some friendship bread to take to them," *Mamm* murmured. "Perhaps the wife will enjoy the recipe as well."

"No wife, *Mamm*." Father smiled. "Only a single man, a doctor of veterinary science, and his hired help."

Chelsea laughed. "Oh no, just what we need in the area…another bachelor to compete with the King brothers."

"He may well have a hard time of it, though, as a vet and an *Englischer*. Everybody loved old Dr. Lapp," Samuel remarked.

"*Jah*," *Mamm* muttered. "He was a good man. Such a sad loss for his family."

Sarah sat quiet and sober. She could find no interest in either her food or *Englisch* neighbors with the thought of her new responsibility at the roadside stand.

Her father leaned close and whispered, "The Lord will help you, Sarah. You will see."

She smiled at him, though her hazel eyes were full of unshed tears.

"*Jah*, Father. *Jah*."

* * *

The red sports car made short work of the bumpy dirt driveway to the Fisher farm, and Dr. Grant Williams grinned in his rearview mirror at the shocked expression on his housekeeper's face.

"Are you still with me, Mrs. Bustle?"

"You know that I am, sir. You might ask Mr. Bustle how he's feeling, though; he tends to get a bit carsick."

Grant glanced at the older man seated next to him in the passenger seat. "Bustle?"

"All is well, sir."

Grant smiled. The Bustles were the type of old-fashioned servants and family friends who were rarely, if ever, seen in the modern world. At nearly a spry sixty-years-old each, they'd been with him since childhood, since his parents had died, and he loved them. But nothing could persuade them from ceasing to call him "sir" or from giving him the formality they believed he deserved as their employer.

"We're here."

In the half-light of the late spring evening, the three-story redbrick farm estate appeared rather austere, though evidence of a cheerful renovation existed in the piles of new wood and machinery that dotted the front lawn. Large fragrant lilac bushes framed the brick walkway that led to the generous porch, and lightning bugs flashed like tiny lanterns of goodwill.

Grant helped Mrs. Bustle from the car and waited for her inevitable comment.

"Looks like it could do with a good cleaning."

Grant chuckled. He expected them to speak their minds, and Mrs. Bustle rarely disappointed.

"I asked you both to move with me to this rural mountainous community from Philadelphia because I couldn't do this without you. Whatever you need to get this place going so I can start practicing…well, you just have to let me know." He was surprised at the emotion in his voice. At twenty-seven, he was focused on accomplishing his goals in life, and establishing a veterinary practice in this area was one of his personal benchmarks. His father had been a medical doctor who was deeply devoted to the Amish people, and Grant felt it was his legacy to continue in serving where his father had left off. Although his father left him enough money in a trust to last two lifetimes, he felt a strange tightness in his chest as he stared up at the old farmhouse that held his name on the deed.

"If I may, sir." Mr. Bustle cleared his throat. "Your parents would have been proud."

Grant clapped the older man on the shoulder and then linked his arms around both of them. "Thank you, both of you."

Mrs. Bustle sniffed. "Could be I'm going to need a hired girl. Maybe one of them Amish girls." She pronounced it *Aim*-ish, but Grant didn't bother to correct her. Everything was new, and it was late.

"Let's go in, shall we?" He produced an old-fashioned ring of keys and helped Mrs. Bustle up the steps. The heavy door swung open once he'd fumbled with the latch, and he moved to turn on the newly

installed overhead chandelier. Cobwebs and dust were
in heavy residence as well as boot tracks from workers on the dusty hardwood floors.

"I had to have electricity put in. You remember I
told you that the house was previously owned by the
Amish."

"As much of the land hereabouts is," Mr. Bustle remarked.

"Yes, we're 'strangers in a strange land,' aren't we,
Bustle? But I mean to build a life here, a life that will
honor my father and mother—with God's help, of
course."

"You'll have to build your bed first, I bet," Mrs.
Bustle announced, returning from her perusal of a
side room.

"That's why we have clean sheets in the car. I'll get
them now, and you…" Grant bent to bestow a quick
kiss on Mrs. Bustle's aged cheek. "You will have the
first bed we build…er, make up. I'll be right back."

He slipped outside into the twilight and noticed the
warm, far-off light from the adjoining Amish farm.
There was something poignant and serene about oil
lamps shining through windows that made him think
of home, though his parents had long been lost to him.
He leaned on the low roof of the sports car and drew
a deep breath of the fragrant night air. Life was going
to be different here; he just knew it. He felt a stirring
of excitement in his soul.

Chapter Two

Sarah slipped outdoors at four thirty into the first hint of dawn. It was her favorite time of the day, if the truth be told. It allowed a full half hour of private time with both the Lord and the kitchen garden before the others were wide-awake.

When she had been a little girl, she could remember believing that God came to walk with her in the garden because she could sense Him the most when she was close to the soil and the plants. And today she longed for His company more than ever. The last week of April had flown by in the flurry of planting and hoeing and weeding, and today was her first day of work at the roadside stand.

She sighed as her eyes traced the faint lines of plants and the shadowy layout of the ground. She let her delicate fingers trail along the leaves of the sweet corn, and she wriggled her bare toes in the damp earth. She fancied that the plants always seemed to rustle in response to her early morning greetings as she carefully stepped over rows of carrots and cress, parsnips, radishes, and salad greens. She breathed a silent prayer for the coming day as her toes met the carpet of moss that she cultured as a natural insulator to keep the fruits and vegetables cool for picnics and Sunday gatherings. She supposed she'd need a lot of moss at the stand to cover the produce and hold in the coolness, for the day promised to be as warm as the one before. She passed the kale and the kohlrabi, stroked the green heirloom tomatoes, and then ventured farther into the flower garden. Careless of her clean apron, she knelt next to the wild roses and curled close to the scented blooms, deep in thought.

Dear Father of all, please help me today. Help me not to be afraid but to bring glory to You in my manners and speech. Give me pleasant words to speak and a quick wit to think. Bless all who come to the stand today. Bless the Englisch *who come, Father, and the new* Englischer *who just moved in across the way. Help us to be good neighbors, and—*

Her prayers were interrupted by the whispered call of her name. It was Chelsea, swathed in her voluminous nightdress, picking her way barefoot through the garden. Startled, Sarah rose. She knew that her sister and brother-in-law had stayed for the night, but she was still surprised to see Chelsea this early.

"Chelsea, *Mamm* will be furious if she catches you out in your nightgown. What are you doing?"

Chelsea's neat teeth flashed white as her gown.

"I'm looking for you, and…" She lowered her voice. *"Wann er schnarit, halt er much waker."*

Both girls burst into giggles at the thought of John Kemp snoring loud enough to keep someone awake. He was so quiet by daylight.

Chelsea caught Sarah's hand, and they turned toward the apricot trees.

"I'm so happy about the baby, Chelsea. Do you know when…?"

"In the autumn sometime, but I didn't come out to talk about that. I wanted to give you some advice about the stand. And I talked with John… If you want, I could come with you this first day, just to see how you get on."

Sarah considered. It would make things easier, but she should begin as she meant to go on. She knew it, and she could not start by hiding behind her beautiful sister.

"Nee, Chelsea, but thanks to you and John. I must do this alone."

They had wandered among the apple trees, and now the first streaks of dawn began to appear over the mountains.

"All right, but quickly then, before we go in. The *Englisch* like to barter for their prices, so banter with them a bit. They will stare at you, perhaps, and your clothes. I always wore my second best to the stand. And I like that wine-colored blouse you're wearing today. Give all the children free tastes or samples, then the *Mamms* will be more likely to buy. And smile…

speak English…and be prepared for odd questions from the *Englischers*. They always want to know things like whether they can become Amish."

The girls laughed together again, though Sarah's heart thumped at all of the hurried information. They wended their way back toward the house just as lights glowed from the kitchen windows and warned them to hurry inside.

Breakfast was a whirlwind for *Mamm* and Sarah during spring, and today was no different. Sarah flew through her chores of gathering the eggs, making the biscuits, setting the table, and then helping to wash the dishes and have the kitchen spotless by 7 a.m., so she would have a whole hour to prepare and gather the necessary items to take to the stand. Father had instructed Luke that he would be the one to drive the wagon of goods the mile up the road to the stand daily and to help Sarah unload before returning to the fields.

Sarah was grateful for the help and now stood in the middle of the kitchen garden with baskets at her feet, staring in perplexity at the array of plants, wondering what to take.

"*Kumme*, Sarah… At least let's dig some potatoes. They always sell." Luke's tone was impatient and snapped Sarah back to attention.

"*Jah*, you gather the potatoes. Dig some onions too, please. Then I will get canned goods from the root cellar… *Ach*, and wash everything clean with the hose, Luke."

Her brother grinned. "Now you sound like Chelsea."

"Good." Sarah took heart at his words and made her way to the outside entrance of the root cellar. Her black shoes and stockings flashed against the whitewashed stone steps as she ventured into the cool, dim interior and made her way to where jars and jars of canned fruits and vegetables stood on shelves in neat rows. She plucked tomatoes, peaches, sweet corn, and mushrooms into a basket, then had to half unload it again because it was too heavy to get up the stairs. By her second trip up, Luke had the small wagon ready, with vegetables dripping clean in baskets. The dark horse, Shadow, stood waiting while eating out of a feed bag.

Sarah peeled layers of moss from the ground and laid them over the open baskets of the more delicate items. Then, on impulse, she scooped up the gray field cat, Grimes, for company and clambered up into the wagon seat next to her brother. She dabbed at her perspiring brow as they started off and hoped her cape would hide any wet stains at her armpits until they dried. They jolted down the dirt road, and Sarah cast anxious looks at the canned goods, but everything held still.

Once at the stand, Sarah paused to admire the workmanship of the long, three-sided wooden building with its four narrow steps. A hearty slanted roof with a generous overhang protected against the elements, and Father had placed heavy tubs of spring flowers on either side of the steps.

Luke helped her unload the wagon, then waved a quick farewell as he drove off, leaving Sarah alone to do the woman's work of "arranging," as he called it. It was hard work to haul the baskets up on the tables and then to spill a few items out enticingly, but she hurried on, speaking reassuring phrases to the cat.

"Now then, Grimes. We'll put the glass jars right up front where the sun can catch their sparkle, and I'll let some of the carrots trail out like this...and then I'll..."

"Hello? Are you open?"

Sarah nearly jumped out of her skin at the sound of the deep masculine voice. She turned with an onion in hand to find a tall, blond *Englischer* poised on the steps leading up to the stand. His dark blue eyes were set in a strong-boned face, and he was smiling, a cheerful, inquisitive flash of kindness.

Sarah felt as though she were watching herself like a character in a book, struck by some invisible force of accord in her spirit when she looked at the man. She moved to put the onion down, felt it miss the table with a disconsolate thump, and watched it roll over to the stranger. He picked it up and offered it to her with a long, outstretched arm; she took it.

"Um, I could come back later, if you're not ready yet. My housekeeper needed a few things for today, and I thought I'd just walk over. I guess I should introduce myself—I'm Dr. Williams, from the Fisher farm. We moved in over the weekend."

Sarah swallowed and supposed he thought her a complete dolt at her lack of response. Her head ached as she squeezed the onion and smiled as Chelsea had instructed her.

"Dr. Williams… *Jah*—yes, of course. Welcome. I'm certainly open for business, if you like."

"Great. Please call me Grant, and you are?" He'd moved up onto the platform near her and she had to crane her neck to see his face, while he ducked his head to avoid bumping into the angled roof.

"I'm Sarah…Sarah King." There. That was nicely said, though Grimes the cat was probably being friendlier by winding himself through the doctor's long legs.

Dr. Williams scooped up the sleek cat. "Ah, a good mouser, by the looks of him. Please let me know if he gets a litter sometime. We've need of a good cat."

Sarah nodded and blushed. She'd grown up on a farm, but it was unseemly of her to discuss litters with a strange man, veterinarian or not. The thought propelled her to replace the onion and slip onto the tiny hardback folding chair beside the small table where Luke had left the money box.

"Please, Dr. Williams…have a look about."

He put the cat down and smiled at her again. "Sarah King. Daughter of Ephraim King, correct?"

"Yes."

"Well, we're neighbors, Miss King—so again, call me Grant—unless… Wait, are you allowed to call me by my first name? I grew up around the Amish as a kid, but that was a long time ago, and I don't know how to address a young woman."

Sarah wanted to smile. Here was an *Englisch* question that seemed strange. "I may. But it might appear... forward. So I won't. I'm sorry."

The doctor nodded. "So then, to appear 'not forward,' I shall call you Miss King. It is Miss, right?"

Again Sarah was thrown by the man's question. Standing among the common bushels of potatoes, it seemed too intimate to discuss whether or not she was married, but she nodded an affirmation, then looked away, pretending to concentrate on the money box. Indeed, when she lifted the tin lid, she saw a note written in Chelsea's hand that read "Smile!" so she plastered a wider lift on her soft lips and hoped the doctor would choose something soon so she could finish setting up before any more customers came.

"This moss is a good idea—a natural insulator. Do you reuse it? You can, you know. Just dampen the root structure again and plant it back in the ground."

"You grow moss, Doctor?"

He laughed. "No, that's just me giving out relatively useless facts; vets do that sometimes. By the way, your English is lovely, very melodic."

Sarah ducked her head and blushed. She'd never been told anything as directly complimentary, and she knew that this was a taste of the world outside. Idle words. It never occurred to her that they might be true.

He lifted a basket of apples and added an onion and several potatoes. "Now I've done it, right?" he asked as he approached her table. "You think I'm trying to make you vain by paying you a compliment."

She shook her head to protest but then decided that would be lying. Her pretty brow knitted in confusion, and she bit her lip.

"Miss King, you are the first person I've met from the area, and seeing as though I value the truth in all its freedom, I want you to promise me something."

She looked up at him and realized he was being sincere, but what could she possibly promise an *Englischer* and one so much of the world?

"If I can, I will."

He plopped the basket on the table, which quivered under the weight. "Good. Promise me you'll always tell me the truth. The whole truth. I need a friend in the area, one who will help me understand more about the Amish—your faith, your ways—or I will never be accepted as a doctor here."

"That's true," she agreed, and he laughed though she couldn't understand why.

He leaned an elbow on the basket. He was so close she could smell his soaping and could also see the tiny gold flecks in his blue eyes.

"So do you promise?" he asked.

"What are you promising, Sarah King?"

Sarah glanced around the doctor's tall frame at the sound of Jacob Wyse's voice; she had been so involved in her talk with the *Englischer* that she hadn't heard her friend Jacob come up the wooden steps. His overly long chestnut hair brushed his broad shoulders from beneath the brim of his dark hat as he came to stand at the doctor's shoulder. She vaguely acknowledged their mutual good looks, one dark and the other so fair...

"Is it your concern, Jacob—whatever I promise?" she asked, then went on before he could reply. "Dr. Williams, please meet Jacob Wyse. He has a horse farm nearby."

The doctor immediately turned and offered a hand in the close confines of the space. Jacob shook it with a tightness around his handsome mouth that Sarah couldn't help but notice.

"Hi... I'm the new vet. Just moved into the Fisher farm."

"Tough business, then. Getting the locals to trust you. The old vet was golden." Jacob's tone suggested that this *Englischer* might fall far short.

The doctor glanced back to Sarah. "Right. That's what I was just talking with Miss King about."

She stared up at the two men until the doctor rocked back on his feet. "So how much do I owe you?"

She glanced at the basket before her—then had a sudden inspiration. She smiled. "You're my first customer, ever, so please just take the things for free today."

"Thank you, Miss King."

"You're welcome, Dr. Williams."

He inclined his head and picked up the basket. He moved to turn, and Jacob was forced to back away to give room for him to go down the steps.

"Have a good day, both of you," the doctor called.

There was something knowing in his brief look back that annoyed Sarah. He must think that she and Jacob were a couple.

She frowned up at Jacob when the doctor had reached the high road. "And what was that about, I'd like to know? You were rude."

"Was I?" Jacob asked, picking up an apple.

"I was just making our new neighbor feel welcome, and you had no right to interrupt. I can make conversation with whomever I choose."

He laid a few coins on the table and took a bite of the apple with his strong teeth.

"I've known you since we were babes, Sarah King, and I know when your eyes shine that you're happy. Don't go getting happy over some *Englischer.*"

"You're *narrish,*" she snapped, opening the money box and depositing his coins.

"I'm not crazy; let's just call it protective." He reached his tanned fingers to brush her cheek and she drew back. He dropped his hand.

"You are my friend, Jacob Wyse, that's all. I've told you…"

He nodded; his hazel eyes, very much like her own, shining with renewed good humor. "And, as my friend, you know how patient I am."

She rolled her eyes, then straightened as a large brown car pulled up and several *Englisch* women in makeup and colorful dresses climbed out.

"Go away," she hissed. "I've got customers."

"All right. But beware of *Englischers* wanting promises…or anything else for that matter."

She sighed aloud as he went down the steps and tipped his hat to the ladies as he passed. The women smiled in return, clearly charmed.

They approached the stand and glanced over the produce. One of them stared at Sarah for a long minute and then asked in a casual voice, "Honey, is there any way we can buy your clothes?"

Sarah's head began to ache once more as she schooled her expression of disbelief into politeness and smiled at her customers.

Grant Williams whistled along the dirt road that led home. He'd found the Amish stand and the young girl charming and decided he'd visit the roadside stand often, at least as long as the obviously protective Mr. Wyse allowed. He had no desire to get off on the wrong foot with any of the local Amish. He was nodding to the workers mixing cement on his front lawn when a terrible banging echoed from inside the house, followed by Mrs. Bustle's abrupt shriek.

He took the stairs two at a time with the basket in his arms and entered the house, letting the screen door slam behind him. The sounds had come from somewhere in the back, and he made his way to the kitchen where Mrs. Bustle was sobbing and Mr. Bustle was patting her back.

"What's wrong?" Grant asked, depositing the vegetables on the counter.

"I was about to light the stove, which is really a pain in the neck, Mr. Grant...when I opened the draught and a mother rat and her babies came tumbling out as cozy as can be. I might have cooked them!" She shuddered. "Now they're running all over everywhere. I can't have rats in my kitchen!" Her voice rose as her ample bosom shook in its household apron.

"Of course not." Grant met Bustle's eye and struggled not to laugh out loud. "Why don't you go into the front room and have a seat while we catch up the rats and...take them out back."

"Mr. Grant, I've known you since you were little, and I'd do anything for you, but please don't expect me to just sit down when those...creatures might be crawling anywhere."

Her eyes grew saucer wide and she didn't contain her scream. "Ahhh! There's one now! Get me up on the table, up, up, uuuup!" Grant and Bustle were helping her up to sit atop the kitchen table when a firm knocking sounded on the back door. Everyone froze until Grant scooped up a cringing baby rat, slipped it into his shirt pocket, and opened the back door with a flourish.

A serious-faced Amish woman in a staid black bonnet stood with hand raised to knock again. She held a linen-wrapped package in the other.

Grant loved the spontaneous, and this was too fun. "Hello, ma'am. May I help you?"

"I'm Mrs. King, from next door. We're neighbors." Her voice was pleasant, though she looked doubtfully at him. He noticed that she didn't try to peer over his shoulder as others might have done, and he appreciated the lack of nosiness.

"Mrs. King, please come in. I just had the pleasure of…" He paused, uncertain as to whether he should mention meeting her daughter in case the girl might get in trouble for socializing. "Of…helping my housekeeper clean up a bit." He held the door wider and the tiny rat chose that moment to peek up out of his shirt pocket.

Mrs. King stepped inside and nodded to the Bustles, who were still frozen. Then she glanced at Grant's pocket and looked to the floor.

Grant patted his pocket and glanced at Mrs. Bustle. "We're having a few guests of the rodent variety, I'm afraid."

Mrs. King lifted her head and offered him the linen package, then she began to roll up her long blue sleeves. "That's friendship bread—it's real tasty. Now I'll help you round up the rats, although that one in your pocket appears pleased to be staying."

Grant laughed, charmed once more. Here was a practical woman who was willing to truly be a neighbor. "I'm Dr. Williams, but please call me Grant. And this is Mrs. Bustle, my housekeeper, and Mr. Bustle, my jack-of-all-trades."

Mrs. King smiled and nodded again. "All right, Dr. Williams. Mrs. Bustle. Mr. Bustle. I think I should have brought you a kitten instead of the bread."

Mrs. Bustle was adjusting her skirt and answered

in a quivering voice, "That would be a blessing, I'm sure."

Mrs. King bent and caught up another baby rat, which she handed to Grant, who deposited it with its tiny sibling in his pocket.

"I'll send one of the boys over tonight with a cat." She glanced at the poor condition of the old stove, then spoke again. "Or we'd be pleased to have you all to supper, if you'd like, and you can take your pick from the barn cats and perhaps enjoy a story or two afterward from my husband. He loves to entertain."

Grant accepted with alacrity. He knew that being invited to supper in an Amish home was a big step toward establishing a relationship with the community.

"Thank you, Mrs. King. We would love to come, wouldn't we, Bustles?"

The older pair nodded.

"*Ach*, here's the mother," declared Mrs. King, grasping a long pink tail.

Mrs. Bustle fainted neatly, and Grant caught her not inconsiderable weight without fuss before she could roll off the table. He met Mrs. King's blank expression and nodded his blond head.

"Have I told you how much I appreciate your neighborliness?"

Chapter Three

Sarah had never been so happy to see her brother as when he pulled the wagon up to the front of the stand at dusk. She felt exhausted emotionally and physically, and even the thought of a good supper with the family did not inspire her.

"How did it go?" Luke stacked empty baskets while Sarah sorted through the few remaining vegetables.

"I sold nearly everything."

"Then it was good, *jah*, Sarah?"

She considered as she lifted things into the wagon and took her seat, holding the cat and the money box.

"It was a long day. I could see the washing hanging on *Mamm*'s line—it made me lonely."

"Not as lonely as plowing while staring at the back ends of four horses."

"Some of the customers were interesting. I met our new neighbor."

"And?"

"He was…nice."

Luke grunted. "Well, we were all glad that you forgot the load of baked goods *Mamm* prepared for the stand. The rhubarb pies were *gut* at lunch."

Sarah let her eyes drift over the fields. She'd also forgotten her own lunch and had to make do with some crisp apples. She would be better prepared tomorrow, though she realized that in addition to her evening chores, she would now have to do an after-dinner baking to take with her each following day. *Mamm* had helped this first time, but now it would be her responsibility. It seemed too hard, and she couldn't believe she'd have to do it all again tomorrow. She also had to find the time to start Chelsea's baby quilt and felt depressed at the thought.

"You'd better hurry up," Luke urged her when the wagon stopped at the farm. "*Mamm*'s got guests for dinner."

"Guests? Who?"

Luke led Shadow into the barn and didn't reply. Sarah wearily straightened her head covering and brushed at her dusty black dress. Even her favorite wine-red blouse was limp in the sleeves, but there was no help for it —guests meant socializing and smiling, and extra work, all of which she needed to be glad to do.

She fixed her shoulders and started to march around the house to the back door, intent on washing her face and hands at the outside pump. She stopped dead at the sight of the red sports car blocking the pump and blinked in the dusky light. If an elephant would have been standing there, she would have been less surprised. She couldn't recall a time when her father had an automobile on the property, except for when the family needed to accept rides from the local van to visit the hospital or go to a funeral too far from home. It could mean only one thing—the guests were *Englisch*, and the remembrance of a sunny pair of blue-gold eyes made her groan in disbelief. She was sweaty and dusty, and she felt unsettled by her reaction to the new vet. She told herself that she had no desire to see him again, and certainly not as she felt now, but she remembered Father's urging from weeks past to be neighborly.

So she inched between the car and the pump, laying a hand on the low door to keep her balance. The sudden screeching alarm made her jump to cover her ears. Luke came running from the barn, the cat hissed, and a flood of people emerged from the back door. She cringed as the horrible whooping sound continued, terrified that she'd done something to break the automobile.

Father and *Mamm* and the boys were running toward the car when Dr. Williams overtook them, pointing his keys in the direction of the vehicle. The sudden silence rang in its relief, but the experience was too much for Sarah's frazzled nerves. She longed to burst into tears and run to *Mamm*, but instead she slipped out from between the car and the pump and hugged her arms across her chest.

"I'm so sorry." Dr. Williams was patting her shoulder. "That's the alarm… I always forget to turn it off."

Sarah's teeth were chattering, and she realized how struck she was to see him again, and to have his large hand on her shoulder. "Then…I didn't break it?"

Dr. Williams stopped patting her. "No, of course you didn't break it."

He looked at the gathered group when Father burst out with a laugh. "*Jah*, you gave our Sarah a good scare. I personally thought that the world was crashing in." His joke broke the silence and everyone talked at once, except Sarah.

Dr. Williams leaned close to her ear. "Tell me the truth, Miss King. Have I given you one too many reasons to be annoyed with the English today?"

Sarah listened to his warm voice and thought absurdly of heated water pouring in languid rivulets down her shoulders and spine. She frowned at the idea.

"If you remember," she returned in a low voice, "I never promised to tell you the truth."

He laughed. "I'll move the car, so you can use the pump in peace."

"No, thank you, Doctor… I'll wash up inside."

She slipped through the throng and entered the kitchen. She washed at the water basin, grateful for the chill of the water after her ridiculous reaction to the doctor, and brushed the damp towel over the back of her neck just as everyone began to troop back in. They all settled at the main table and the adjacent smaller table that *Mamm* used for guests, forming an "L" shape that made it easier to serve. Chelsea and John Kemp had left earlier in the day, and Sarah recognized two new English faces as guests.

"Sarah, Mr. and Mrs. Bustle are visiting us also," Father pointed out from his position at the head of the main table. Dr. Williams was seated in James's place at Father's right hand while the Bustles were at the adjoining table.

She smiled in greeting and turned to help *Mamm*, who hurried from the stove with a platter of potato cakes, delicately fried.

"Sarah, *danki*—thank you, but take your place. You're tired, I'm sure." *Mamm* brushed past her, and Sarah slid into her spot. Dr. Williams smiled at her across the table and she nodded vaguely.

Father bowed his head to pray once *Mamm* had returned with the large platter full of sliced ham, and the table quieted. Sarah darted a look at the doctor and was pleased to see his head bowed and eyes closed. After prayer, the meal proceeded in a pleasant manner. The boys had been trained to make social conversation, and there was a spirit of goodwill in the air that soon revived Sarah's flagging spirits.

Father looked at her when she laughed quietly at something Luke had said. "*Ach*, Sarah, and your first day at the stand—how did it go?"

"Fine, Father."

"More than fine," Dr. Williams interjected. "I was her first customer, and I got a full basket of vegetables and fruits. You are fortunate to have such a daughter, sir. And such a family as this."

Sarah flushed, but Father was pleased; she could tell.

"Thank you, Doctor. I am blessed."

"Will you tell me how it is that you have such an abundant array of vegetables and fruit?" the doctor asked.

Father smiled and Sarah had to still her feet to keep from bolting from the table; she knew how Father loved to tell stories. "It's our Sarah, here. *Der Herr*...the Lord has given her a wondrous garden since she was a little girl. Much of what you're eating was canned from our abundant harvest last fall."

Dr. Williams laughed. "So your daughter has a green thumb."

Father pursed his lips, then smiled as he deduced the *Englisch* expression. "A green arm, I would say."

Everyone laughed but Sarah, who had no desire for the attention to focus on herself, gardening or not.

"I'm a bit of a gardener myself," Dr. Williams went on. "Just an amateur, really. But I would love to get a garden going for Mrs. Bustle to use, and for myself— herbs, you know. Sometimes herbal medicines are the best for the animals I treat."

"*Jah*," Father agreed. "I use some herbs as well on the dairy cows, though I cannot seem to always cure their feet. Perhaps you might have a look at them, Doctor."

"I'd be glad to."

"And Sarah will be glad to come over with one of the boys this Sunday after church meeting to help start your garden. *Jah*, Sarah?"

"Of course, Father," she murmured, knowing she'd been looking forward to an afternoon of rest from the stand, but intrigued nonetheless at the prospect of seeing the doctor's home. She resolutely ignored the voice in her head that whispered she'd also be interested to see the doctor again.

Dr. Williams shook his head. "I can't let you do that, Miss King. Surely you have better things to do on a Sunday afternoon?"

"I may," she admitted, ignoring Father's glance. "But I love to plan new gardens. It would be my pleasure."

Father smiled in approval. "*Gut*—good!"

She glanced down at her plate, then up again, intrigued by the blue-gold eyes that held her.

"On the contrary," said Dr. Williams with a tilt of his glass of milk. "The pleasure will be mine."

"And," Mrs. Bustle interjected with appreciation, "it would be my pleasure to learn how you make potato cakes, Mrs. King. They're wonderful!"

Mamm smiled and nodded, and Sarah was grateful for the turn in the conversation.

After dinner, Father walked outside with the guests to give them a cat from the barns, and Sarah listened as the odd sound of the car engine broke the night's silence. Father came back in as Sarah and *Mamm* finished the dishes.

"They are fine people and will be good neighbors," Father pronounced, and Sarah's heart gave a peculiar leap to hear this affirmation of Dr. Williams.

"*Ach*, I think so too," she enthused, her eyes shining.

"Which brings me to a certain point, my daughter." Father came to stand before her. "I could not help but notice that Dr. Williams seemed a bit taken with you and perhaps you with him?"

Sarah couldn't help the blush that stained her cheeks at her wayward thoughts about the doctor. It was one thing if Father noticed, but she hoped she hadn't been as transparent to everyone.

"You are old enough and wise enough to have your own mind, of course," Father continued. "But I think that you know that it would never be our desire for you to date an *Englischer*."

"*Jah*," *Mamm* chimed in. "A girl sometimes has a funny way of marrying the man she dates."

Sarah shook her head. "I don't want to marry anyone."

Mamm clucked her tongue disapprovingly. "*Jah*, and poor Jacob's heart is broken because of it."

"Jacob Wyse aside," Father continued. "We want you to know that we trust you, Sarah, and we will trust you to manage your future, with *Der Herr*'s help, of course. We love you and want what's best for you, but marrying an outsider, no matter how good a man, would result in you being forced to leave our community...and our family." He reached to squeeze Sarah's shoulder reassuringly. "Now, enough about this. What will you make for tomorrow's stand?"

Sarah tried to push the embarrassing conversation out of her mind and considered the merits of apple tartlets over whoopee pies.

"And before I forget…" Father smiled. "Sarah, you worked hard all day. We're proud of you, and it is not fair that you should have all of your chores and still keep up with the stand. The boys will take over your morning and evening work so that you may do your gardening and baking."

"*Jah*," *Mamm* added, reaching to brush a gentle hand against the curve of Sarah's cheek. "And I'll wash the dishes, breakfast and dinner. You just wash up after you bake."

"Oh, *Mamm*—I can't let you do all that."

Mamm laughed. "Do you think I'm too old for such work?"

"No, of course not. I just feel…"

"Sarah," *Mamm* said seriously. "Tell me what this saying is: *Alli mudder muss sariye fer ihre famiyle.*"

Sarah sighed. "I know."

"Tell me."

"'Every mother has to take care of her family.'"

"*Jah*," *Mamm* continued. "And I'll take care of you while you take care of all of us."

"Thank you," Sarah murmured, her heart full.

"And…" Father drew some bills from the money box she'd left on a side counter. "Your wages for the day, little Sarah." He offered her the money, and she put her hands behind her back, shaking her head.

"Father," she said, shocked. "I cannot take your money."

"You are not a child anymore, my daughter. Take the money each day and save it or spend it as you see fit. You have good judgment and you've earned it." Father's eyes twinkled.

Sarah took the money and slipped it into her apron pocket. She'd never had money of her own before and could not see the need of it, but she wouldn't disappoint Father or *Mamm*.

"Thank you both."

Father smiled and *Mamm* nodded.

"Now, what are you going to bake for tomorrow?"

Mamm's question brought her back to the practicality of the moment and Sarah smiled, feeling renewed, despite the awkwardness of a few moments before. "I thought I'd make whoopee pies…"

She got no further for all of the "whoops" that the boys let out from various places in the sitting room where they'd been listening.

"Make extra please, Sarah," Luke called.

"See, Sarah, you're earning your money well." Father laughed, and Sarah could not contain her own mirth as she reached for the large yellow mixing bowl and brought down the cocoa powder. It was not going to be as hard as she thought, and she breathed a prayer of gratitude to the Lord as she assembled the eggs.

* * *

The Bustles discussed the evening at the King farm with pleasure while Grant concentrated on not missing the minor turn in to their lane. The lack of streetlights made it difficult to navigate the roads. He swung into their lane and soothed the cat they'd been given, which was meowing excitedly on his lap, as if it sensed that it was to become something a bit more than a barn cat.

"Ah, the poor little thing," Mrs. Bustle clucked. "I'll take it inside and get it some food."

"Not too much, dear," Bustle interjected. "We want it to be hungry so that it can catch—"

"I understand your point," Mrs. Bustle interjected, still not quite recovered from her escapade with the rat mother.

Grant pulled in and everyone climbed out. He noticed some FedEx boxes in the shine of the porch light.

"Supplies! Great. I can't wait to get things going." He picked up the boxes in one strong arm and caught the screen door on his lean hip knowing Bustle would have held it.

"I'm good, Bustle. I'll just take these back into one of the rooms and have a look. I bet it's all meds; I ordered some penicillin."

"Very good, sir, and will you be requiring anything else this evening?"

"No, my friend. Both of you enjoy your rest, and maybe let the cat prowl around a bit."

"Very good, sir. Good night."

The Bustles went one way, and Grant went another,

down a narrow hallway, close to where he expected to set up his office. He hummed as he opened the boxes, thinking about Sarah King's hazel eyes. Then he stopped as he pulled plastic-wrapped, size-eleven beach flip-flops from the package. He looked at the address and saw that the zip code was one number off and groaned. Somewhere, a big-footed man was staring down at vials of animal antibiotics. He just hoped it wasn't somebody who'd take it into his head to sell them as street drugs. And then he laughed aloud at the thought. He was too used to living in the city, not that he didn't think that drugs weren't an issue out in the middle of nowhere. And though the sandals obviously didn't belong to an Amish man, he'd bet there were probably many an Amish youth who experimented during their *rumspringa*, or time of "running around" as he knew it. He thought of the beautiful Miss King and couldn't imagine her doing anything more wild than eating a peach out of season, and then he laughed again at himself—he was thinking too much of the girl.

He moved to the next box, expecting to find at least some of the meds, and instead withdrew a lodge comforter with bear paw prints and an indistinct moose on it. Clearly the postal service was a bit lax in this rural area, but he decided to see the humor in it. "All things for a purpose," he remarked to the cat, which had followed him down the hall.

"I know you'd rather be outside, but I promise

there's plenty of food running about." He scooped the animal up and made his way up the stairs, depositing the cat on the landing outside the Bustles' door.

Chapter Four

"It appears that there's a colony of bats living in the attic, sir." Bustle's voice was bland and low.

Grant smiled, looking up from his book. "Naturally. Does Mrs. Bustle know?"

"I thought it best not to…"

"You're right, of course. When the colony flies out tonight, we'll go up and seal all the entry holes in the roof. The bats will find another place to roost."

"Excellent idea, sir."

"Not really…just an old trick from one of those *Farmer's Almanac*s I've been reading. It's amazing how much information is relevant for renovating an old farmhouse."

The two men were sharing breakfast as the morning light poured in through the washed windows. Mrs. Bustle had eaten and was hanging out a washing of cleaning rags on an old clothesline out back. The newly acquired cat, dubbed Fisher after the

estate name, was prowling about, having successfully
moused twice that morning.

Grant rose and tidied up his place, much to Bustle's
disapproval, then went through the myriad rooms and
passages to where his office and treatment rooms were
to be housed. He eased open the wooden door with its
old-fashioned, varnished knob and sighed to discover
that the workers had not yet gotten to this part of the
house.

When he'd bought the estate, it had been a hurried
affair, and Mr. Fisher had been anxious to leave the
area. He wasn't clear on all of the details, but Fisher
had left nearly everything behind when he'd gone,
right down to the green velvet window drapes and the
hand-tooled, massive desk that he now placed a lean
hip against. He mentally compared the room to the
simplicity and lack of decoration that he'd seen at the
King farm and wondered at the difference. The Fishers had been Amish too, but perhaps they were of a
more liberal frame of mind. He glanced down at the
scattered papers on the desk and saw receipts for large
chain stores, as well as a crushed Avon bag. He mused
over this as he thought about Sarah King's fresh-faced
expression and the way the light played across her
unadorned, creamy cheeks and brow. Clearly the
girl needed no artificial enhancement to improve
her beauty. He smiled to himself at his meandering
thoughts. He'd had numerous girlfriends throughout
his training, but none ever struck his fancy for any
length of time. He decided he must check out the local

dating scene if an Amish girl in all her plainness was causing him to think about such a thing as the use of makeup.

"Women!" he exclaimed and set about clearing out the room.

By Thursday, Sarah had begun to get the rhythm of working at the stand and realized that she could do something with her hands in the idle minutes between customers. She decided to begin Chelsea's baby quilt with some trepidation and had gone to the vast attics of the farm to find fabric scraps, once she'd chosen a simple patchwork design. She hid her bundle of cloth and needles in a basket, not wanting *Mamm* to know what she was about—since she would be sure to have something to say about Sarah quilting again, as was proper for any Amish girl, in *Mamm*'s viewpoint.

Sarah had just finished serving her first morning customer and had taken out the quilt squares she had cut beforehand when a buggy turned briskly into the stand's parking area. Sarah glanced up and felt a sinking in her heart when she recognized her Aunt Ruth and *Grossmudder* King, obviously out and about for a surprise visit from their farm some twelve miles away.

Sarah gathered the fabric squares and stuffed them back into her basket, rising to greet the two ladies. Aunt Ruth was about forty-five and patiently kind as she helped Sarah's grandmother down from the buggy. *Grossmudder* King was in her eighties but got around reasonably well with the help of a cane. It was her tongue that was as sharp as any young person's though, and it always gave Sarah grief. The woman could find fault like a dog could find a duck, but none of these thoughts showed in Sarah's polite smile. She moved to assist Aunt Ruth as she helped the old lady navigate the stairs to the stand.

"Move off, Sarah King. I can make my own way," *Grossmudder* snapped, gesturing with her cane.

Sarah smothered a sigh. "Of course, *Grossmudder*."

"Sarah, how are you?" Aunt Ruth gave her a hug.

"She'd be better if she was married," *Grossmudder* muttered, poking at some apples with a bony finger.

Aunt Ruth rolled her eyes at Sarah, who had to suppress a laugh.

Grossmudder stepped by them both and went to where Sarah's basket was beneath the small checkout table. She prodded the basket with her cane. "And what are you quilting here? I saw you when we drove up."

Sarah felt as young as thirteen again when she faced the shrunken woman from whom she descended, but she reminded herself that she was doing the quilt for Chelsea, who would love it no matter how it turned out.

"I'm making a quilt for Chelsea's *boppli*."

"*Ach*, that's nice," Aunt Ruth exclaimed.

"Hmm…" the old lady declared. "It'll only be nice if you've managed to improve your quilting skills, which I have to doubt since you've not attended a quilting for years."

"Well, *Grossmudder*," Sarah returned serenely, "it is true that not everything improves with time."

Aunt Ruth turned a laugh into a cough while *Grossmudder* King's eyes flashed. "Don't be sassy, miss. You remind me of your mother when she was young!"

"*Danki*," Sarah murmured.

Grossmudder huffed. "Well, let's go down to the farmhouse, Ruthie. I haven't got all day. Sarah, I'd give meditation to the ways of your tongue; it's probably why you have no husband as of yet."

Sarah smiled politely and resisted the desire to point out that somehow her grandmother had managed to marry in spite of her own tongue. She watched the two women drive off with a sigh and considered what excuse she might use to be absent from supper that evening. One meeting with *Grossmudder* King in a day was more than enough.

She turned her attention to a basket of sweets she'd made the night before. She'd begun to find it pleasant to do the baking after dinner each evening and experimented with different desserts and pies as these seemed to sell the best, especially to the *Englisch*, who appeared to have a strong liking for sweets.

The night before, she'd made peanut brittle in *Mamm*'s largest cast-iron skillet, mixing the brown sugar, molasses, and freshly shelled peanuts until they reached just the right consistency. She'd also had to fend off her brothers when she'd cooled the brittle on cookie sheets and had started to break and bag it. It seemed she had more willing tasters than true helpers, and she'd soon shooed them all away, finishing each beribboned bag by herself. Now she arranged the bags in neat piles in the early morning sunshine at the stand and smiled in satisfaction as she took her seat to wait for her next customer.

She knew that Dr. Williams would be along at some point; he visited the stand each day, much to her discomfiture. She couldn't get away from *Mamm* and Father's talk and felt that every time her eyes strayed to his tall form, she was betraying a trust. She'd never found it difficult to obey her parents before, but there was something so engaging about the doctor that she seemed to forget all of her best intentions whenever they talked. She expected his visits would stop, of course, when he'd developed his practice in the area, and then she could go back to even footing in her mind. And of course, Jacob made it a point to stop by whenever he could, but he and the doctor had not met since that first day.

A horse and buggy trotted to a brisk stop before the stand, and Mrs. Loder, a neighbor of *Mamm*'s age, climbed down from the buggy and flung the reins over the hitching post. She wore her visiting bonnet, which was rather askew, and the blue blouse typical of housewives her age, along with a black overdress and apron.

"*Ach*, Sarah…*guder mariye*." She climbed the steps to the stand and looked about hurriedly.

"Good morning," Sarah replied. "Is something wrong?"

"*Jah*...I was supposed to go to a quilting for my sister-in-law today and was to bring a sweet, but I set my youngest girl to watching the cinnamon bread so it wouldn't burn while I put out the washing, and *ach*... sure enough, Lucy got busy playing and the bread burned."

"I'm sorry. It's so hard to be small and to pay attention." Sarah couldn't contain her thoughts, knowing little Lucy from various frolics and picnics.

"*Ach*, I know that... She cried and I didn't scold because she felt so badly, but I still need a sweet in a hurry."

"Well." Sarah rose and opened a bag of peanut brittle. "Why not take several bags of the brittle? Just put it onto a platter, and you'll be ready to go. *Sei so gut*... Please, take them with my blessing."

"You're a good girl, Sarah, but I need to pay you."

Sarah smiled. "*Nee*...no. We're neighbors; it's my pleasure."

Mrs. Loder smiled at her and patted her shoulder. "*Danki*, Sarah. I will take it and hurry!"

Sarah put six bags into a box and handed it up to the older woman when she'd taken up the reins to the buggy. Mrs. Loder expertly turned the horse, and Sarah went back to the steps to wave good-bye.

The sound of the horse's hooves had just ceased to echo when a car came driving fast from the opposite end of the high road. Loud music blared from the tan automobile as it pulled into the parking area near the stand in a cloud of dust. Sarah resumed her seat and waited. She had not had to deal with any *Englisch* teenagers yet, and her stomach fluttered as two lanky youths got out of the car.

One was smoking a cigarette and flicked ashes into the dirt at the roadside while the other mounted the steps to the stand.

Sarah offered a faint smile, but then swallowed and looked to the wooden floor when the boy began to come toward her.

"*Guder mariye*, Sarah King."

Sarah's head snapped up at the proper pronunciation and vaguely familiar voice. She met the cold brown eyes of the boy, trying to place how the *Englischer* knew her name.

"Don't you know me, Sarah King? You should. You had no problem remembering me at the picnic at the Loders' last spring. You knew me well enough to avoid me when I might have held your hand by the creek." The youth laughed and his friend began coming up the steps.

Comprehension dawned for Sarah just as the boy who'd spoken insolently bit into an apple he'd grabbed.

"Matthew Fisher?" she asked.

"*Jah*, Sarah. Sarah the proud. Sarah the snob." He spit out a seed and turned to his friend. "Sarah King here and her family were key in running my father off his land. I say I owe her a debt."

The other boy had torn open a bag of peanut brittle and was chewing. "Maybe we should collect, then."

Sarah's heart was pounding and she was praying in

the back of her mind as quickly as a running stream. "We didn't do anything to harm you, Matthew," she managed. "Or your family."

"Liar," he hissed, slamming the apple on the wooden floor so that it splattered. "You didn't call it shunning; that would have been a bit too much, right? But you thought you were better, didn't you?"

His companion had come to stand next to Sarah's chair and pulled on her *kapp* string with dirty fingers.

"She's pretty, Matt. Let's have a little fun." He leaned close, and she could smell the lanky teenager's foul morning breath mixed with the smell of the peanut brittle.

She tried to draw a calming breath. "What do you want?"

The boy laughed and squeezed hard at the nape of her neck. "What do you think?"

"Aw, let her alone already," Matthew rejoined in a sullen tone. "She's too much of a priss."

"I bet I could loosen her up," his friend said, keeping a firm grip on Sarah's neck.

Sarah felt as though her heart would beat through her chest, though her clear eyes remained steady. The youth moved to kiss her and she jerked away, knocking over her chair and rising to press herself into the small corner of the stand.

"Sarah, is it?... Not shy, are you?" The boy was moving closer and she screamed while he laughed— then his laughter was suddenly cut off and he grabbed for his throat.

Sarah pressed shaking hands to her lips as Dr. Williams drew the boy backward, until he finally shook him like a dog shakes a rat. He flung him down the steps where Matthew was scrambling to rise.

"Let me make one thing perfectly clear," Dr. Williams said in an even tone. "Should you ever take it into your heads to stop by this stand, or this area again, let's say even within ten miles of here, I will find you—and you will be deeply, regrettably sorry."

The boys scrambled to their feet and ran for their car, gunning the engine, then screeching out in a furl of dust.

Sarah tried to slow her breathing, thanking the Lord for sending help, even as the wood floor seemed to rise up to meet her spinning head.

The doctor replaced her chair in its proper position and helped her to sit down. Then he broke the seal on a jar of spiced apples and syrup and held the glass to her lips.

"Drink this, Miss King. It's sweet and will revive you."

She obeyed, letting the thin syrup slide down her dry throat. He next offered a white handkerchief that she clutched, pressing it to her lips.

"Now, no harm done—just a dreadful scare, right?"

Her hazel eyes filled with tears, and she tried to focus on answering.

The doctor straightened her head covering, waiting for her to speak.

"If you hadn't come along…"

"You would have planted him a facer and he'd have slunk off like the dog he obviously is."

She shook her head and swiped at the tears that fell now. "No, I probably wouldn't have... I couldn't think. It was Matthew Fisher...the Fishers, you know, from your farm."

She met his eyes and saw that his face appeared drawn and white, though his blue-gold eyes blazed with intensity.

"I see. Obviously there are some mixed feelings there," Dr. Williams said with a look of concern.

"I don't know what that boy with Matthew might have done..."

Dr. Williams replaced the lid on the apples. "It won't happen again, Miss King. They're cowards and won't be back around."

"When Father hears of this, he won't let me work at the stand."

"Is that wishful thinking?" The doctor laughed. "I say your father has greater faith than that."

Sarah had to smile at his "wishful thinking" comment. Somehow this *Englischer* seemed to know her thoughts so well. She lifted her chin and drew a single sniff.

"May I offer you some peanut brittle, Doctor?"

"Only if you agree to join me."

And because he seemed so calm, she did.

A bag and a half of peanut brittle later, Dr. Williams jumped to his feet. "Hey, I nearly forgot in all that ruckus—I brought you something."

Sarah concealed her surprise. She had never had a "something" from a man before, and certainly not from an *Englisch* man. She wondered what *Mamm* would say, then bit her lip as she realized the doctor was repeating himself.

"I'm beginning to recognize that look. Are you permitted to receive something from an *Englisch* friend, Miss King?"

"Ye-es," she said, trying not to appear too excited by the wooden box he'd produced from beside the steps of the stand.

"Well, good then. I was cleaning out my office this morning and taking some things up to the attic. We've got a colony of bats hanging up there, incidentally." He went on while she wrinkled her small nose. "Anyway, I found this box up there and when I opened it, well, I just thought of you... Here."

He proffered the box and she took it onto her lap, letting it fill her arms. She hesitated in sliding the wooden lid open when she considered the visitors in his attic.

"No bats, I promise."

She smiled and opened the box, then gasped in surprise and faint dismay. "They're beautiful!" Her slender fingers pulled handfuls of colorful fabric squares into the light of day. There were cottons and silks, worsteds and flannels, layer after layer of unusual and pretty material of varying weights and colors.

She fingered an iridescent green piece of cloth and considered his words. He thought about her when he saw the fabrics? She just didn't feel like she matched up, especially because he probably assumed that she could quilt.

"Did you know," he queried, bending his long legs to hunch down beside her, "that the hummingbird is the tiniest bird in the world?"

"Yes." She nodded, confused as to where he was going with the conversation.

He reached a long finger to stroke the iridescent fabric square she held. "And did you know that hummingbirds can flash their bright colors, as well as hide them when necessary?"

"Yes, I knew that. I like birds, and hummingbirds often come to the garden," she admitted.

"Well…" His finger briefly whispered a touch against hers before he withdrew. "You're like a hummingbird to me, Miss King…like this material here. Tiny, curious, always darting busily around and hiding your bright colors…except when you smile with your eyes."

She blushed and shook her head, thrusting the shiny material beneath a stack of others.

Grant laughed. "Too worldly, right? Just think about it."

"I can't. It's vain…almost."

"No, it's a compliment, given truly and without device. You can choose to accept it or not."

She swallowed, not wanting to hurt his feelings, but not wanting to believe words of the world, words that rung with intimacy as well as friendship. She decided to put aside her indecision and awkwardly said the first thing that came to mind.

"I know that hummingbirds like to perch... They have weak feet."

He looked into her eyes.

"Knowing that you are probably not being ironic, thank you, Miss King. I think you just made my day."

She thought for a moment, then slid the lid closed on the box. "I can't take these from you."

"But you said that you could accept..."

"No," she interrupted. "It's not that." She sighed. "You asked me to tell you the truth. Well, the truth is that I'm not a quilter, not like other Amish women." She reached past his knees to pull a handful of squares out of her basket. "I'm struggling just to make a baby quilt for my sister." She glanced at him and offered the box back.

He smiled at her. "I suppose quilting was somewhere in the back of my mind when I saw the material, but the truth is what I told you. The squares are beautiful just as they are."

Sarah let the box rest on her lap and realized that he didn't care whether she quilted or not. It was a liberating thought. "Thank you, then. I'll keep them."

"Great." He got to his feet and started to pack the remaining peanut brittle in a basket.

"Come on. I'll walk back with you to your father's farm for lunch and tell him of your visitors. I don't want him to be alarmed."

Sarah stood, holding the wooden box of fabrics. For

a few minutes, he'd made her forget all about Matthew Fisher and his friend, but now she shivered.

If the doctor noticed, he didn't say anything; he merely slung up the basket of peanut brittle and waited until she'd gotten the money box and gone down the steps.

"By the way…" His deep voice made her peer up at him in the bright sunlight. "I'm buying this lot of peanut brittle. Mrs. Bustle, and don't repeat this, can create a meal out of two sticks, but she is not a candy maker."

"You'll make yourself sick," Sarah cautioned, eyeing the bags in the basket.

"I'll take my chances."

Sarah dreaded going into the house, knowing that her grandmother was there, but there was no help for it. She sensed the tension immediately when she walked in with Dr. Williams at her heels. *Mamm* smiled politely, but the corners of her mouth were tight, and Father rose from the table with a furrowed brow, while her brothers paused in eating their lunches. Aunt Ruth and *Grossmudder* King were in bentwood chairs by the woodstove, drinking tea, and suddenly stopped their rocking. It was one thing to have the doctor over for supper, but it was quite another to bring him unannounced into the intimacy of the family kitchen, when Father and her brothers were taking a break from the fields to eat lunch.

"Sarah, why are you home from the stand so early?" *Mamm* questioned.

"I had a little problem," Sarah said lamely, sliding the wooden box of fabric squares out of sight behind the counter.

"I suggested that we walk back together," the doctor interceded, putting down the basket of peanut brittle. "Miss King had a bit of trouble at the stand with some teenagers, and I happened to come along."

Mamm came to Sarah's side. "Are you all right?"

"*Jah, Mamm*, thanks to the doctor."

"What happened exactly?" Father asked.

"It was Matthew Fisher, Father, and an *Englisch* friend of his. Matthew was angry at me, at us, for his family's leaving. He... They..." She faltered, and the doctor took up the story.

"One of the boys forcibly tried to kiss your daughter. I gave them a good shaking and a warning not to come back around."

Father came around the end of the table and extended his hand to the doctor. "Then we must thank you, Doctor, for helping our Sarah. We must be vigilant of the Fisher boy."

"I'm glad I could help." Dr. Williams returned the handshake.

"Who are you anyway?" *Grossmudder* King inquired loudly from her chair.

"*Ach*," Father said with a harried look. "You must meet my mother and my sister."

The doctor went to shake hands while Sarah

watched, wondering what her grandmother might say. She didn't have long to wonder.

The old woman gave the doctor an unceremonious poke in the knee with her cane. "Well, you're tall, but Sarah should have been able to use her wits to manage the boys herself. I don't believe that a woman needs rescuing."

"Unless it means marrying her," Luke joked from the table and his brothers laughed.

"In that case, Luke King," *Grossmudder* said with her normal tartness, "it seems that you'll never be in the position to rescue anyone."

Sarah threw a pleading glance at *Mamm*, who interceded. "Doctor, won't you sit down to lunch with us? And, Sarah, how about a cup of tea?"

"I'm sorry," the doctor said, his voice laced with humor. "I need to be going, but thank you just the same." He nodded to the room at large and then to Sarah and made his way to the back door.

"*Ach*, don't forget your peanut brittle," Sarah called and hurried to him with the basket.

He took it from her with a smile. "Thank you, Miss King."

She saw him out the door, then turned back to the kitchen.

Father cleared his throat. "A good man. A good neighbor to us."

"*Jah*," Samuel replied. "But we should have words with Matthew Fisher just the same."

Father stroked his beard. "We will see, but for now

we must thank *Der Herr* that Sarah is well and ready to go back to the stand after lunch, *jah*, Sarah?"

"Of course, Father." *So much for getting out of the work at the stand*, Sarah thought ruefully.

"I wanted some peanut brittle," *Grossmudder* King complained. "Forgot to get it this morning. Now I suppose that *Englischer* walked off with the lot."

"It's bad for your teeth, *Mamm*," Aunt Ruth objected.

"When you're eighty some years old and you want peanut brittle, Ruthie, don't tell me that you won't be having it! Why, the time was that I..."

Sarah let the diatribe flow over her head and hastily swallowed a cup of tea, then she escaped back into the sunshine and the roadside stand.

Later that night, in the cool comfort of her little bed, she thought about the peanut brittle she'd made and smiled. God used it to help a neighbor, feed an enemy, and share with a friend. She pushed aside the doctor's complimentary words from the afternoon about the fabrics, even though the wooden box was now tucked beneath her bed. As the stray pines whispered through her open window, she drifted off to sleep beneath the patchwork quilt *Mamm* had pieced for her as a child and thought of the doctor's eyes and the colorful flick of a hummingbird as it darted across a golden blue sky.

Chapter Five

Grant, poised with a flashlight, and Mr. Bustle stood ready on the top attic step. Seeing the bat colony hanging upside down in eerie repose was enough to give anyone the shivers, but Grant especially had problems with bats. Although he loved all animals, he'd been bitten by a bat as a young boy and had never quite gotten over his fear of them. He'd been helping to carry the groceries in at night from the back of the family's station wagon and had gone back out alone to retrieve a candy bar he thought had fallen from the bag. He saw a shadowy lump on the backseat and grabbed for what he thought was his chocolate, instead coming up with a handful of misguided baby bat. He'd screamed louder than Mrs. Bustle, shaken the thing off, and then run, still screaming, in to his mother. It was one of the last times before her death that he could recall going to her for comfort.

All this flashed through his mind as the last rays of sunlight sank beneath the level of the small attic window, which had a distinct hole in it, large enough for an adult bat to fit through. Almost as one, the colony began to awake, and Grant doused his light, feeling his skin crawl, but once they'd stretched their wings and called in high-pitched shrieks to one another, they began a mass exodus through the hole. It took a full three minutes, and Grant estimated the colony to be in the high hundreds. When they'd gone, he looked over his shoulder at Bustle in the flash of his light and saw that his friend was pale.

"Come on, Bustle, we've got to get that glass replaced before they get back."

"Yes, sir."

Grant marched across the attic floor, ignoring the piles of bat droppings he was stepping in, and made for the window. He had the old piece of glass out and was fitting a new one when Bustle spoke.

"Sir? Did...the almanac mention anything about the babies?"

"The babies?" Grant edged the glass in with satisfaction. "What babies?"

"The bat babies, sir. It appears that they like your shirt."

Grant turned in growing horror to look over his shoulder and let out a faint groan. At least twenty bat pups clung to the back of the flannel shirt he'd thrown on and seemed to be as happy as could be next to the warmth of his body.

"Give me the other glass pane back, Bustle."

"But, sir..."

"We'll get a professional, and a veterinarian is definitely not it."

He switched the glass back so that the hole was once again present and began to ease out of the shirt. The baby bats squeaked in protest.

"Bustle?"

"Yes, sir?"

"Don't let the cat up here... They'd eat him alive." Grant joked. "And let's not mention this whole escapade to Mrs. Bustle."

"Quite, sir."

Grant dropped the shirt on the floor and ran, Bustle at his heels, until he'd slammed the attic door. He took off again until he got to the shower he'd had installed the week before. He stayed there for a nice ten minutes, and that night he wore boots to bed with a long-sleeved shirt, jeans, and a hat, just for good measure.

Sarah had heated water at the stove and used the hip bath in the secluded comfort of the blanketed-off kitchen the night before, so this morning all she had to do was dress and wind her waist-length hair into its intricate coil to stay beneath her *kapp*. Church meetings were held every other Sunday at the home of a different family in the community, and there were enough families so that the Kings need only host several times a year. This morning the Loders were hosting, and *Mamm* wanted to bring fresh root beer for the after meeting meal, so Sarah hurried down to the kitchen to help. She wanted to finish in time to gather

her seeds, for Father had said that Luke might take the lighter buggy to drive her to the doctor's home after luncheon to help him with his garden.

Mamm wished her a good morning as she plunged down the narrow stone steps to the cellar where the crocks of root beer had been placed days before. Sarah had helped to funnel the cane sugar, baker's yeast, and root beer extract along with the fresh spring water into the narrow necks of the crocks, and now she hooked a finger into each corked crock and lugged them back up to the kitchen. She'd learned that displacing the cork, even a bit, could result in an explosive outpouring of carbonation, and she had no desire to change her apron. She left *Mamm* to settle the jugs in a tin bath full of ice and asked if she might gather her seeds from the attic for her visit to the doctor's.

"*Jah*, Sarah, but *bass uff, as du net fallscht* on those attic stairs."

"I will not fall, *Mamm*, *danki*."

"Here." *Mamm* handed her a fresh biscuit filled with spicy brown sausage. "Eat this, or you'll feel like fainting in service."

Sarah took the food, though her stomach was jumping with nerves. She was usually excited on church meeting days, but she was especially happy today at the thought of sharing her knowledge of gardening with the doctor.

She climbed through the familiar rabbit's warren of staircases to the topmost attics of the old farm. A wasp droned at a small windowpane, and she pushed open the glass to set it free as she chewed the last of her biscuit. Far below her she could see the plowed and growing fields like the furrows on *Grossmudder* King's aged brow. She closed the window, though; she had no time for idle thoughts today. She turned and navigated the orderly rows of trunks, some of which held the time of the journey to America from Europe. Others, she knew, contained *Mamm*'s simple blue bridal dress and various knitted baby items from all of the family. And still others were filled with Amish quilts, patterns, and color squares, layered with cedar shavings to keep pests away until it was airing time.

She passed through the large main attic room and bent to slip through another narrower passage into one of the wings. Here, the light was brighter because Father had enlarged the window, but the air was very cool, being insulated by the heavy stone that formed the walls. Sarah straightened and went to the giant pigeonhole desk that looked as though it belonged in a bank and not on a farm. Sarah knew it had been her great-great-grandfather's, who had built it up there, finding solace to do his ledgers away from his brood of thirteen children.

Father had used its many drawers to house feathers and to tie flies for fishing for a long while, but when Sarah's accumulation of seeds had outgrown the spice cabinet downstairs, he'd officially given the desk over for her sole use to store and label seeds.

"It's our heritage she's preserving," he'd admonished when one of the boys had complained. "The seeds are part of our relationship with the land, with *Der Herr*, and Sarah is a faithful steward. She shall have the desk as her own."

She'd been fourteen then and could hardly believe that her father would trust her with such a treasure as the desk, but he did. He'd moved his feathers and pins out accordingly, and gradually, over the years, Sarah's seeds and labels and journals on gardening had taken over nearly all of the space. Sarah knew of the *Englisch* fascination with the so-called heirloom seeds, but she did not know if they valued a seed as a treasure, a heritage, a wealth. She could not judge, though, and she would bring her very best seeds to the doctor. She ignored the pang of excitement that shot through her at the thought of sharing her ideas on gardening with someone who seemed genuinely interested, and she concentrated on the seeds.

Choosing from among the wooden drawers was more fun than choosing from the fabrics at the dry goods store when it was time to sew a new blouse. She handpicked, parceled and labeled, and then tied all with a piece of string just as she heard the faint call of her name from downstairs. She closed the drawers and flew down the steps and outside, straightening her *kapp* and climbing with Luke and *Mamm* into the lighter buggy. Father and the boys were crowded into the wagon with Shadow and Hairs at the pull. Father slapped the reins as soon as Sarah was seated, and Luke clicked to the dark brown Morgan, called Light-foot, and they all moved briskly forward. The Loders' farm was nearly five miles down the road, and families came as far as twenty miles off to attend services.

"Where's the root beer?" Luke asked, and *Mamm* gestured to the tin washbasin ahead of them in the wagon, ensconced between several pairs of black-clad legs. The weather was cool, and the horses made short work of the miles. Father made sure the animals were well rested and impeccably curried for the Sunday drive; he had a particular disdain for other Amish men who did not take as much care with their horses.

The air was sweet and fragrant with the burgeoning of summer, and Sarah breathed in the mingled scents of lilac and laurel and let her gaze drift to the gently rounded curves of the Allegheny Mountains, which encircled their community. Before she knew it, they were pulling into the Loders' lane, where many other buggies were unloading. Sarah saw that the large black covered "bench wagon" had already arrived, bringing the necessary seating for the worship. Every other week it was driven to the hosting family's home and dutifully unloaded and reloaded by the men. The Loders' front rooms were not large enough to house everyone, so the meeting was to be held in the barn, which was common for the smaller farms.

Sarah smiled at friends, nodded to Jacob, and then slipped into her section with the unmarried girls. Father and the married men sat in another section while *Mamm* and the married women did the same. The young, unmarried men and teenage boys tended to stay in the back rows, where they could "eye" ev-

erything, as Luke put it. Sarah was just glad to have a
place to worship. Though the three-hour service could
sometimes be long in the heat of high summer, it refreshed her soul to listen to the sermons and to sing
from the hymnal, the *Ausbund*, the unchanging musical core of her faith. She wondered what the doctor
would think if he could hear their plain singing, unadorned by harmony or musical instruments so that
their worship might be without vanity. She jerked her
thoughts up when she knew that her attention was
drifting but nonetheless patted her apron pocket to
make sure the packet of seeds was nestled there.

Then she realized that one of the elders had called
upon Luke to lead the singing of the traditional second
hymn, the *Lob*. Sarah tensed as she half turned to look
at her brother's pale face. It was an honor to be called
upon to lead a hymn, especially *"Das Lob Lied,"* but
Luke had not yet had the privilege conferred. He rose
to his feet and walked to the front of the congregation.
Sarah could tell he'd like to throw up; he'd had the
same expression on his face when he'd gotten into a
ground wasp's nest and had been stung more than two
hundred times. She knew he'd rather take the stinging
all over again rather than risk the *Lob*. The song was
twenty minutes in length, and if a young man didn't
get off on the right foot on the first syllables, it was
all over.

Sarah saw Luke's Adam's apple work reflexively,
and she closed her eyes and prayed for him as hard as
she could. Then she heard the first warbled syllables,

the "OOooOOooOOooOO" dribble out of his mouth. She thought he'd never looked so young, but he hung on, moaning and droning until the restless shuffling from the back row let her know that her brothers were not being easy on Luke. Infinitely later, Sarah's neck was sweating and Luke had led them all through the fourth and final verse. There was a distinct moment of silence as he made his way, heavy-footed, back to his place, looking grim. The service went on, but all Sarah could think about was Luke's face.

After the meeting, things broke up as the women began to set out food, using the backless worship benches as both seats and tables. Sarah knew it wasn't proper, but she sidled her way closer to the young men and was at Luke's elbow before *Mamm* could notice her missing.

"You were...unique," Sarah whispered.

"Go away," Luke whispered back, and she did, but not before she heard her older brothers' good-natured teasing and Luke's reluctant laughter. She smiled to herself and resumed her place to eat a rushed luncheon.

"Why the hurry?" Jacob asked, as he straddled the bench where she was eating.

Sarah glanced at him, the light green of his shirt picking up the mixed color of his eyes. She had no desire to tell him of her afternoon plans because she could imagine his reaction.

"How about a buggy ride?" he asked when she didn't answer right away. "I've got a new colt that's a little wild. I know you like to drive." He smiled at her, and she ignored the thrill in her chest at the thought of driving a colt that wasn't fully broken. She'd done it many times with Jacob, and it was exhilarating.

"I can't. I have other plans. My father asked me to do something for him." There. That wasn't a lie.

"What?"

"Hmm?"

"What are you going to do?" he persisted.

She took a sip of her lemonade and knew he wasn't going away until she told him.

"Oh, all right. I'm going to Dr. Williams's house to take him some seeds. Luke is driving me. It's not a big deal."

His eyes flashed. "No big deal, huh?"

"*Nee.*"

"Guard that heart of yours, Sarah. It's too trusting."

She frowned at him. "I trust myself to know what I want and what I don't."

He laughed. "*Jah*, but the problem is that you know, and I know, that you're wrong half the time. Remember the summer you wanted to raise potbellied pigs and you lost a whole radish growth to wilting? Don't make the mistake of trading a passing fancy for long-term growth."

She smiled sweetly at him. "Potbellied pigs and radishes will get you everywhere in conversation with a lady."

He got up and stared down at her. "Just remember what I say."

"How could I possibly forget?"

"Well, that colt won't wait. I'd better be going." He turned and walked off, and Sarah sighed at his broad, retreating back. She had no desire to hurt Jacob; she valued their friendship a great deal. She'd known him forever, and she also knew that he was handsome enough to have his choice of any girl. Last year, when he began to show his intentions toward her, she'd backed away, and he'd patiently persisted. Maybe today would change his mind, she hoped. She rose to find her brother, meeting Father on the way.

Luke wasn't ready to go, though. Having gained some notoriety for his impromptu performance, he bantered with his friends until Father approached them, holding Sarah's hand.

"*Ach*, Luke, your sister needs a ride, and now I know, should one of the cows go missing, that you'd be the one to sing her along back home at night." Father didn't smile; he simply patted Luke's back, squeezed Sarah's hand, and moved off into the crowd.

"Come on," Luke said, and Sarah followed happily.

Mrs. Bustle had discovered a plastic bag lined with peanut brittle crumbs and had strived to outdo any possible question of her baking skills. She outfitted the tea table with a mountainous chocolate cream cake, finger sandwiches, petits fours, and crystal tumblers of Moroccan iced tea.

"There," she declared, just as the clock struck three. Grant stood near the picture window he'd just had installed and watched the dust stir from the horse and buggy coming up the lane.

He turned to smile at her handiwork. "Thank you. It's lovely, but I don't think they expect all this."

"All the better." She nodded, heading off to do another round of battle in the kitchen.

Mr. Bustle answered the knock on the front glass door, and Grant came forward to greet his guests.

He was struck anew by the purity of Miss King's gently curved face and clear eyes and her brother's skin, though tanned, which also shone with good health.

"Welcome." He shook hands with Luke and then with Sarah, glad that she seemed willing enough to do so. "Please come in and excuse the carpentry mess… Mrs. Bustle's put on quite a tea in your honor." He led the way into the dining room and grinned at Luke's boyish whistle of appreciation upon viewing the table. Sarah frowned at her brother and looked as though she'd like to scold him.

"I'm sorry," Grant said. "But I just have to understand, Miss King—do you want to lecture Luke on the whistle or just in general?"

Sarah frowned as Luke laughed. "Caught," he told his sister.

"Yes, I am." Sarah sighed. "If you must know, it's that my *bruder* is like all the boys—he could eat forever. He just ate less than an hour ago… *Ach*, that sounds ungrateful… I'm making a mess of things…"

She spread her hands with a helpless gesture as Luke grinned.

Dr. Williams waved an arm toward the table. "Please, both of you, come and sit... And please, eat or don't eat, as you like."

He drew out a chair for Sarah, who took it with gracious thanks.

Grant filled Luke's plate and let Sarah choose as she liked, then he took a piece of cake himself. He moved the beautiful flower arrangement off the table and onto the floor, the better to see his guests' faces.

"Sorry," he explained. "I want to look at you as we talk. Your own table was so pleasant in its simplicity."

"Thank you," Sarah murmured, toying with her ornate fork.

"Well, if you'll excuse my ignorance, I'd like to hear all about your kitchen garden and about what you might grow for healing or natural remedies—for both animals and people."

"I brought your seeds." Sarah produced the paper packet from her apron pocket.

"*Ach*, Sarah, not from the desk?" Luke groaned.

"Yes, from the desk."

Grant raised his brow and she continued. "I sort my seeds in a big old desk, though most are not truly mine. They're from my *Grossmudder*... Excuse me, please, I mean my grandmother and her mother before her."

"Aha," Grant exclaimed, pleased that he could contribute. "Heirloom seeds!"

"Well...the *Englisch* call them heirloom seeds, but maybe for a different reason than we do."

"Not just because they're old?" Grant ventured.

"There's that, but also the word *heirloom*... It's an older word, in English, *jah*? So I truly think of each seed as an heirloom, a valuable piece of history that—"

"*Ach*. And we're off," Luke muttered, helping himself to more cake.

"Let your sister be," Dr. Williams adjured good-naturedly.

"You haven't got her talking tomato varieties yet... Just wait."

"Tomato varieties? I thought there were only a few."

"Oh no." Sarah's eyes glowed, and Luke shook his head.

"There's the ox-heart variety, the striped tomato, and the phantom tomato, or white tomato. And, you see, an heirloom plant usually has time as well as a story behind how each seed came into a garden."

"I'm intrigued," Grant exclaimed, pushing aside his plate.

"And I'm happy to go and pace off your garden for you, Doctor, while Sarah explains." Luke rose. "I brought some shovels and a pick. Do you want it right outside the back kitchen like we have?"

"Yes, and if you don't mind, tell Mrs. Bustle what you're doing. She'll give you some more direction. Thank you, Luke."

When he'd gone, Sarah fingered her seed package, then gave him a direct look. He marveled at the way her hazel eyes seemed to change colors depending on what light she was in. Now they were a translucent light brown, like the early coat of a young fawn.

"Please, go on, Miss King. I'd love to hear some of the heirloom stories."

"Well, there are the husk cherries, we call them *juddekaershe*… They've been grown for nearly five generations in my family. Sometimes they're called ground cherries or winter cherries. The seed comes from a distant relative who moved here from Schoeneck, Pennsylvania. In Pennsylvania Dutch, *Schoeneck* means 'beautiful corner,' and these pretty fruits are related distantly to the tomato family. They look a little like tomatillos, and we use them in pies, jellies, and jams. When the boys pull them up at harvest, they pull the whole plant and hang them upside down in the attics. The winter cherries have to ripen and slip out from their little husks. They also can be harvested all winter and their vines spread out nearly three to four feet on the ground." Her eyes danced as she described the plants, and he watched as she became aware of how animated she'd been.

"Please, don't stop," he encouraged. "I love to hear you speak, and I do want to learn. You see, I can remember kitchen gardens from my childhood. I'd go with my dad on calls to the Amish farms and get to wander around. I always liked the profusion of the gardens and ate more than one ripe tomato straight off the vine."

"Your father was a vet too?"

"No, he was a medical doctor, a general practitioner. He had many Amish patients and was deeply devoted to the Amish people. He passed that on to me, I guess."

There was a brief silence while she seemed to consider his words, then he smiled.

"So tell me about some other seeds before Mrs. Bustle thinks we're not enjoying tea."

She slanted a curious glance his way, then went on. "Well, there are also peppers—the sweet yellow stuffing pepper... You might fill it with spinach or a chicken salad, and the pimiento pepper, which is truly as sweet as an apple. *Ach*...and I brought seeds for pretzel beans, which really do look like green pretzels when they mature, and the purple burgundy lima bean. It makes a better stew, I think, than just the lima bean itself."

Grant listened, fascinated by her lilting voice until it seemed more charming than the aged crystal they drank from.

"And there are a few flowers, but useful ones...like the oyster plant, which looks pretty, but we use its roots for a mock oyster soup." She spilled a single seed out into the palm of her small hand to show him. "Then of course, I brought some herbs. The specific ones you like I can give you as time goes along. I'm not sure of all of the medicinal uses as far as animals go."

"I'll find out... I've also enjoyed finding out how much a steward of the land you are, Miss King. You and your family, of course. And I respect what you say about the seeds. If you'll show me how to plant them correctly, I'll cherish them. You have my word."

"Thank you." She smiled.

Mrs. Bustle came into the room to clear the table, and Sarah rose as if to help.

"No, thank you, dear. You go on outside with the doctor and see what your brother's got dug."

Grant gestured toward the kitchen and Sarah went along, her dark shoes and dress seeming to match the timeless quality of the antique oriental runner Mr. Bustle had just laid that morning.

Sarah noticed that the kitchen was still in haphazard condition while Mrs. Bustle explained that she was still adjusting to the stove and relative lack of space. The back screen door was open, and Luke dug heartily. He'd paced off a fair rectangle of land with three neat paths and overturned the sod.

"So how do I go about planting the seeds?" Grant asked, as he and Sarah walked outside and surveyed the rich soil.

"Well…" Sarah knelt near the edge of the dirt and he did the same, making her pulse jump with his closeness. She opened her hand, which still held the oyster seed, and reached out to give it to him. The seed stuck to her hot palm and he clasped her hand until his warm fingers slid it free. She looked at the earth and tried hard to think of what Father had told her. He trusted her, but she was beginning to not trust herself when it came to this charming *Englischer*.

"You just stick the seed in a hole in the dirt and cover it," Luke interrupted in a laconic tone, leaning a boot on his shovel.

Sarah glared over at him, half-embarrassed. "There's more to it than that."

Luke shrugged and turned his back, going back to his digging. "Whatever."

"So what else is there?" the doctor asked with a faint smile.

Sarah slid her slender fingers through the rich earth, its coolness restoring her calm, until the doctor placed his hand over hers, following her movements in the ground.

"Like this?"

"*Jah*," she murmured.

He threaded his fingers through hers, and she could feel the weight of his large hand. "And then the seed?"

"Yes… Point down, if it has one."

"All right." He still held her hand in the cover of the dirt and used his other to push the seed into the small opening.

"And then we… You just cover it." She swallowed as she watched their twined fingers moving through the rich earth. She let her hand relax against the pressure of his own and felt her breath come out in a rush when the hole was filled and he still held her hand against the ground. She looked over at him and felt like she might drown in the intensity of his eyes. She dropped her gaze to his firm mouth and wet her lips.

"Water," she managed.

"Hmm?" His voice was a deep, timbered rumble.

"You need to wet the ground." Luke declared, pouring water from a tin watering can over the clasp of their hands. They both jumped, pulling apart.

"*Danki.*" Sarah looked up at her brother, who regarded her with a frown. She rose and the doctor did the same, clearing his throat.

"If you would allow me, Miss King, I'd consider it a privilege to see your own garden sometime."

She nodded and was about to speak when her brother James came around the back of the house.

"Dr. Williams, if you could come, please—the bishop's favorite cow is down; he'd appreciate you making a call."

Grant nodded, then turned to grin at Sarah. "My first house call here," he murmured. "Pray for me. I'll get my bag." He hurried off and she avoided looking at Luke, who'd come to stand beside her.

"You're playing dangerous games, Sarah," Luke announced, shouldering his shovel. And when she would have protested, he shook his head. "And no, I'm not telling Father and *Mamm*. I like the doctor too, but you—you'd better stick to a good Amish man." He started to walk away.

"Where are you going?" Sarah found her voice at last.

"To ride with the *Englischer* to the bishop's." He grinned back at her. "He'll need directions."

* * *

Pray for him. Pray for me, she thought. She could not be trusted, even though her parents had told her that they believed in her. And then Jacob's mocking words and Luke's warning... It was all too much. She was just being neighborly, she rationalized. Yet she found the doctor so unlike anyone she'd ever met in the community. Yes, he was worldly, with his electricity and casual talk, but he was also kind and sincere.

She rubbed her shoe in a patch of the earth and thought of how to pray for him. Then she began to walk around the perimeter of the unplanted garden, moving and praying at the same time. She asked for blessings on the doctor's home and on his work. And she prayed unbidden words from her soul that he would be healthy and happy, and greater still, accepted by the Amish community around him.

Chapter Six

When the red sports car swung onto the bishop's lane, Ezekiel Loftus, Grant was amazed to see more than a dozen buggies assembled outside the large farmhouse and barns.

"Church meeting?" he asked Luke.

"New vet."

"Ah."

He grabbed his bag and a box of generalized "downed cow" equipment and headed for the largest barn. It was stuffed to capacity with Amish folk, a few onlooker animals from side stalls, and one hapless ill cow, proclaimed as Tweet, lying bloated in despair in the middle of the barn floor.

Milk fever; stage three, Grant thought with a silent groan, and he had no idea of what steps had already been taken to "help" the cow. He'd discovered early in his studies that finding out what a client had already attempted was not always easy. He'd pried information out of self-prescribing, helpful owners that ranged from dandruff shampoo to garlic bologna and everything in between. He'd learned not to blink an eye. Most of the time, the cures were odd but harmless, and he usually was able to intercede in time, but this was different.

Luke had explained succinctly on the brief ride what the bishop meant to the community. "He's the head of everything, next to *Der Herr*, the Lord."

"Great."

"*Jah*, really great."

Really great, Grant thought as he faced the man who seemed half his size and three times his age. Here was a typical Amish farmer who surely must be close to ninety. His wizened countenance was not exactly dour but neither was it hopeful, and Grant extended a hand only to have it grasped by a firm grip and a welcoming smile of relief that threatened to split the wrinkled face in two.

"Dr. Williams, thank you for coming so quickly. Tweet here, well, she's my favorite…practically the mother of the herd…" The little man bobbed his head, and Grant saw tears sparkle in his coal-black eyes.

It was not the first time he'd seen a grown man cry over a cow. He recalled a Mr. Boon from vet training who'd proudly displayed a tattoo of his favorite cow on his rugged forearm and had wept openly when she had to be euthanized due to old age. He thought about sharing the tale but decided tattooing, cow or otherwise, was probably out of the realm of the bishop's appreciation. In any case, he now had the chance to help a true animal lover, something he enjoyed. It was also an opportunity to make or break his practice in the community, he thought. If the bishop's cow should meet with an unfortunate end, he could just picture the bleak, empty months of no calls and a failed try at a life's dream. But if the cow responded to the classic treatment for the ailment, it might mean a more ready acceptance. He clapped the bishop on the shoulder in an attitude of comfort.

"She'll be fine. Now what have you done so far to help her?"

The bishop pursed his lips and the gathered crowd rustled a bit. *Here we go,* Grant thought.

"I tried to watch her after she calved this last time."

"Calved? How old did you say she is?"

The old man's face held a deep fondness. "She's a little different than other cows, hasn't given out, hasn't given up—she's sixteen."

Grant nodded, feeling a sinking sensation in his chest. An older-than-old cow calving was a surefire prescription for milk fever and its often deadly results.

"Please go on."

"I doused her good with Epsom salts."

Grant smiled. Not a bad homeopathic cure; mixing the salts with water did produce an electrolyte rich solution, but it still lacked the necessary calcium.

"I used the tar oil."

The bishop lifted the cow's muzzle gently and Grant saw the familiar staining of "tar oil" around the cow's mouth. The Amish, he'd read, had a curious reliance on the black oil, some strange mixture of herbs and something like corn syrup, as a cure-all for both man and beast, but the stuff tasted so bad, neither would usually swallow it. He considered briefly, then asked to see the bottle.

"*Jah*." The bishop hurried through the crowd to a tool bench and came back with a clear, unlabeled bottle full of black syrup, which he handed over.

Grant popped the cork and sniffed at the contents. He'd learned during his training that tar oil was harmless, but he had never used it to treat an animal before. Curious about the herbal mixture, he wanted to experience it. So he took a brief swig and forced himself to swallow.

There was murmur from the crowd and an anxious gasp from the bishop.

"Are you feeling sick, Doctor?"

It was some moments before Grant could speak, so he nodded, then choked out a response. He'd surely heard the worst of it by now, but the bishop continued.

"And last, the raw onion in her ear." He indicated the right ear and Grant bent to stare at the offending vegetable, while trying to catch his breath. The bishop sniffed. "I know it's odd, but *Mamm* always said there's nothing like a raw onion." Grant nodded and pulled the onion out, finding his voice.

He handed the onion over. "Good work. Now I'll just finish up for you, if I may."

"*Jah*," the little man replied, visibly pleased with the commendation.

Grant slipped a looped rope from his box and gently put one loop around Tweet's neck and the other around her back foreleg. She rolled a miserable eye at him and he hummed soothingly as he worked. He drew up the solution of calcium, phosphorous, and dextrose into a giant syringe, then squirted a bit out, ignoring the grave silence of the crowd.

"That'll hurt her a bit." The bishop wrung his small, work-worn hands, eyeing the giant needle.

"Not much, I promise."

Grant knelt and found the vein in the damp neck of the animal, dispensing the liquid. Tweet began to shiver and shake, the muscles beneath her skin rippling with the influx of calcium. She began to drool and Grant continued to hum.

"She's looking a bit worse, *jah*?" The bishop had dropped beside him and fretted, close to tears again.

"This is normal," Grant soothed even as he prayed. *Dear Lord, let this old cow live.*

He finished the injection and waited. It normally took only seconds, but she wasn't getting to her feet. Instead, the giant eyeballs rolled backward in the sockets as she continued to shake. He felt the palpable dissension of the crowd at his back, but he had to wait.

"Looks like you've done more harm than good," a dry voice pronounced, and Grant looked up to see Jacob Wyse leaning against a support timber.

"We'll give her a few more minutes," Grant said levelly, while the bishop stroked the straining neck of the animal. Grant felt sweat dampen his brow, then a thought occurred to him and he rustled in his bag.

"One more injection," he murmured.

"More than likely to put her out of her misery," Jacob asserted, but Grant ignored him.

"It's magnesium," he said low to the bishop as he found the vein. "Sometimes it can really make a difference."

Grant sensed the almost immediate change in the animal's disposition when he'd emptied the syringe and slipped the rope off her neck and leg. He moved back a bit, motioning the bishop to do likewise. He waited, and suddenly Tweet made a scrambling attempt to rise, causing the bishop to jump to his feet and Grant to join him.

"*Kumme*, Tweet. *Kumme!*" the bishop encouraged.

Grant smiled and breathed another prayer, this time of thanks. The cow staggered to her feet and stared around at the onlookers, letting out a perplexed "Moo!"

The bishop shook Grant's hand, and the onlookers smiled with goodwill; he smiled back. Jacob Wyse seemed to have drifted out of sight. There was a sudden air of festivity as the members of the community shared in the joy of the bishop. The little man wrung Grant's hand again, as did many other of the men.

"Now, Doctor, please, name your fee," the bishop commanded jovially, but Grant shook his head.

"I've got more than enough worldly goods, sir. God

has blessed me financially from my father, all the way back to my great-grandfather, so I want to offer my services for free to the Amish hereabout; it's my offering to the Lord."

"Then we are doubly blessed," the bishop announced, sealing Grant's acceptance for the moment. "A new vet, and one who works for *Der Herr*!"

There was a murmur of approval from the crowd.

"Now," the bishop continued. "We will have something to eat, *jah*? And you will stay, Doctor, as my guest?"

"Oh, certainly."

"And then we'll play volleyball. Do you know how to play?"

Grant ignored the fact that he'd been captain of his team in college and nodded. The community was accepting him, and the feelings that engendered were too close to a heart sore for him to examine at the moment. He could only grin and be part of the crowd as they swarmed into the house for an early supper of cold ham, potato salad, apple butter, and fresh bread.

Afterward, he was amazed at the rousing game of volleyball that the men got going in their full dress and hats. He had to stretch his long arms many times to get the ball over the net as he also found them to be cunning with a light tip of the ball. He had more fun than he'd ever had in school, even though Jacob Wyse stared grimly at him through the barrier of the net. He didn't care at the moment; here was a group of men, some older than sixty, some as old as the bishop himself, who loved to play as well as work together, and he realized that it was all part of building a better and stronger community. He found himself grateful to be able to participate in a way of life that seemed to surpass any security he'd found in the world and knew that the Lord had led him here.

Sarah had heard from Luke when he came home to do chores that the bishop's cow had revived, and she was glad that the doctor would probably be absorbed into that house's Sunday afternoon doings. She wandered outdoors into the shade of the day and found her favorite place beneath the wild rosebush. It was only on Sunday late afternoons that she might have a bit of time to herself in daylight hours and she savored the opportunity now, listening to the far-off laughter of her brothers as they played kick the can in an adjacent field.

She stroked the delicate pink and white petals of the roses until a welter of blossoms fell down and about her, sticking to her *kapp*. She felt for each one to remove it and then settled back against the ground to stare up at the blue and white sky, tracing the outline of the mountains and finding shapes like a child in the clouds. She felt a restlessness that was unfamiliar, especially in the midst of her garden. She closed her eyes, then opened them when the sound of a car engine made her bolt upright. She adjusted her head covering and brushed at her apron and skirt. She wondered at the thrilling sensation that filled her chest, then drew a deep, steadying breath and made her way through the rows of vegetables to the entrance of the garden.

Dr. Williams had parked his automobile in front of the pump as *Mamm* came out to greet him. Sarah listened to his voice, half hiding herself among the cantaloupe vines that grew on a trellis near the open path.

"Will you have some lemonade, Doctor? I heard the good news about the bishop's cow," *Mamm* said politely.

"Actually, if you don't mind…I wanted to look at Miss Ki—Sarah's kitchen garden," Dr. Williams said. "She said I might get some ideas for my own garden."

Sarah wondered what *Mamm* would think about him asking for her.

"*Jah*, certainly. I'll call her. Sarah! Sarah." *Mamm*'s tone was level, and Sarah slunk out from her vines and walked the few steps needed for them to see her.

"*Ach*, there you are, child. *Kumme* and show Dr. Williams your garden to give him ideas for his own. I will ask Luke also to accompany you…in case he might offer any advice."

Sarah glanced at the doctor, wondering if he'd realize that they were being chaperoned, as *Mamm* hollered for Luke. The doctor wore an expression of good humor and was obviously about to speak when her brothers rallied from the field and tried to persuade him to come join their game.

He held up his hands in mock protest. "Maybe in a bit… I just finished volleyball at the bishop's."

They backed off, and *Mamm* stood with a faint frown on the porch. "Luke, go with the doctor and your sister to see her garden," she called.

"*Mamm*…" Luke began to protest.

"Please," *Mamm* said in a way that brooked no response, so Sarah had no choice but to extend her hand to the garden as Luke brought up the rear. "If you'd like to come this way, Doctor."

"Thank you, Miss King."

They entered the garden, and Luke shoved a way-ward vine out of his way. "I'm not babysitting the both of you," he whispered. "Sarah, just behave yourself. I'm going to the apple trees to have a nap, and don't bother telling *Mamm* either."

"I won't," Sarah snapped, mortified at her brother's words.

"I didn't think you would," Luke quipped and saun-tered off.

Sarah couldn't bring herself to look at the doctor until she heard his laugh.

"So are you in the habit of misbehaving with men in your garden, Miss King?"

She glared after her brother's retreating form. "I could wring his neck."

The doctor stepped closer. "You still haven't an-swered my question."

Sarah breathed in the delicious smell of him and sought for a clever answer while attempting to rein in her senses and her convictions. "I have never shown another man my garden, other than my father and brothers," she admitted.

"Then I'm the first? I'm honored." His voice deepened, and then he reached a long arm to lift something from her head.

"Have you been frolicking among the roses?" He held a pink petal in his open palm and she frowned.

"Of course, and I lie atop the potato hills too," Sarah quipped. Then realizing that she was bantering with the doctor— an *Englischer* she hardly knew—the way she did with her older brothers, she blushed.

"I see." He smiled and traced the petal down her warm cheek, then tapped her on the nose with it.

She looked away, feeling unstrung and breathless inside, but having no desire to reveal it.

"So what would you like to see first?"

"Back to safe footing, Miss King? Very well. Why have you got these cantaloupes all netted up like this?" She saw him slide the rose petal into the front pocket of his jeans as he studied the mosquito netting that supported each fruit up and along the vine.

"To prevent bottom rot. I do it too on some of my heavier tomatoes. Although you can still have bottom rot without the fruit touching the ground."

"You'll have to teach me what to look out for."

She nodded, then stepped deeper onto the path. "Over here are the salad greens— they're easy to reach and are closer to the porch for supper."

"Wait," he said. "Just...wait."

"What is it?"

He was staring out over the full stretch of the garden, his handsome face intent. He looked down at her. "You don't see it, do you?"

She looked back at the plants trying to place something out of order. "No…"

"It's beautiful," he explained. "Breathtaking, want to lie down here and die, beautiful. You've captured a patch of heaven in your hands."

Sarah was shocked. "Please…don't."

"Oh no, not this time. This time you're going to see something through the jaded eyes of the world, Miss King. This time you're going to know what you do in this space of dirt brings something to my heart and mind that I've been starving for." He lowered his voice. "But maybe I never knew I was hungry, until now."

Her heart thumped as her gaze dropped to his mouth, but then she pulled herself up short. "Would you like some fruit?" she asked coolly.

He lowered his heavy lids on the gleam of blue-gold and shook his head. "No, thank you."

She glanced out at the refuge of her garden, wondering how to proceed with the conversation when he laughed, breaking the moment. "Come on, show me your favorite plants, and please excuse me for being… sentimental."

"*Jah…*" She walked on, feeling both relieved and discontented somehow. She would have to go over the conversation in her mind later. "My favorite plants for this moment are the pumpkins."

"Great. I love pumpkins. Do the Amish celebrate Halloween?"

"*Ach*, no! It's an *Englisch* holiday and doesn't have the best meanings, *jah*? Do you…celebrate it?"

"Well, I have carved a pumpkin or two in my time, but it's not my favorite holiday."

"What is your favorite?"

"Christmas," he replied.

"*Jah*, me too."

"Ah, finally we agree."

"Do we…disagree a lot?" she asked.

She watched him kneel to feel one of the Long Island cheese pumpkins, running his hand over the rind that resembled a wheel of cheese. He looked over his shoulder at her.

"I'm *Englisch*, remember?"

She bit her lip. "Of course… I just meant… I…don't know what I meant."

"I can relate." He rose and stepped between the rows until he reached the white pumpkins. "What are these?"

She followed him. "The gooligan whites. We cut off the stem, scoop out the seeds, and add maple sugar, brown sugar, butter, and a sage leaf. They're very *gut*…good for eating."

He nodded and glanced out to where the largest pumpkins lay, growing shadowy in the oncoming of twilight. "What about those giants?"

She laughed. "This is the large Yellow of Paris pumpkin. It is the giant original from which all giant pumpkins have come. Sometimes it grows to over one hundred pounds."

"An heirloom seed?"

She shook her head. "From the seed catalog."

"Ah."

He turned and she followed his gaze, watching as the last of the sun's rays cast one stretching glance over the field, catching it and them between shadow and light, poised and motionless, until the orange light surrendered and sank behind the mountains.

"I'd better be going," the doctor sighed.

"Certainly," Sarah agreed, though she felt a little hurt without quite knowing why.

He moved close to her and bent over until she could see the golden gleam of his eyes in the dusky light. "Don't think that I want to go," he murmured.

"I don't think…"

"Neither do I; not around you… That's why I'm going. Thank you for sharing your paradise." He ran the back of one hand down the curve of her soft cheek, then dug his hands into the front pockets of his jeans.

"You're welcome," she said with sincerity. She watched as he walked away, his long shadow stretching back to touch her own. She listened for the turn of the engine of his automobile, then heard him pull away and down the drive, leaving her alone with a pounding heart, damp palms, and feelings of uncertainty. She drew a deep breath and marched off to the apple grove to wake her errant chaperone before *Mamm* came looking for them.

* * *

"Blamed fool!" Grant exclaimed to himself as he ground the gears of the car, fleeing the King farm like he was being pursued by a winged nightmare. He didn't know how or when or why, but he'd gotten his heart entangled with the pretty little vines of Sarah King, and he wasn't sure how it sat with him.

He recalled a girl he'd dated somewhat seriously during his first year of college. She'd seemed to take a special pride in being territorial with him, often hanging on his arm when other girls were around or taking time to tell everyone within earshot that he "belonged" to her. He hadn't liked it a bit, but he sure wished Miss King would exercise even a drop of that possession. Instead, she tended to avoid him, or when she did respond, she felt so guilty about it afterward that it made him feel guilty too. But, he reasoned, he had no right to be thinking these thoughts. She was Amish; he was an outsider to her no matter how much acceptance he might feel from the community. And he knew that they could never be together—an Amish woman who married outside her faith risked being shunned by the entire community. He sighed aloud at the thought.

He pulled into his own lane and decided that he was bone-tired. When he unlocked the door, the cat ran a ring around his legs, and he bent to pet it. Then he made his way upstairs to the room he'd chosen as his own.

He'd shied away from the master bedroom, finding it too large and oppressive, and had picked one of the smaller rooms that must have belonged to the brothers, because bunk beds were still in residence. His clothes were unpacked into a hand-hewn bureau, thanks to Mrs. Bustle, but there was no closet—something he'd noted in each of the bedrooms. He'd read that the Amish would hang their clothes on nails or hooks on the wall beside the bed. He found such a hook and hung up his shirt, then lay down in the bottom bunk.

He slept fitfully until he finally had a dream, but it was troublesome, and he tossed against the images in his mind. Sarah King was at the roadside stand, but she was wearing *Englisch* clothes, a denim skirt and a blouse. Her hair blew in long, loose tendrils, and he felt like he could touch one stray curl if he could just reach it; but he couldn't make it up the steps. His legs kept collapsing beneath him, again and again, until she turned away. He knelt on the steps as she leapt down from the side of the stand and began to walk away. He called out her name in desperation, but she did not turn.

He woke to find his hair damp with sweat and his body shivering in the bunk; he half rose on one elbow to gasp into the dark. When he realized it was nothing but a dream, he kept his eyes open, staring upward at the wooden bed slats above him, until dawn began to break through his window and he rose to greet the day.

Chapter Seven

Sarah knew her community had an incredible "grapevine," as the *Englisch* would say, and news traveled fast, though there were no phones but the emergency ones in the shanty sheds in the middle of fields. Within several weeks of saving the bishop's cow, she was hearing Dr. Williams's name mentioned at hymn sings, sewing circles, and picnics, and it was all in good favor, which gave her a curious warmth in her heart.

They'd finished his own garden the Sunday afternoon before, with both Luke and Samuel in attendance to help lay the plants. *Mamm* had come along to visit Mrs. Bustle and to show her how to make friendship bread, while Father had stayed home to read his Bible.

Sarah had sketched out a map on a brown bag and then presented it. "Here's a simple map of an Amish kitchen garden."

"Is it like yours?" Grant asked, glancing at her from gold-flecked eyes.

"*Jah*… I mean…well…it's rather close."

"Miss King," he chided.

"My garden has had more time to build. Yours will be lovely, I'm sure."

He caught her hand. "Your garden has the special touch of the hummingbird, and that cannot be duplicated." He gently rubbed the calluses on her palm, then laughed when she pulled away. Luke and Samuel seemed not to have noticed as they trotted the seedlings Sarah had assembled from the wagon to the plot. "And I'm going to need a greenhouse put up to get any progress out of these plants once the fall sets in; that's something you've probably never used," the doctor observed.

"No," she admitted. "I like the changing of the seasons in the garden."

He took the proffered map and studied the neat drawing. Each part of the garden was labeled with a letter that corresponded to a legend of plants written below. He was amazed at the foresight and variety of what she intended and handed the map back.

"Miss King, please, I defer to your expertise. Would you conduct the layout?"

"*Ach, jah*…thank you." She appeared delighted and he felt an odd thrill in his chest, like the exhilaration that came when he was able to counter an animal's hurt with his medicine and God's help. He knew from their brief discussion on her inability to quilt well that she probably used her garden as the sole outlet for her sense of creativity among purposeful work, and he was glad to give her the opportunity to shine.

He watched as she stood poised on the edge of the plot. Luke rolled his eyes, then sighed.

"*Ach*, go ahead, Sarah…we're ready."

She clasped her hands in front of her, crumpling the map as if she didn't need it, and her cheeks took on the bloom of a new rose. Grant smiled to himself, thinking that she truly did resemble a conductor, preparing to bring great music to an appreciative audience.

"*Jah*, but first the trellises; we need three. You forgot."

Samuel said nothing but headed back to the wagon.

"Please, Miss King…you're going to have to let me pay for all of this," Grant exclaimed.

"*Nee*, you're our neighbor. This is a pleasure for us, *jah*, Luke?"

"*Jah*," came the dry response.

Grant hid another smile as Samuel returned, carrying three cross-worked, wooden trellis pieces that he and Luke proceeded to bury without fuss across the back width of the plot.

"Now, we'll start," Sarah said. "In the back far left of the plot, on either side of two of the trellises, we'll put the Amish canning and paste tomatoes." She looked at Grant. "The paste tomatoes look like teardrops when they come and are meaty with flavor. The others grow fruits that are almost all similar in size… They're good for canning in the fall." She skipped along after her brothers and Grant followed, watching as she double-checked the placement of each plant, her small hands capable and steady in the soil. Then she stood by the nearest trellis and shook it slightly, testing its firmness.

Luke sighed aloud.

"Next, the Amish snap peas need to go on the trellises. They'll give peas for more than six weeks, if you pick them regularly."

"I'll be sure to tell the Bustles—or maybe I'll do some picking myself," Grant acknowledged.

She glanced at him doubtfully, and he tried to look capable in return.

Luke and Samuel set each one of the pea plants while Sarah coaxed the leader tendrils of vine onto the lowest levels of the trellis. She was humming and Grant watched the tenderness with which she placed each baby green curl. He understood that what she was doing was planting with love, and he thought that it was something he could watch forever.

She moved to the third trellis. "On either side here, the Brandywine tomatoes. These are spicy, and one tomato can grow as large as to weigh one pound."

"Or less, with worm rot," Luke offered and Grant watched Sarah dart him a daggered look. For all their wonderful simplicity, even the Amish crossed cultural lines in their dynamics between siblings, and it provided fun observation.

Sarah stepped back to the front of the first trellis. "Now, the Amish ghost tomatoes…these come out all white but sweet, and we also need the vernandon bush beans. These must have room but are worth it. They are like slivers of green richness in a salad."

Grant felt his stomach as well as his mind become engaged in the activity as Sarah moved between the second and third trellis. In truth, she was like a darting hummingbird, her green-brown eyes sparkling, stray tendrils of gold escaping from her head covering, and her hands moving in quick time to match her directions.

"*Ach*...now one of my favorites—the white wonder cucumber."

"Not green?" Grant asked. "I've never seen any but green."

"Perhaps there is much that you have not seen," she shot at him sassily, and he laughed aloud in surprise. "*Nee*, but they are white-skinned, and they grow best when the weather is the hottest. We make fancy pickles out of them."

She paused in the middle of the plot, wiping her hands on her clean apron, careless of the dirt. Samuel and Luke waited as she considered the next planting. And then she was moving again.

"I think we'll do a miniature white cucumber here, in front of the bush beans." She leaned down to pat the soil.

"Two types of cucumbers?" Grant asked with a smile.

"The miniature ones grow only as long as three inches, and you don't need to peel them. They can simply be washed, cut, and put directly into your salad."

Grant realized that the days of Mrs. Bustle's elaborate roast beef meals would probably go by the wayside in the face of all of the kitchen produce Miss King was planning. He patted his already lean stomach and wondered if he could grow used to salad for breakfast.

Sarah was pacing along, pointing out two areas about five feet apart. "You will need some peppers, Doctor, for seasoning and spices... We'll put the Alma paprika pepper here and the Beaver Dam pepper over here."

"Beaver Dam?"

She laughed, the sound spinning into his chest as he watched her face turn upward to the sun.

"I don't know why it's called Beaver Dam... I know it is Hungarian, and we slice it and eat it raw in sandwiches with cheese. It's not too hot—do you like hot?"

"Hot is good with me."

"*Gut*—good..."

"Sarah." Luke's tone was impatient.

Sarah rolled her eyes at the doctor. "My *bruder*... the only Amish man who is in a hurry."

"Maybe he's got a date," Grant suggested. "Or a girlfriend."

She laughed and so did Luke and Samuel. "*Nee*, he hurries too much to even have an *aldi*...a girlfriend."

Grant laughed with them and felt like he belonged; it felt good.

Sarah was at the plants again. "The lavender-rose eggplant here and the purple dragon carrot over there."

Grant shook his head at the outlandish names and wondered what Mrs. Bustle would do with purple carrots.

"Back to the herbs," Sarah instructed. "Luke, will you and Samuel go get that last lot from the wagon?"

Her brothers walked off but not before Sarah saw them exchange glances. Dismissing it, she continued her stroll. "We need some chamomile for the stomach and to sleep, the basil for soup, and lavender to soothe and relax, and just to be pretty. Do you know lavender?"

Grant nodded, thinking of laundry detergent. She must have noticed his look because she danced close with a delicate strand of purple and held it up to his nose. He smelled the plant, but he also smelled her, a sweet, soft scent like mint and something long-forgotten from his mother and childhood. He pretended to study the lavender while enjoying her closeness and took the plant piece when she turned, easing it into the front pocket of his jeans just as Luke and Samuel came back.

"We're nearly done for now," Sarah encouraged. "We'll have the spinach and the hailstone radish… These really do look like small pieces of hail."

"I've never seen actual hail," Grant stated.

Samuel laughed. "Isn't there any hail in Philadelphia?"

"Not that I've seen." He paused, then amended himself. "Not that I've noticed."

It was true; he'd spent the last years of his life so buried in books or animal anatomy that he probably couldn't even tell what day it was, let alone what season. But here was a group of people dependent on the seasons, the mercurial weather, and dealing with the threat of things like hail that could hamper their financial existence. It was all the more reason to have a faith in God's presence as they did, and it made him respect their culture even more.

"Well, you'll notice hail here," Luke broke into his thoughts. "Bet you'll get to be delivering cows in it too." Again the mutual laughter, the gentle teasing. Grant felt something shift inside of him, and his throat worked against a rush of emotion.

"What next?" he asked.

"Only three more things for now," Sarah stated, a small dirt-stained finger pressed against her lips as she thought. "The lettuces, onions, and garlic." The brothers produced the plants, and Sarah gave a final pat to the earth. Then they all four stood back to consider.

"There," Sarah announced, her hands clasped once more before her.

For Grant, it was as if the climax to some great symphony had just concluded. He saw the garden, not in its tender beginnings, but in the full-blown profusion to come. There was a balance, a purpose, and a function for each plant, but there was also a threading of beauty running through each row. He had the strange thought that Sarah's garden, for he could not think of it as his own, was a living quilt with each plant a square and each leaf a stitch.

"It's like a quilt," Sarah proclaimed, startling him with the similarity of their thoughts.

"I was just thinking that."

Samuel and Luke had gathered their few tools and headed back around the side of the house while he called his thanks. He was left alone with her, and the garden, and their shared thoughts. She must have become aware of the gentle quiet, because she self-consciously began to tuck her hair back.

"Please don't."

"It's vain to have my hair show."

"No, it's beautiful…just like what you've done here. How can I ever thank you?"

She shrugged. "They're simple plants."

He stepped nearer until he could see the threads of gold that shot through a single tendril of her light brown hair in the sunlight.

"I don't mean the plants, I mean watching you do this for me. It was a gift."

She bent her head and he caught up one of her dirt-stained hands into his own. She allowed it, causing him to catch his breath.

"Sarah," he whispered, raising her hand to his lips. He unfolded the fingers of her hand, like the petals of a new flower, and pressed his mouth into her palm, closing his eyes. He expected her to pull away and was trying to savor as much as he could of the taste of earth and warmth and something distinctly woman. But she didn't struggle, and he lifted his head and opened his eyes to stare down at her.

She was looking up at him, mesmerized, and he watched awareness swamp back into her eyes as she pulled at his grip. He let her go and she turned, hugging her arms about herself, her head down.

"Sarah…Miss King, I meant no disrespect. I just wanted to say thank you. I know it's not proper in your world…" He floundered and had to clench his hands into fists to keep from touching her again.

"Not proper," she repeated in a choked whisper. "What is proper?"

"What do you mean?"

"A kiss is proper in its time."

He shook his head, feeling out of his depth.

"Talk to me, Sarah—please. Tell me the truth of what you're saying."

She turned back to face him, and he was troubled to see tears damp on her cheeks.

"Oh, Sarah, please don't cry. I promise I'll never do anything that makes you uncomfortable again."

She lifted her eyes to his own. "I'm telling the truth, Doctor. It was not uncomfortable or unpleasant. It was too pleasant. I—I've never had anyone kiss me but my family before."

"Oh. Not even growing up? A boyfriend, perhaps?"

She smiled without mirth. "You mean Jacob Wyse, don't you? No, not even him as a friend."

Her words shook him as vapid images of his own

life rose up to confront him, casual kisses with girls through high school, a parade of steady girlfriends through college who would have been all too glad to do much more than kiss. Girls dressed in short dresses and shorter skirts. Easy hugging and hand-holding, touches that meant nothing and more than nothing when he thought of his moments with this simple Amish girl. He swallowed hard.

"Then you've given me two gifts today—the garden and the kiss."

"You think I'm strange," she said resignedly.

He didn't touch her; he couldn't. He used his voice instead. "Sarah...I think myself strange. The world's never made so much sense as when I see it with you."

She nodded. "It's our way to 'be in the world, but not of the world.' If I am showing you the world so that it makes sense, then I am failing *Der Herr*...my faith."

"I'm not explaining myself right. And I'm not back-pedaling or trying to fool you about what I mean. I mean that I have clarity, a clearness when I'm with you that I don't have at other times." He rubbed his shoe in the dirt. "I remember when I was ten, right after my parents died, I went to a frozen lake near where I lived. The ice was thin on the shoreline, so I broke off a big piece and put it in front of my face. I could still see the lake, but everything was blurry and far off. I felt safe behind that ice. In a lot of ways, I've lived like I still had that ice in front of me—a shield, a protection…but with you—you make me put the ice down; you melt it. And I'm alive again."

She shook her head. "It's the Lord; He's doing this for you. Not me."

"It is God through you, Sarah King, working through you because you permit it. Thank you."

She studied him, visibly weighing his words. Finally, she quietly said, "*Gern gschehne*—you're welcome."

The bang of the screen door caused them both to start as Mrs. King came down the back porch steps with a faint frown.

"Sarah, are you finished?"

"*Jah, Mamm.* I'm done." She did not meet his intense look. "For now."

She watched the doctor go around the back of the house after he mentioned going on a promised call, until she realized that *Mamm* had spoken to her.

"I'm sorry, *Mamm*—what is it?"

"I just hope that you are using wisdom in your doings with the doctor, Sarah. Don't forget what Father told you."

"I know, *Mamm*," Sarah spoke, hoping her eyes would not betray her thoughts, then immediately regretting the deception. "What did you want me for?"

Mamm frowned but went on. "I asked Mrs. Bustle if she might need some help dusting and cleaning, and she said that she'd be grateful. Are you willing to help?"

"*Ach, jah*, certainly."

"I'll get the boys to muck out the barns. I don't know what was in Mr. Fisher's head, but it had little to do with his farm."

Sarah said nothing, thinking of the anger in Matthew Fisher's eyes at the stand.

Mamm patted her arm. "Come along, child. I didn't mean to make you think of unhappy things. Let's just help Mrs. Bustle."

Sarah nodded and followed *Mamm* indoors. Parts of the house were indeed still in a muddle. Sarah got a brown bag and began to gather newspapers from the floor of a still-cluttered room off the kitchen. The various ads for clothing or fast food stared up at her, and she tried not to look too hard as she rolled the papers to be burned later. There was no doubt that working at the stand had made her more observant of the *Englisch* ways of dress and their mannerisms, and sometimes she found a particular pair of shoes or a blouse that a woman customer was wearing to be very attractive. And very worldly, she reminded herself.

She thought it odd that the Fishers took in such papers, for normally the *Budget* was the only major newspaper read in nearly all Amish communities. Still, there must have been a reason. She went into the kitchen, found a dry rag, and set to dusting the hardwood furniture that the Fishers had left behind, all the while feeling a tingling burn in the palm where the doctor had kissed her hand. Her hands had been dirty, but he'd kissed her as though the earth was part of her, and somehow, she took this as a sincere compliment. It was not one of words but one that acknowledged in some way her oneness with the land, the gift of the Lord. And she felt that it was the closest she had ever let anyone come to seeing her true heart, the one that loved the growing things yet worshipped the Creator of them all.

Her thoughts were interrupted by Mrs. Bustle's loud cry. Both *Mamm* and Sarah ran into the kitchen to find the elderly woman perched atop the kitchen table.

"Another rat?" *Mamm* asked.

"No...it's the cat," she stammered. "It's got something there that's...not quite dead!" She shrieked once more, then pressed her hands to her quivering lips.

Sarah went over to the cat and bent down. "I don't think he means to hurt it; I think he's bringing it to us." She opened the cat's mouth and took out the squeaking item. "*Ach, Mamm*, look—it's a baby bat."

Mrs. Bustle moved as if to faint and Mrs. King caught her, hastily spritzing her face with the water bottle she'd been using to clean with. Mrs. Bustle came to immediately.

"Oh, Mrs. King, I'm sorry, but a bat!"

"It's just a baby one," Sarah said, cradling it in her hands. "You must have a colony living in your attic."

"What?! Bustle! Mr. Bustle!" Mrs. Bustle let out a delicate roar, and *Mamm* and Sarah looked at each other in fascination.

Mr. Bustle hurried into the kitchen. "What is it, my dear?"

She pointed a shaking finger. "Do you know anything about a bat living in this house?"

Mr. Bustle had the grace to flush. "Not a single one, no."

"A colony, then? In the attic?"

Sarah had to hide a smile at the interchange between the couple. Mr. Bustle was doing his best to appear calm in the face of his wife's near hysteria.

"Maybe a bit of a colony…ahem, not a colony, a group rather…"

"A group of bats in our attic? And you've known about this for how long?"

"Ah, well, that's difficult to say…"

They bantered on while *Mamm* went back to dusting and Sarah found a warm rag to wrap the baby bat in. She found it amazing how the *Englisch* displayed their emotions in front of others. She couldn't recall *Mamm* and Father ever having such a loud discussion in front of neighbors. She slipped out of the kitchen and found her way upstairs to the attic, taking the gray little mite with her. She entered the darkness without preamble or any thought of turning on the light and gently reattached the baby to the wall near some sleeping adults. She was back downstairs within minutes.

"What did you do with it?" Mrs. Bustle asked, still quivering on the tabletop.

"I put it back with the others; it'll be fine."

Mrs. Bustle rolled her eyes, but Mr. Bustle regarded Sarah with a respect that she found hard to fathom but appreciated nonetheless.

Chapter Eight

Sarah squinted against the sun as she tried to concentrate on her stitches for Chelsea's baby quilt. She'd come to more greatly realize and appreciate beautiful things, like quilts, among the plainness of her culture. And now, although she still struggled with her precision, the quilt's small details seemed intensified against the vivid darkness of her skirt. Just like life, she considered, or a flower bloom against the dirt. Quilting was becoming an art for her, one that touched her soul in a place that only growing things had up until now.

She had just bundled her work away and sold her last half-moon pie when she saw the doctor walk down the high road and cut across to the stand. He was visibly upset about something, and she clasped her hands in her lap as she sat back down in her chair, waiting for him to speak. She didn't have to wait long.

"Tell me, Miss King, are you familiar with a place called Becker's Beasts and Birds?"

Sarah thought for a moment. "*Jah*, about eight miles away up the road, on the left."

"Have you been there?"

"No—it's a tourist attraction for the *Englisch*, I believe."

He dropped angrily down on the top step of the stand. "That's right and *Englisch* owned. It's a pigsty."

"I thought it had all different kinds of animals."

Dr. Williams tilted his head back to look at her and rolled his blue eyes. "A figurative pigsty."

"*Ach.*"

"Yes—*ach*. They've got a sun bear in there. Do you know what that is?"

Sarah shook her head and he glanced back to the high road.

"It's a very rare and beautiful animal. I did a project on them in high school. It's the smallest of the bear family…reaches only four feet in height. It's got sleek brown or black fur and it comes from Malaysia, but the coolest thing about it is this horseshoe-shaped marking around its neck, muzzle, and eyes; it looks like it's been touched by the sun with bright yellow or sometimes tan markings. It eats honey…doesn't hurt anyone…" His voice lowered. "Come to think of it, that report…the sun bear is probably why I decided to become a veterinarian. To find out about the strange and wonderful creatures God made."

She waited, pleased that he would share such an intimate part of his life with her.

"Anyway…Becker's sun bear hasn't seen the sun,

which it needs, for years. It's living in its own filth, in a cage it can't stand upright in. I just...I just was so angry with those people, I walked out. I should have tried to buy the thing, but I wanted to grab Becker's neck even more."

"Father has great trouble himself when he hears of an Amish man who doesn't treat his horses right," Sarah said.

"Yeah...I guess it's all over...*Englisch,* Amish, whatever."

"So what will you do about this sun bear?"

He swiveled to look at her. "What?"

"Are you going to pray about it? I'll pray with you."

"No, I'm not going to pray about it... I'm angry!"

"That's why you should pray."

He frowned at her, but she held his eyes steadily.

"Don't tell me, Miss King, that you never get angry, and don't you dare cite 'righteous indignation' to me. Don't tell me you don't have moments when you'd just like to grab ahold of someone and rattle them until..."

"I'm having one now," she replied sweetly.

He stared at her, then burst into laughter, shaking his head. "You never cease to amaze me."

She bent her head at the compliment and he rose to walk near her chair. "I can't ruffle your feathers with all of my fool blustering, and all you need to do is give a gentle word and you turn me inside out. Why is that?" He reached one long finger down to trace the warm curve of her cheek, and she resisted the urge to turn her face into his hand.

"Are you asking me or yourself?" she said instead, allowing him to lift her chin until she met his gaze.

"I don't think I know," he said hoarsely. Gone was the anger in his eyes, but the intensity was still there, blue-gold and blazing. She bit her soft bottom lip.

"You have the sun in your eyes, Dr. Williams."

"Do I, Miss King?" He bent his long back and lowered his head until his face was bare inches from her own. "You have the earth in yours."

She watched his heavy lashes drift downward as he moved closer still. She forgot to breathe for a moment, then jumped when the blaring of a horn from a passing car broke the moment. Teenagers shrilled and whistled and the doctor straightened, walking to the top step of the stand, his back to her.

Sarah tried to get her heart to settle and realized where she was—in broad daylight, nearly kissing an *Englischer*. Why, anyone could have gone past! She rose anxiously to adjust some jars of jam.

"I think I'll walk on a bit and talk to your father about Becker's. He…ah…might have some more answers for me."

"Yes, of course." She didn't turn and let out a deep, tense breath when she heard his footsteps go down the stairs and head out onto the rocky lane that led to the farm. It seemed that no matter what her intentions were when she met with the doctor, she always ended up weakening her resolve within minutes of being in his company. She blindly turned the jam jars once more and was relieved when the brisk trotting of a horse warned her that a customer was coming. Mrs. Loder turned in to the stand, and Sarah drew a breath and prepared to greet her neighbor.

Grant could see Luke King as he knocked on the clear glass of his front door. The younger man was becoming more and more of a fixture at Grant's home and had a keen and natural knack for understanding animals and their care. Indeed, it was through Luke that Grant found most of his calls, and the Amish community was becoming receptive to seeing the *Englischer* and the young Amish man come riding across the fields together in the red sports car. The *Ordnung*, or the unspoken rules that governed the community as determined by the local bishop, allowed for an Amish person to ride in a car if invited, so long as it was for a good purpose and destination and not for pleasure. An Amish youth or adult may not own an automobile; however, Grant could tell by the way Luke's eyes would stray to the dashboard and all of its finer points that the rides were a treat for him, albeit a cautious one.

Grant opened the door, expecting a routine call. Instead, Luke removed his straw hat and twisted it between his hands.

"What's wrong?"

"I hear tell that the only beast Mr. Becker is missing from his business is a woodchuck. I might know where there is one."

Grant frowned, knowing his friend was saying

something important but not quite sure what. Miss King must have told her brother about the sun bear, but what was this about a woodchuck?

"Will you come in?"

"*Nee*… But you could come out a bit."

"All right." Grant stepped out onto the porch. He was amazed to see the other two King brothers and their father standing on his front lawn. They all looked solemn, and Grant had a sudden image of himself bending to steal a kiss from Miss King. Was there to be some old-fashioned retribution from her family? He felt his neck grow cold at the thought. Then he noticed the large wooden crate with air holes drilled in it in the back of the family's wagon, and his imagination ran wild.

"Gentlemen, from what I can gather…you have a… woodchuck in that crate?"

Mr. King shook his head and stroked his gray beard in apparent thought. "*Nee*, the crate is empty, for now." They laughed among themselves, and Grant straightened his spine.

"Well, what can I do to help you? I'm afraid I don't understand."

Luke spoke from beside him, slowly, as if to a child. "It seems that the only beast Mr. Becker, from Becker's Beasts and Birds, is missing, is a woodchuck. We might know where to find one."

"Am I…the woodchuck?" Grant whispered back, and all the men burst into hearty laughter.

Mr. King took a step up and poised below Grant.

"No, son, you're not a woodchuck; you're a man. Didn't anyone teach you this when you were studying veterinary science?"

Again the laughter, and Grant started to lose his temper, feeling like a fool.

"Look, I don't understand... I think I'll go back in to my dinner."

"*Ach*, don't lose your spirit now. We're just fooling with you. The truth is that Mr. Becker has been a sore on our community's back, but it's not our way to fight against his kind of mean-spiritedness. But I had a visit with our schoolteacher, Miss Lapp, and she explained that a sun bear might do well in a climate like Hawaii. Is that so?"

Grant stared at him. "Yes... Hawaii's climate is similar to Malaysia."

"*Gut.* And do you think there also might be zoos or other places that would take in a creature like a sun bear...or a woodchuck...if one were to appear on its doorstep?"

"I suppose. It is possible to airmail animals, but the rates are astronomical. What woodchuck?"

Mr. King smiled. "If you haven't seen yet, Doctor, the women are gathered over across the way. They have it in mind to have a paint *vrolijk* this evening in your kitchen, with your permission, of course."

Grant now noticed the group of capped women standing in the distance of the drive, with Miss King at the forefront of the group.

"A paint...frolic?"

"A frolic, a party or time of work and enjoyment. Would the Bustles mind, do you think?"

"Ah, no…Mr. Bustle's rented a car and they've gone for the weekend back to Philadelphia to visit family."

"Do you mind, Doctor?"

"No…I don't mind."

Mr. King clapped his hands with a smile and waved over to the women. "We're going!" he called.

Grant saw the women start to move forward in a merry group, and Luke gestured for him to come along to the wagon.

"We're going? Where are we going?"

"To swap the woodchuck, just like you said, Doctor," Mr. King exclaimed. "Surely you remember suggesting it?"

"I don't…well…I don't really get it." He paused as Miss King and a horde of Amish women and girls passed by and started up the steps to his house. He met Sarah's gaze for a moment, heard stray giggles, and still wondered if he were off to some Amish festooning of would-be kissers at the hour of sunset.

He found himself in the back of the wagon sitting with the brothers and the large crate between them. He realized upon closer inspection that the crate had a This Side Up stamp and was air-postage prepaid with an address of Hawaii Zoo on its label. The weight was 190 pounds. A little less than him, some more than a sun bear. He met Luke's gaze across the crate, and an idea began to stir in his head.

Across the secret furrows among the corn and

wheat, they plowed on toward Becker's, stirring up crickets and the earliest twinkling of lightning bugs. And in the quiet interior of the wagon, Grant compared his short-sleeved light blue polo and jeans to the dark pants, blue and aqua shirts, and suspenders of his fellow passengers and felt like he'd fallen out of step with a time that was more dependable than his own. The King men were silent for the most part, eyes steady, only occasionally making a comment here and there to each other in rumbling Pennsylvania Dutch about the height of the field or the stray passing of a bird.

Grant decided to regain some of his footing. He knew the strict beliefs of the Amish to abstain from violence at any cost, but he couldn't help feeling like he'd been railroaded into something, and he figured he knew how to play cat and mouse as well as the next man.

"So are you going to shoot Becker?"

Mr. King gave a gratifying jerk to the reins and three pairs of eyes met his own with mixed shock and bewilderment.

"You know, maybe just in the leg, truss him up, put him in the crate, mail him to..." He peered closer at the label on the wooden box, fingering an air hole. "The Hawaii Zoo?"

Mr. King glanced back over his shoulder and his eyes met the doctor's with a faint twinkle. "Was it not just awhile ago, Doctor, that you thought it might be you going in that crate?"

Grant shrugged. "Never can tell. One full crate's as good as another."

Mr. King slapped the reins. "Boys...the good doctor can give as well as he can get. You'd better be warned."

Grant grinned at Luke, who frowned back, then ignored the gazes of the others as he pretended to study a passing hawk beginning a last nightly round.

In truth, he had no idea about how things would play out at Becker's, but that just made life more interesting. He closed his eyes, letting the bump of the wagon lull him, and smiled as he thought about Miss King frolicking with paint in his kitchen.

"What color have you chosen, Sarah?" one of *Mamm*'s friends asked as the women trooped into the doctor's kitchen. Since Sarah had organized the paint *vrolijk*, the women allowed her the privilege of choosing the color.

Sarah glanced around the kitchen. Mrs. Bustle had visibly done her very best to clean, but the dilapidated stove and the faded wallpaper drew all the heart from the room.

"Light blue," Sarah replied, ignoring the desire to say that it matched the doctor's eyes.

"Light blue?" Mrs. Loder questioned. "Are the *Englisch* used to a blue kitchen? I thought they might favor yellow or something else."

"*Ach*, I'm sure it will be fine," *Mamm* interjected,

rolling up her sleeves. "We'd better get started, though; I don't expect it'll take long up at Becker's."

The women laughed, sharing the joke, and then each began to work in earnest. Sarah smiled as she pulled down strips of flowered wallpaper; it was called a frolic for more than one reason. It was a grand opportunity to get together to help a neighbor, but it was also a time to joke and laugh together, to update one another on happenings at home, and to generally be merry as they worked.

They soon had the wallpaper down and bundled away and then set to cleaning the walls. Mrs. Loder, *Mamm*, and Sarah slid the heavy refrigerator, the only gleaming new piece of furniture in the room, out from the wall, being careful not to dislodge the electric plug from the outlet.

"There are hardwoods under this old linoleum. Wide fir, I believe," Sarah said, bending over the cord in order to see where there was a gap between the wall base and the floor.

"Hmm… I wonder why the Fishers never uncovered them?" the bishop's wife asked. "Maybe the wood's warped."

"We could find out," Sarah announced and then glanced around at the group. "If—if you'd like."

Mamm laughed. "'*Es fenschder muss mer nass mache fer es sauwer mache*'—One has to wet the window in order to clean it."

The others agreed and helped heave the refrigerator and stove up by inches so that Sarah could slide

out the old linoleum. A wide fir floor was indeed revealed, scratched but in hearty condition.

Sarah clasped her hands in glee and then complimented the women who already had one of the walls
painted. The light blue was very Amish looking, but
it brought serenity to the center of the house that she
hoped Mrs. Bustle would like, as well as the doctor.
Although, she worried, perhaps the *Englisch* did not
consider the kitchen to be the heart of the home. She
shrugged off her concerns and scrambled up a footstool to reach the white trim around the top of the
walls. With a steady and artistic hand, she had a fresh
coat on two walls within minutes. Then she skipped
down to pass around cups of lemonade that *Mamm*
had brought, and they all paused to savor the delicious
sour-sweetness and to admire each other's handiwork.

"Looks good so far," Mrs. Loder remarked.

"*Jah,*" Sarah agreed, glad that she'd been able to
persuade *Mamm* to organize the frolic despite her res-
ervations. "I just hope the doctor will *kumme* home
happy."

Mamm gave her a sharp look. "If we want him to
come home happy, we'd best get back to work. There's
still a lot to do," she chided. "We must do a *gut* job.
'Whatever you do, do as for *Der Herr.*'"

The doctor was, in actuality, having rather a rough
go of it. He'd found himself standing outside the ramshackle attraction of Becker's Beasts and Birds, facing

an irate Mr. Becker, with no true idea of what to say beyond a few awkward words.

The King men stood behind him in a quiet semicircle, seeming to blend in with the stillness of the land and the evening. Grant was back to feeling the fool and tried once more to speak to Mr. Becker.

"I'm here for the sun bear. I'm—we're taking it out of here."

Mr. Becker laughed. "You are, are you? Well, don't expect those dolts behind you to help any. They don't go in for fighting, and that leaves just me and you, Son. And I'd say that those woman's hands of yours are in for some trouble."

Grant didn't mind the personal slur, but the prejudicial ugliness of "dolts" was enough to get his back up on behalf of the Amish men.

He glanced over his shoulder at Mr. King, who still had a twinkle in his eye, and then looked back to Becker. Something clicked in his brain and he found himself repeating what Luke had first said to him back on his own porch.

"Mr. Becker, it appears that the only animal you've got missing from your collection is a woodchuck, and we're here to tell you that we might know where to find one."

If Grant had hit the man with a full uppercut, he couldn't have looked more suddenly dazed by the strange words. It was as if Becker was a balloon that had just lost all its air. He went from angry to visibly anxious in a matter of seconds. Grant was fascinated.

Clearly, Becker believed some mysterious folklore about a woodchuck. At the moment, Grant didn't care. He just knew that he was within hand's reach of a suffering sun bear.

"Hey…hey, I don't want no woodchuck. There's no trouble here," Becker was mumbling. "I'll sell the bear, if you're interested."

Grant decided to test the power of superstition against cold cash.

"No paying for anything," he ordered in a deep voice. "It's the bear at no cost, or—it's the woodchuck."

"All right. All right." Becker frowned. "The bear's been a mite sickly, and I'd be glad to make room for a monkey I've got my eye on. Just come on in and wrestle the bear out. I'll help." He was unlocking the double barn doors as he spoke and then pushed them wide open. The stench of wildlife and its droppings came clear and fetid to the senses on the evening air, and Grant felt renewed pity for the caged animals imprisoned inside.

The sun bear was lying disconsolately on its side, its hair matted, its eyes blank and listless. Grant paused a moment.

"I'd like to line the wooden crate with some clean straw and set up a water bowl and some food… I'm not sure how it'll take the flight." He spoke in a low undertone to Mr. King.

"Already done. And our postmistress is Amish. She

booked it overnight express…so not too long in the crate."

Becker was looking for the key to the rusted lock, and the sun bear began to stir, sensing something was up.

"You should have told me to bring my bag… I could have given it a mild sedative," Grant whispered to Luke.

"Got all the sedatives you need right here," Becker commented, indicating a dusty table piled with junk and dirty syringes. "Valium, Ativan… They all work the same on people and animals."

Grant snorted in disgust. "Never mind, we'll move her as is. She shouldn't put up too much of a fight as weak as she probably is."

Becker swung the door open, and the sun bear took one lunging jump straight at Grant's chest. He fell backward, covering his face against the potential for scratching, but the bear lumbered off of him and sniffed around the ground, staggering to stay on its shaky feet.

"She's cage lame," Grant growled, rising to tower over Becker. The man held his hands up in supplication.

"I told you; I don't want no trouble. Just herd her out to the crate."

The King brothers had lowered the crate out of the wagon and onto the ground, and Grant saw an ample supply of fresh fruit, a sun bear's weakness, in the dim back of the box. The sun bear made straight for it, the only sound being her enthusiastic slurping of a watermelon half. James and Luke slid the crate lid down and secured it in place with four pins, then Samuel and Grant joined them and hauled the crate back up into the wagon. They all climbed up to resume their places, and Mr. King picked up the reins. Grant stared down at a subdued Becker and was still amazed at the turn of events.

"Go on with you," Becker entreated.

Grant shook his head in disgust. Mr. King lightly slapped the reins and they were off, sun bear in crate, veterinarian in perplexity. When they'd gone about half a mile, Grant broke the silence in the wagon.

"What exactly is a woodchuck? Is it code for 'we'll deck you,' or what?"

Luke grinned at him in the growing twilight. "'How much wood would a woodchuck chuck if a woodchuck could chuck wood?'"

The wagon riders took up the refrain in an instant. "'He'd chuck as much as a woodchuck could, if a woodchuck could chuck wood.'"

"Nice," Grant complimented them. "But that still doesn't answer my question."

"Becker's a superstitious man, according to local talk. A woodchuck can bring the worst of luck, so the stories go, for those who believe such things. We just thought we'd remind him." Mr. King explained as the horse continued its leisurely pace and Grant began to slap at the night's mosquitoes.

"Well, are there any woodchucks around here?" he demanded of his silent crew.

Luke laughed. "*Nee*, but there's a sun bear sure enough, and that beats a woodchuck cold."

All of the brothers laughed, and Grant joined in. He understood that they had bonded together to back him up in a quest that really mattered to him, and the warmth of gratitude began to permeate his thinking. It was like having a small army behind you, and he'd never had the security of brothers or sisters.

"Thank you," he said gruffly, and Mr. King clicked to the horses and glanced around to peer at him in the fast falling moonlight.

"*Nee* thanks yet, Doctor. You've got to take this sun bear down to the post and have Edith get it out for you tonight. You can borrow the wagon, but we've all got to get to bed."

Grant smiled. "No problem."

The next morning Grant marveled at his gleaming, refreshed kitchen as he grabbed an iced coffee from the fridge on the way to a call about a colicky horse. He had scratches on his tanned forearms from hauling the crate to the minuscule post office by the dark of night, but he felt joyous at the encounter. Edith had turned out to be a riot, a thin Amish woman in a postal shirt thrown over a night robe, who had parceled the crate onto the loading dock with him as if they were mailing Christmas presents. And he'd discovered through a few late-night phone calls that one of the curators at the Hawaii Zoo was a former vet school classmate who was only too glad to prepare for an incoming sun bear.

When he got to his early morning vet call, the elderly Amish man greeted him with a toothy grin and shook his hand.

"Got a horse with a bit of a bellyache, Doctor."

"No problem. Let's have a look."

"See the scratches there on your arms."

"Yes…a late-night call."

The old man laughed. "Guess that's what you get for trying to mail a cow."

Grant didn't miss a beat. "On the contrary, it was a woodchuck… Two of them, actually."

The man's grin disappeared and he made a lame gesture toward the barn.

"*Jah…jah…* Right this way, Doctor. No trouble here."

Chapter Nine

Sarah noticed the change in the *Englisch* clothes as the summer days slipped seamlessly into early September. She'd grown used to girls wearing shirts with no sleeves and boys wearing no shirts or denims with strange knee holes torn in the fabric. But now, the visitors to the stand were more young women, holding babies on their hips or the hands of bright-haired toddlers, clad in collared shirts and denims, skirts, and blissfully colored blouses. Occasionally, when a woman's hair shone vibrant and free in the sunlight, Sarah allowed her gaze to linger a moment too long and then had to pray against the sin of vanity, knowing her own hair, once unbound, hung shimmering below her waist. She tucked any stray brown tendrils that dared escape her *kapp* ruthlessly back inside and sold caramel apples, kettle corn, and licorice pipes, realizing that she was becoming too familiar with the ways of the *Englisch*.

Sarah had finally finished the baby quilt top and

was working on the actual quilting of it. Her mind had swum when she'd actually gotten to the point where she needed *Mamm*'s help, and her vocabulary grew over mysterious quilting words like *pressing*, *seam allowances*, and *batting*. But now she felt relatively adept, at least to complete Chelsea's quilt, and she'd grown to love listening to visiting Amish women who shopped at the produce stand and always had a good quilting quip when they saw her working. Sarah's favorite traditional verse was "At your quilting, maids, don't tarry; Quilt quick if you would marry. A maid who is quiltless at twenty-one, never shall greet her bridal sun."

She was just smiling over reciting the verse when Jacob pulled in at the stand with a magnificent brown Morgan at the pull of his buggy. Sarah paused in her stitching to admire the movement of muscle beneath the sheen of the horse's coat and had to admit that no one took better care of horses than Jacob.

"He's beautiful," she said when Jacob came up the steps.

"*Danki*. He was trouble at first because of some cruelty from the previous owners, but he's as gentle as a lamb now. What are you working on?"

She'd forgotten her quilting and glanced with surprise at her lap. "*Ach*, just a quilt for Chelsea's *boppli*."

He took off his hat and leaned against a table piled with vegetables. "I thought old *Grossmudder* King scared you out of quilting once and for all." He smiled at her, and she recalled that it was Jacob to whom she'd run when she'd been so stung by her grandmother's comments as a teenager. In truth, she'd run to Jacob for many things as they were growing up, and she realized now how much she'd held herself off from him since he'd tried to change their friendship into something more.

She looked at him and thought that she missed that closeness of childhood and adolescence; she could have used someone to talk with about the doctor and the feelings she'd been having.

"What?" he asked curiously at her gaze.

She shook her head and looked down. "It's nothing—just—you've been such a good friend to me."

"Always friends," he sighed. "I think I put too many years into that role."

"They weren't wasted."

He laughed ruefully. "That depends on how you look at it."

She pursed her lips and pushed her needle through the quilt.

"Look, do you want to go for a ride?" Jacob asked.

"I have to stay here to work; you know that."

"Come on, Sarah. Just leave a box for money and let it run on the honor system. We can be back in half an hour."

She bit her lip in indecision.

"Just to appreciate the horse," he coaxed drily. "Not me."

"Stop it. All right; I'll go, but only if we can stop

by the schoolhouse. *Mamm*'s been wanting me to take some jams over to Lilly Lapp for her and her mother."

"No problem." He smiled and put his hat back on while she left a note and an open box for customers to pay. She filled a basket with a variety of jams and jellies, and they went down the steps together. She felt especially happy when he didn't try to help her up into the buggy. Maybe things could be normal again between them, she considered.

She spent an exhilarating time enjoying the ride and the familiar way that Jacob had only to speak and the horse pricked up its ears and obeyed. They drove to the schoolhouse and discovered the children out for lunch and running about. They all clustered close to see the beautiful horse, and Jacob got down to hold the bridle while they took turns petting it and offering vegetable pieces from their lunches. The schoolteacher, Lilly Lapp, stood in the doorway of the small schoolhouse, and Sarah was struck anew by her dark-haired, blue-eyed loveliness. Lilly and her mother lived alone since old Dr. Lapp, the former vet to the area, had passed away the previous year. The entire community worked together to help care for the widow and her household, though, remembering to bring food goods and to do work around the small Lapp farm.

"Thank you for this, Sarah." Lilly smiled, indicating the basket of preserves. "That's a beautiful horse."

"*Ach*, come and see it and say hello to Jacob."

"All right."

The two girls walked among the gamboling children and approached the Morgan.

Jacob tipped his hat. "Miss Lapp."

Lilly nodded and reached a tentative slender hand to the muzzle of the horse.

Jacob laughed. "He won't bite." He took the schoolteacher's hand in his own and stroked it down the glossy coat. Sarah watched a blush stain Lilly's cheeks, and the children giggled at their teacher. Jacob dropped her hand after a few moments and Lilly stepped back.

"Lunch is over, children," she announced to a collective moan of small voices. She smiled at Sarah and Jacob. "Enjoy your ride together." Sarah watched her walk to the schoolhouse with the children in attendance and climbed back into the buggy. Jacob joined her and picked up the reins, and the Morgan was off.

"Lilly Lapp is a beautiful girl," Sarah commented.

He made a noncommittal grunt. "I can't understand why someone would want to keep spending time in school as a teacher."

Sarah laughed. "That's your father talking; he never did want you in school when you could have been working around the horses."

"Well, he's right. Too much book learning and not enough life learning isn't good for anyone."

Sarah made no comment as she knew it was something they'd long argued over. Instead, she talked idly about this and that, and he made no disagreement when she told him they had better go back.

He pulled the buggy up to the stand and Sarah glanced sideways at him. "Can't it always be like this, Jacob? I've missed you."

He stared straight ahead. "That's something, anyway."

"Jacob, please…" She lay a placating hand on his arm just as she recognized a familiar whistle. She glanced back and saw the doctor walking down the high road to the stand. "*Ach*, it's a customer. I'd better go." She prepared to hop down from the buggy when Jacob caught her arm.

"Sarah, even if you don't want me, I see you. I know you. You're being a fool to think that you could have anything with an outsider."

She wrenched away and got down from the buggy, her conscience pricked at his words. "Thank you for the ride," she said stiffly. She watched him shake his head, then turn the buggy to drive past the doctor without returning his wave.

She met the doctor at the steps.

"That was a beautiful horse, though I seem to rub its owner the wrong way," he commented with a grin. "Did you have a good ride?"

"It was fine. I made some pecan tarts last night," she went on hurriedly. She had no desire for the doctor to think that there was anything between her and Jacob, and she ignored the pang of conscience that said she shouldn't care what he thought.

"Great."

She had to admit later, as she watched the doctor

walk away, that he didn't seem to think anything of seeing her with Jacob. He was just as pleasant and cheerful as always, and she felt more confused than ever about the increasing place the doctor was occupying in both her mind and her heart.

One blue-skied Sunday in September, Sarah decided to go to the woods on the paths beyond the farm to gather the various items she needed to make the stand better supplied for fall and to have a chance to reflect upon her feelings of late. She took a large basket and a few things for lunch and set out with *Mamm*'s admonishment to be back before dusk.

The deep floor of the Allegheny Mountains was pillowed with a light coating of fresh orange, red, and yellow leaves, though the trees themselves were still fairly thick with color. Beneath the bright colors under her feet was a decaying eternity of dark brown— hemlock, pine, birch, and maple, as well as dogwood and oak—all worked together to cushion and nearly silence her steps. The trail lines remained, though, trails much older than her own people, she knew. Trails of the Susquehannock Indians, the tall people who once inhabited what she now called home, and she breathed a prayer for the long-extinct tribe.

She was startled from her thoughts by the rustling footsteps of someone coming up on the path. She had a vague feeling of uneasiness, aware of how alone she was. She'd nearly decided to turn back around, when a familiar blond head appeared and the doctor hiked up the trail toward her.

"Miss King—what a pleasure."

She stared at him like he was some sort of apparition of all her desires, and despite all of her recent convictions, she couldn't contain her joy at seeing him. She also knew that her parents would be upset to have her walking with him in the primal intimacy of the woods, but she promised herself that she would be coolly polite and nothing more.

"What are you doing here?" she asked, frustrated that she sounded breathless.

"Oh, I had a bit of free time and thought I'd walk to the creek and have lunch. These paths are great, and it's a nice place to think among the trees."

"*Jah*, you're right."

"What about you?"

"What?"

He smiled. "What are you doing here?" He gestured toward her basket.

"*Ach*." She latched onto the safe topic. "The *Englisch* ladies seem to like wreaths. I thought I'd make some from leaves and berries and perhaps a few pinecones. Then I'll make some leaf and pine garlands and boughs; Chelsea, my sister, you know, told me in a letter to do some leaf arrangements in canning jars, and I need teaberries and maybe there are a few late blackberries or raspberries for jam—they hide like the deer in patches of sunlight and continue to ripen, though the year grows late."

"You manage to capture all the secrets and intimacies of the woods."

She bit her bottom lip at the huskiness of his voice.

"You know, someone might think that white teeth pressed against a red mouth might be an invitation for someone else to look at those lips."

She stopped her chewing and he laughed, the sound causing a rustling among the leaves on the ground as a chipmunk squeaked in protest and darted up a birch tree.

"Well, since we're here, shall we walk together? I can help you gather the things you need."

"*Jah*...of course."

They started down the path together, and Sarah glanced sideways at the tall man beside her. For just a moment, in the seclusion of nature, she wanted to pretend that they were pioneers together ready to work the land. Or, she smiled, she could pretend that he'd been born Amish and—she tripped over a root at the thought and he steadied her.

"Careful."

"*Jah*," she agreed, both disappointed and relieved when he dropped his hand from her arm.

"Your father and brothers are so busy lately; the harvest is the hardest time of the year for them, isn't it?"

Sarah considered. "Not hard—work is good. The Lord has given us purposeful work in each of the seasons; there's just more to do at harvest."

"The Amish don't seem to separate work from everyday living."

She bent to select a pinecone, checking to make sure it was without rot. "What do you mean?"

"Oh, the *Englisch* say 'I'm going to my job or my work,' and then they think of home as something separate and better sometimes. It's rare to find an *Englisch* person who truly loves his or her work."

"I still don't understand... How can home be separate from work? It's all part of the same. How can an *Englisch* man think if he divides himself over and over each day?"

"We just do it."

She stopped and looked up at him with concern. "Don't you like your work, Doctor?"

"Who me? I love it. God has blessed me incredibly."

She nodded, satisfied, and continued along the path. "I feel blessed too."

"I know; that's why it's so peaceful to be with you."

She regarded him primly, trying hard to think of him as a polite friend. "*Danki.*"

He caught a stray falling red leaf and ran it down the arm of her black, serviceable, hook-and-eye coat. She shivered, despite herself, and he smiled, twirling the leaf in his long fingers. "You're quite welcome."

Grant resisted the urge to look down at her as they walked. He had difficulty controlling his impulses when he was around her, always finding a way to sneak in a touch here or there, like with the leaf. He knew he made her nervous at times, but he also sensed that she was interested in his attentions, even if she fought against herself in the process. If he were smart, he should probably just back off, since he knew that if Sarah returned his affections, she'd risk being shunned by her community. But he couldn't help himself. He suppressed a sigh and heard the nearby sound of the creek.

"Hey, let's go to the creek for lunch." He patted the pockets of his brown leather coat. "Mrs. Bustle handed me enough for two."

"I have a sandwich."

He grinned. "Then we won't go hungry."

"*Nee.*"

Pine Creek in the early autumn was at its best in terms of secret pools and gently swirling leaves, lazy gurgles and the stray dart of a dragonfly. The moss-covered rocks seemed to invite time and life to be still for a moment, to listen to the relaxing fluidity and to forget the cares of the world.

He extended a hand to help her across the water and wasn't surprised when she jumped like a young deer, barely touching his fingers as she gained his position, and they both sank down by unspoken agreement on the large rock in the middle of the water.

He emptied his full pockets, revealing treasures of egg-and-ham salad on fresh bread along with miniature vanilla crème brûlées and tiny, purpled wine grapes. She brought forth an apple pie in a child-sized patty tin and a roast beef sandwich. They both bowed for a moment of grace, with no seeming need to speak a word, as the hand of the Father seemed so present in their meal.

"This is nice," he said, thinking what an understatement it was.

"I've wanted to ask you…" She broke off with a shy glance.

"Anything," he prompted. "Remember, I'd like there to be the truth between us." *And that thought*, he nagged himself silently, *makes you a liar, because you'd rather talk about how beautiful she is than anything else that might be on her mind.*

"I wanted to ask you," she continued. "If it's not too forward…about how your *mamm* and father died."

If she'd knocked him across the head broadside, she couldn't have rattled him more. He never talked with anyone about his parents, about *how* it had happened, anyway. He stared down at the water and felt the pull of something deep within him.

"More ice melting," he told her.

"I didn't mean to bring you pain. I just thought about…well, how young you were and how hard it must have been."

He shook his head. "My parents died in an automobile accident."

"*Ach*…I'm sorry."

He went on as if she hadn't spoken. "A great tribute to the evils of automobiles, I know, but there's a bit more to the story. You see…they swerved to avoid hitting a deer. Mother lived for a few hours, long enough to tell me how beautiful the animal was."

"They should have hit it," she cried, and he shook his head.

"No, I know your farm sensibilities tell you that, but we were all animal lovers. Mother would swim brown recluse spiders out of the pool and Father kept three dogs—in his office."

"You told me once...your father was a physician?"

"Yeah, but he would have been just as great a vet, though."

"And he'd be happy for you in your work?"

"Very happy. Very happy that I'm using my work to serve the Amish people, just like he did."

"Why did he care so much about the Amish?"

Grant smiled. "He admired their sense of community, I guess. He thought your people got things closer to the first-century church than anyone else, and I think God called him to care for the Amish community like He's called me."

He tore off a small piece of sandwich, throwing it into a set of circles where he'd seen a fish jump the moment before. A brown trout promptly took the bread, and he tore off another piece, glancing at her sideways.

"I'm glad He's called you here," she whispered, her eyes matching the rich brown tones of the surrounding trees.

He abandoned the bread and reached across the food to cover the hands she'd folded in her lap. "Thank you. You don't know how much that matters to me—what you think."

She looked down at his hand in her lap and rubbed her small thumb across the pads of his fingertips, and he felt his heart begin to throb in his throat.

"I feel the same way too—about what you think," Sarah admitted.

He would have spoken but there was a nearby rustling of the dense foliage, loud enough to make him jump to kneel protectively beside her, when a majestic white-tailed buck cleared the bank and leapt into the stream, not more than ten feet in front of them. Grant stared at it in wonder, sinking backward with his arm around her shoulders.

The deer returned his gaze, its many pointed horns glistening in a flash of sunlight, then it gave another splashing leap and majestically mounted the opposite side of the bank until it disappeared into the woods.

"It was a deer, for you, from *Der Herr*… In memory of your parents," she whispered and he looked down at her, feeling the truth of her words. He bent his head, intent on the soft line of her lips when his nostrils flared and his eyes narrowed alertly.

"I smell smoke… Do you smell it?"

"*Jah.* It's probably from a nearby farm."

"No… I don't think so. Stay here for just a minute, will you?"

He was taking the rocks in great strides, puzzled by the sense of urgency that drove him on. Something didn't feel right. He broke through the dense overgrowth near where the buck had gone and came into a sudden clearing. A figure in a blue-hooded coat hunched over a pile of damp leaves, trying to start a fire.

"Hey!" Grant called.

The person turned and he caught a glimpse of a clean-shaven male face before the man took off into the woods, leaving the smoldering leaf pile behind. Grant gave chase but then thought of Sarah and turned back to stamp at the pile, surprised by her sudden appearance at the edge of the clearing.

"I heard you call." She watched him finish stepping on the leaves. "What's wrong?"

He walked over to her. "Someone was trying to start a fire."

"An Amish?"

"I don't know. He had a blue parka on and no beard. He ran off when I called."

"Probably an *Englisch* teenager up to tricks."

"No... I don't think so. I'm not sure why, but there was something wrong, I think. And a fire in these woods would be no trick; it would be a disaster."

"*Jah*, you're right. I'll tell Father when I return."

"All right." He smiled down at her, wanting to dispel the strange feeling he had of danger. "Let's get your things for the stand first."

She agreed and turned ahead of him to walk out of the clearing, but he looked back, unable to get over the feeling that someone stalked their going, and he hurried to catch up with her slender figure.

* * *

The beautiful day continued despite the disruption of the almost fire. The mountain paths revealed their secrets like walkways of strewn jewels. Delicate mushrooms, shy teaberries, pussy willow stems, and rich ferns all made their way into their baskets. They paused in a pine glen to gather seeds and Grant made a casual observation.

"You know, you've never ridden in my car."

Sarah bent to select a large pinecone from the ground and he did the same.

She glanced at him as she hunched on the ground, smiling to see him plop two dissimilar cones into his basket, then brush his hand on his denims.

"There's been no need, Dr. Williams."

"Don't you think we've progressed to you calling me Grant—at least when we're alone?"

She shrugged, embarrassed, not wanting to think about how many more chances they'd have to be alone.

"If you like."

"I like, and, as I was saying, there's apparently always a need to ride in a car... You'd be surprised."

Something in his tone made her curious.

"*Ach*?"

"Oh yes, *ach* indeed." He loved to repeat her Pennsylvania Dutch, but this time she didn't feel amused as he went on. "Let's see, there's been the young Miss Loder, needing a ride to the market. A Miss Stolis wanting a ride because night was falling and there was a storm closing in." He furrowed his handsome brow. "A Miss Adams, *Englisch* you know, who just wanted to know more about the field of veterinary science, and a Miss—"

"That's fine, Doctor. I get your point." Sarah's voice was tight, and she had a burning vision of yanking Deborah Loder's blonde hair and giving Anna Stolis a walk in a storm she'd not soon forget. She slapped a half-eaten pinecone in her basket, then turned toward the grapevines that Father grew near the creek.

She drew a deep, shaky breath and realized that she was jealous. She'd never felt the emotion with such intensity before, and the overwhelming feeling of the sin nearly made her sick at her stomach. She was jealous of others spending time with a friend, which made her the least desirable of friends. She didn't deserve to spend time with him herself; she needed to go home.

She'd just turned again when she caught his blue eyes regarding her amusedly while he snacked on late black raspberries. The dawning awareness that he was teasing her did nothing to slow her from gritting her teeth and swinging her basket in an unladylike arc back over her arm. She shook her head at him, then turned to go, wanting to stomp but deciding she'd not give him the satisfaction.

He caught her arm, then jumped back a step when she swung her basket at him. "Don't forget, Doctor, that there were three brothers before you who really liked to tease a little sister. Stay back, or you may find yourself in need of your own care."

"I thought the Amish were against violence," he replied in an injured tone, and she ignored the pulling in her heart at his cajoling.

"I'm going home, Doctor. Good afternoon."

"There's only one girl I want to take for a ride in my car, Sarah King, and in your heart, you know that." His voice stopped her. It was true. She knew it. He cared about her. She had the power to make him care more, without regard to the future. She turned, trembling, to face him.

"I do know it," she whispered, her anger fast melting into unwanted tears. "I don't want to know. I cannot. It's not done."

"What's not done?"

"Now you know what I mean." She swallowed hard. "An Amish and an *Englischer*…as more than friends. It's not done."

The smile left his eyes and he stared at her. "How could it be done, then?"

Chapter Ten

"Sarah...Sarah King? Have you chosen? I don't have all day."

The impatient voice of Mrs. Stolis echoed through the crowded dry goods store as Sarah stared at the bolts of fabric for the twelfth time. She could not forget her conversation yesterday with the doctor in the woods. She hadn't answered him; she couldn't. Somehow she had led herself into an intimate talk with an *Englisch* man she barely knew, and she knew that she had to stop it. The Bible said to "flee from temptation." And so she had fled, losing him through the tree- and shrub-lined paths until she was back at the farm and hidden in prayer by her own bed.

She'd pled to *Mamm* that her stomach was upset when she'd been called to come and help with dinner. *Mamm* had allowed that she was ill, and Sarah did not feel that she'd harbored a lie since her stomach was truly knotted in anxiety. She'd fallen into a restless sleep, dreaming that she was running through the woods being chased by herself.

And today she'd woken and dressed, forgetting that it was the day of her birth until she'd come downstairs, intent upon slipping into the garden for her dawn rendezvous, when she saw *Mamm* in the kitchen beating a bowl of frothy whiteness with a wooden spoon.

"*Guder mariye*, Sarah. May the Lord bless you on your birthday. *Wie geht's?*"

"I'm much better, *Mamm*, *danki*. I—I had forgotten that it was my birthday."

Mamm laughed. "I did not. It's been twenty-one years since I carried you, and I still remember your coming…in the garden, of course, right in the middle of picking berries for jam. The midwife said we'd found you under the blackberry leaves instead of the cabbage…your head was stained purple for two weeks where I touched you."

"I love that story."

"*Jah*, and you will also love your gift from Luke today. He's going to watch the stand so that you and I may have a free afternoon to ourselves."

"*Ach*, *Mamm*, really?"

"*Jah*, your father agrees."

Sarah had smiled her gratitude and smelled the batter for her cake. Then she'd slipped away to the garden to pray but had not found peace. Her thoughts were too jumbled to center properly on *Der Herr*. And now she stood before the bolts of fabric thinking how well the aqua blue would make up a shirt for the doctor.

"Sarah! If you're not going to choose, then let me go ahead," Deborah Loder snapped, shifting her wicker basket. "I want to buy that sky blue for a new blouse."

"Which would look lovely with your hair," Sarah remarked glumly.

Deborah looked at a loss for a moment, then went on in a kinder tone. "*Danki*, Sarah. May I go ahead?"

"*Jah*, please do."

Sarah sighed and drifted back to where *Mamm* was examining some small teaberry candies for cookie toppings. It had been *Mamm*'s idea to come to the Stolises' dry goods store as a celebration of Sarah's birthday. Sarah still had all of the money she'd earned from the stand, and *Mamm* had thought it a nice idea if Sarah might buy herself some fabric for a new blouse. Her wine-colored one was getting worn, but the colors of the materials had swum in bland unison unless she was matching them against a pair of blue-gold eyes.

"I need nonpareils and dried teaberries for those sugar cookies the boys like. Should I get both today? And, Sarah, where is your fabric?"

"I could not choose."

Mamm shot her a sharp glance. "Are you still ill, child?"

"*Nee, Mamm*."

"Yet you are not yourself. I think that..."

She was interrupted by the bang of the screen door and the appearance of Mr. Loder, who looked sheepishly around at the cluster of women. He nodded to his daughter and cleared his throat.

"Word is that they've sent for the midwife over at John Kemp's farm."

Sarah clutched her mother's arm in excitement; Chelsea's baby must be coming! Mr. Loder left in the same abrupt manner, his duty done, and the women began to buzz about *Mamm* and Sarah as they were hustled to the front of the store to complete their purchases.

"Are we going to Chelsea's, *Mamm*?" Sarah asked in a low tone as they finished paying.

"*Jah*, we will *geh…*"

Sarah had to grab her mother's basket, which she left on the counter, and then scurried to loosen Shadow's tether as *Mamm* appeared ready to take flight, post and all.

Sarah held on as they navigated around the other buggies at the store, then set out at a good trot.

"If Mr. Loder knows, then Father and the boys will know too." Sarah's heart pumped with excitement. "*Jah*, they will know by now."

Sarah realized the truth of this as word spread fast through the fields where the telephone houses were permitted to be used for good reason, and childbirth was considered reason enough as the community rejoiced in each new life.

It was warm, and the confines of the closed buggy seemed hotter than usual as they took to the high road.

After a moment of studying *Mamm*'s tense profile, Sarah laid her hands over her mother's on the reins.

"Please, *Mamm*… Let me drive. You're worried."

Mamm gave the reins over with a sigh and leaned back in the buggy.

"*Danki*, Sarah. You are a good girl. I know that all will be well, and that *Der Herr* is in charge, but it seems… I can remember Chelsea being as tall as a footstool and today she's giving birth…" *Mamm* wiped at her face with a clean handkerchief. Sarah clicked to Shadow who, she knew, was already doing his very best. The most a horse and buggy could travel was eight miles an hour, and the Kemp farm was some ten miles west of the Stolises' store.

Sarah was concentrating on the road and the passing *Englisch* vehicles when she heard an automobile coming up fast from behind. The red sports car sped past and pulled onto the dirt off-road about an eighth of a mile ahead. *Mamm* made a surprising sound of relief in her throat, as Sarah's heart began to pound even more furiously.

She had no idea what to say to the doctor and could not delay the moment as Shadow's fine feet took the distance in no time. Sarah turned the buggy off the road where the doctor and her brother James stood waiting outside the car.

James caught Shadow's bridle and scratched the horse's nose while the doctor hurried to help *Mamm* down from the buggy.

"I heard the news of your daughter, Mrs. King. I

thought maybe I could help with a ride. Your husband agreed and sent James to take Shadow and the buggy back."

"*Ach*...this is good. Thank you, Dr. Williams." *Mamm* smiled warmly at him for the first time, Sarah noted with satisfaction.

The doctor offered a hand to Sarah, and she touched him lightly as she jumped down but did not meet his gaze. *Mamm* had approached the automobile and stood waiting by the passenger door. The doctor hurried to open it for her and held her arm as she slung herself into the low seat.

James laughed aloud. "*Ach, Mamm*... If only you could see yourself. I wish Father were here. You look right at home!"

Mamm shot him a dark look. "Stop your foolishness, James King. *Ich kam sell neh geh*—I cannot tolerate that!"

"Indeed," the doctor rejoined. "Your mother is very brave to ride in a sports car...and your sister, of course."

He'd gone around to the driver's side and levered back his seat to reveal the minuscule back interior and swept his hand before him with a gallant air.

"Please, Miss King, if you will."

Sarah hurried to move, but her skirts got caught on the door and he bent to loosen them while she pulled at the fabric in embarrassment. He leaned close enough for only her to hear. "Miss King—in my car. Why does this subject seem familiar?" He straightened and

Sarah met his eyes for the first time, finding them dancing in amusement. She let out a sigh of exasperation and jumped into the back, uncaring of the ball she'd made of her skirts. The doctor began to whistle and put his seat back, folding his long body to fit behind the wheel.

Sarah felt as trapped as a mouse and tried to shift her weight.

"Seat belts, ladies. If you don't mind." He helped *Mamm* fasten the belt and cast a look in the back. Sarah was ready for him and had the belt snapped despite the fact that it tightened in the jumble of her clothing. He met her gaze in the rearview mirror and she knew he was smiling, so she turned her head to study James as he gave them a happy wave.

Sarah watched *Mamm*'s aged hands tighten on the low dashboard as the doctor pulled out.

They made it onto the high road, and Sarah began to enjoy the quick, fluid movement of the vehicle and the almost purr-like sound of the engine as the miles to the Kemp farm flashed by in a whirl of colored trees, harvesting neighbors, and the backdrop of the rolling mountains. Sarah had to suppress a giggle as Mr. Zook gave the car a second glance from his perch on the corn harvester, surprise etched on his face to see *Mamm* in the passenger seat. *Mamm* took it in stride and raised a passing hand in salute while Sarah looked around to see the man's expression of disbelief.

The Kemp farm came into sight, and Sarah thought how pretty it was with its rows of maple trees lining the dirt drive and the farmhouse's white gables and light green shutters. She'd only visited the farm once before, shortly after Chelsea's wedding. The young couple had moved into the main house and John Kemp's mother had moved into the small *doddy* or grandparent house as was the custom when there was an only son who married.

The doctor pulled up before the steps and then hurried around the car front to help *Mamm* out. Sarah tried to fool with the seat lever but could not make it move, so she waited and watched *Mamm* take to the steps. Dr. Williams came back to Sarah's side and moved the seat lever to release her. She clambered from the back, ignoring his outstretched hand.

"Miss King," he chided. "Is this my thanks for the ride?"

Sarah craned her neck to look up at him and her *kapp*, which had lost a few pins in her exiting the car, blew off in a gust of wind. She gasped and reached to cover her head while he stretched long fingers to catch the delicate thing by its strings.

"Please," Sarah gasped, her slender fingers unable to contain the massed bun of light brown hair and its stubborn strands. She felt him put the *kapp* back on her head, and she grasped it with relief, pulling tightly on the strings. She saw him bend down to the ground, gathering stray pins, and she waited, feeling miserable.

"Here you go." He handed her the pins and she took them, haphazardly stabbing them into her hair.

"I'm sorry," she murmured, starting to move to the steps.

He caught her arm. "Wait... Why are you sorry?"

She stopped, still holding her hands to her hair. "Because it's sinful to let any man see my hair unbound, except my husband."

"Your hair is beautiful."

She shook her head and pulled away, running up the steps and inside the screen door, letting it slam with finality.

Grant sighed and turned back to the car, intent on leaving. He felt sadly out of step with the slip of a girl who'd changed his world over the last months, and he wasn't sure how to proceed. He heard the squeak of the screen door, and he looked up hopefully.

A young Amish man with coal-black hair and a neat, curling beard stepped outside. He was visibly distraught but came down the steps with a hand outstretched.

"Are you Mr. Kemp?"

"John...please. And you're Dr. Williams?"

"Yes. How is your wife doing?"

The young man shook his head and swallowed hard. "It's our first, you know. *Frau* Knepp has been with her for hours... I don't know."

"*Frau* Knepp is the midwife?"

"*Jah...*"

"Well." Grant tried to encourage him. "First labors always take awhile. It's normal."

"*Jah.* Please…will you come inside?"

Grant considered; Sarah would probably have a fit. "I'd better not," he said with regret. "I've got some calls."

"Just for a bit… I could do with some menfolk's company."

"All right…for a few minutes."

John sighed in gratitude, and Grant followed him to the dark screen door.

When they entered the home, they stepped directly into the large kitchen, which was in a state of utter chaos. Sarah stood at a counter, scraping up sugar trailing from a large bag. Fresh apples, in all stages of dissection, were mounded in bowls and kettles while the stove boiled madly. Canning jars stood at the ready but had not been touched while the heavy smell of burnt brown sugar and spices hung thick in the air.

John turned to smile at him. "My wife and my *mamm*—they were making some apple butter when the labor began."

"Ah."

"*Danki*, Sarah," John went on. "I know it's a mess in here."

"It doesn't matter." Sarah smiled back, though she would not meet Grant's eyes.

Everyone jumped, including Grant himself, when a strangled moan echoed from behind a nearby closed door.

"*Ach*…" John said, moving automatically to the

door, where he then stopped and looked back in desperation.

"Go in there," Grant said before he realized the words were out of his mouth.

John Kemp's face took on a whole new light, as if he'd just been waiting for someone to tell him to go to his wife, and he nodded his head with a broad smile. "*Jah*...I will go." He hitched up his suspenders like he was girding for battle then straightened his shoulders and opened the door. There was a flurry of female voices, but as the minute lengthened they subsided, and John did not reemerge.

"Why did you say that?" Sarah asked, as she emptied more sugar back into the bag.

"Because that's where he belongs; he'll probably help her make it go faster."

"Birthing is the work of the midwife; it's the work of the husband to wait."

"Why? I bet your brother-in-law has delivered hundreds of animals on the farm."

She looked shocked and he went on. "I'm not comparing animal birth to that of humans, just making a point that it's a natural process. John was there in the beginning; he should be there in the end." He helped himself to a Granny Smith apple and watched her, waiting for her response.

She gave him a searing glance. "You are too worldly."

"No, I'm matter-of-fact. I'm a doctor, remember? It's not worldly, Sarah, to say the truth."

"Some truths don't need to be said aloud."

"Really? Which ones? Like the one I asked about yesterday?"

"Yes," she snapped, then bit her lip.

He moved to stand beside her. "I see you've repaired your hair covering."

She looked back down at the sugar. "*Jah*, of course."

He let his gaze sweep around at the mess, then stepped back, giving her some room. "All right…for your sister's sake, let's make the apple butter and declare a truce."

She smiled then, revealing a dimple, and he felt his heart jump in response.

"Do you know how to make apple butter, Doctor?"

He straightened his long back and grabbed a browning, peeled apple. "How hard can it be?"

She rolled her eyes and took the apple from his hand. "First, we must stop the browning. We need to mix vinegar and salt with water." She glanced about and he read her thoughts.

"Do you need a clean kettle? I'll wash one." He rolled up his sleeves as he spoke, peering into various pots to find the least full. He chose one from the stove that was encrusted with dark brown sugar and wondered if they had a green-textured scrubber like he'd seen Mrs. Bustle use.

Sarah handed him a piece of steel wool and he took it wordlessly and began to scrub.

"I'm making a mess," he confessed after a minute, and she laughed.

"Turn the pot over another that's boiling…here." She stretched to help him. "The steam will loosen the burnt sugar." Her blue sleeve brushed his bare arm and he forced himself to step away, concentrating on the overturned kettle instead.

"What's next?"

"We sterilize the canning jars. I'm not sure if Chelsea had finished all of them."

"Another clean pot?"

"*Jah*…please."

They worked together for a few minutes, and Grant breathed in the companionable peace. He admired her deft movements about the kitchen, bending here and there to clean and straighten or easily peeling more apples to go into the anti-browning mixture for a dip.

"This is fun," he remarked and felt her glance of surprise. "What?"

She shook her head. "You seem to enjoy whatever you do."

He lowered his voice. "When I'm with you, yes."

She snapped a dish towel in the air between them. "Truce, Doctor…remember?"

"You have a feisty side."

"Feisty?"

"Yep." He smiled smugly, transferring jars from the stove to the counter with long tongs.

"What do you mean…feisty?"

"Oh, you'd call it sassy, I suppose."

She stood stock-still. "I am not sassy. That's behaving without respect."

He leaned close to her. "Maybe to your *mamm*; but to me, it's fun."

She backed against the counter and turned, reaching for a bag of spices. "It's time for the cinnamon and allspice."

He returned to the canning jars and whistled, ignoring her turned back.

He sensed when she turned back to him and he pretended not to notice. "All right...last jar. Now what?"

"We stir the mixture on the stove and stir and stir... Otherwise it will burn."

"I'll stir, then."

He took up the long wooden spoon and stood over the large pot, whistling and stirring, enjoying the warm feel of the steam on his face.

"Do you want me to take over?" she asked.

He grinned at her over his shoulder. "Nope. I'm having fun."

He ignored her sigh and continued to stir, all the while concentrating on her gentle flurry of movements behind him as she continued to clear up the kitchen. He wondered if it would make any difference in her behavior if he backed off in his attentions; he smiled as he considered the innate curiosity of a hummingbird.

Sarah concentrated on the sandy grains of brown sugar as she scraped the counters clean. She didn't want to think about the fact that the doctor was so close behind her that she only needed to take a step and her skirt would brush his long legs. She closed her eyes against the sudden desire to turn and touch his back, to rub her fingers against the pale blue cotton of his shirt, which matched his eyes. She shook herself and decided that she was flustered in her excitement over Chelsea, not the doctor...or Grant, as he'd asked her to call him.

Then she became aware of the sudden, palpable silence in the room and sneaked a glance over her shoulder to find him staring at her.

"It's done, I think."

"Take it off the heat, then," she instructed, her voice strained.

He smiled at her, a knowing look. "Yes, we definitely need less heat."

She couldn't look away. She watched him close the single-step distance between them and extend his arms to reach the counter on either side of her. She was caught, trapped by the warmth of his body and her own yearning to press herself closer to him.

"You have apple butter on your cheek," he murmured, and she tried to reach a hand between them to wipe her face.

"Don't."

She froze, somehow knowing what he wanted, and she arched her neck upward.

He put his mouth on her cheek, and she blinked at the sensation, knowing that he tasted her skin. He pulled back and she felt like crying out at the loss of his touch, but she watched as his thick lashes lowered, and he bent his head. He brushed his mouth across hers, and she thought of sunshine, and green leaves, and boiling maple syrup. She responded, a tentative foray of her lips that provoked a small sound of approval from the back of his throat. She moved her mouth with abandon, wanting him to make the noise again, when the rattle of a doorknob forced them to turn from each other in haste.

The bedroom door opened wide and Mrs. King emerged, her face wreathed in smiles, just as Sarah managed to grasp to the counter, clutching its edge with white-tipped fingers.

"Mamm…how is Chelsea?"

"Wunderbar… And you are now Aunt Sarah to a *boppli* boy…and on your birthday too!"

Grant looked over his shoulder at her. "It's your birthday?"

"Jah."

Mamm nodded in satisfaction. "Our first grand-child…John Kemp Jr." She turned her comfortable frame back to the door. "You may come in shortly, Sarah."

She shut the door behind her and only the sound of the slow bubbling apple butter broke the silence between them as they faced each other once more.

Grant cleared his throat and spoke hoarsely, "Happy birthday."

She looked at him and reached trembling fingers to her lips to savor the sensation of the kiss.

"You…kissed me."

"You kissed me back."

"*Ach*," she exhaled. "This cannot go on; it cannot. I am Amish; you are *Englisch*."

"Are we so different, then, Sarah?"

"No… I mean, yes…we are. I cannot have you, not without losing my faith, my home. I will not do that."

He pursed his lips. "I don't want you to lose anything."

"Then why kiss me?" she whispered in desperation. "How many *Englisch* girls do you kiss like this? Is it your way?"

"No, I don't go around kissing just anyone. I'm going to talk to your father."

"What?" she hissed. "Are you *narrish*? *Nee*, you will not talk to Father."

"Why not? You know I care about you, and I think you care about me. Why shouldn't I tell your father, so we can stop hiding what is the truth?"

She dropped her face into her hands and gave a faint sob.

"Don't cry, Sarah."

"I don't know what else to do."

"I don't want you to cry; I want…" He stopped as the front door opened and Luke and Mr. King entered.

"Well, little Sarah…you are now Aunt Sarah! And Dr. Williams, you're here to share the good news as well!" The older man exclaimed jubilantly, and Sarah watched as Grant moved to shake his hand.

"Yes, sir. It's a boy."

"A boy…a grandson!" Mr. King reached to embrace Sarah, then stretched out an expansive arm to encompass the room. "*Jah*…it's a good day for the King family and for the Kemp house. *Der Herr* blesses us, eh, Sarah? What more is there to ask for?"

Sarah tried to avoid Grant's eyes as he smiled wryly at her. *What more indeed?*

Chapter Eleven

"*Ach*, Dr. Williams," Father clapped his hands. "I forgot in all of the excitement—the Bilder farm sent word. They've a sick old dog at their place and wondered if you might come."

"Of course. I'll go at once." Sarah watched him unroll his sleeves, trying to ignore the sight of the strong, tanned forearms splattered with apple butter. She scuffed one small toe of her shoe at a flour spot on the floor.

"Congratulations again, sir! Uncle Luke...Aunt Sarah." She looked up to meet his eyes, but he'd already turned and was headed out the door. In a few moments, the sound of the automobile receded into the distance.

Sarah concentrated on filling the sterilized jars full of the rich apple butter and setting the seals while Luke ran an appreciative finger around the hot edge of the pan. She slapped his hand away and listened to Father's cheerful pacing before the closed bedroom door. Then she checked the paraffin, which was melting in a double boiler. When it was done, she ladled the hot wax over the warm apple butter, making sure that the wax touched all sides of the glass jar to ensure a proper seal; then she screwed on the brass tops and lids and carefully dried each jar. The familiar process soothed her for the moment, and she felt like she could breathe again without thinking of Grant.

Mamm soon emerged from the bedroom carrying a bundled armful and went straight to Father. Her eyes were filled with happy tears as Sarah and Luke clustered around to see; John's *Mamm* soon joined them from the master bedroom. Father took the baby and gently lifted the quilt Sarah had made with his workworn hands to reveal a pink, sleeping face with a rosebud mouth and a thatch of black hair.

*"Ach...*Mama, how *Der Herr* has blessed us."

Sarah watched the loving exchange of glances between her parents and knew that she longed for such a relationship for herself when she'd been married as long as they had. She slipped away from the group admiring the baby and went to Chelsea's doorway. John Kemp's head was bent over her sister's, and his shoulders shook as he cried tears of happiness while his wife stroked his hair. Sarah drew back, not wanting to interrupt when *Frau* Knepp saw her and thrust a bundle of sheets and quilts at her.

"Sarah, *danki*... These need to be washed."

There was no tomfoolery with *Frau* Knepp, so Sarah turned with the staggering load and headed out back to the washtubs and wringer. Long laundry lines were strung between two oak trees and a handful of carved stick props leaned against a nearby shed. Sarah sighed as she began by pumping the water from the nearby pump to fill the aluminum wash bins. She put several sheets in to soak, then added crumbles of handmade oil soap. Chelsea's soap held the rich scent of both almonds and berries that was pleasant to smell, so the scrubbing seemed to go by more quickly than usual. She'd just run her second sheet through the wringer washer when *Mamm* came out to join her.

"Sarah…you are a good girl, but I didn't forget that this is your birthday too. Go in and visit with Chelsea for a few minutes before she falls to sleep. I will do the washing."

Sarah was only too glad to relinquish the task as her hands were already freezing from the pump water. She skipped indoors to find Luke and John talking at the kitchen table while Father rocked the precious bundle with a look of peace on his wrinkled face. Sarah dropped a kiss on his forehead and patted the baby before going to her sister's room. *Frau* Knepp had gone, and Chelsea appeared to be dozing, her long chestnut-red hair unbound and flowing against the pillows. She opened her eyes at once when the door squeaked and smiled wearily at Sarah.

"Come in, Sarah, please."

Sarah approached the bed on silent feet. Chelsea's face looked pale but luminous, and Sarah felt she was in the great presence of new life, a new touch from the Lord's merciful hand.

"How was it, really, Chelsea?" Sarah whispered.

Chelsea grinned. "Hard…but worth it. Did you see him?"

"*Jah.* He is very handsome."

"Come and sit down. You make me feel like I'm ill. And I want to thank you again for his first quilt. I know how much you labored over it." She patted the edge of the bed beside her and Sarah perched gingerly.

"I actually grew to love the time I spent doing it; I'm so glad to give it to you."

"*Danki.* Now, tell me what's bothering you, little *schweschder.*"

"Me?" Sarah was shocked. "I don't want to talk about me. It is your special day."

"It's your birthday, remember? Go over to the top drawer of the bureau and open it. You'll find your gift inside."

Sarah rose and went to the wooden bureau. She opened the topmost drawer and withdrew a brown-paper-wrapped package tied with a red ribbon. She went back to sit on the bed as she unwrapped it.

She withdrew a bound leather book embossed with the words *For Thoughts* on the outside. She flipped through the pages and found them to be lined but empty.

"It's a journal," Chelsea explained. "I had one before I married. I used to write all sorts of poems and thoughts inside. I thought that you might like to do the same since you loved writing in school."

Sarah hugged the book to her chest, then clasped her sister's hand. "*Danki*, Chelsea. I will use it."

"But who will you write of?" Chelsea's smile was knowing.

"No one special, of course."

"Ah well, perhaps you will use it for your plants."

Sarah frowned at her sister. There was no doubt that Chelsea knew something, and if Chelsea knew it, then others might suspect too.

"What do you know?"

Chelsea attempted a casual stretch, then winced so that Sarah hurried to straighten the bedclothes.

"Well?"

"I know you, little sister. And your eyes are never so big, not even for your garden. John told me that he asked Dr. Williams to come in. I've heard that the doctor is quite good-looking for an *Englischer*."

Sarah could not contain her blush and stared down at the journal, unsure of what to say.

"Sarah, I wouldn't tell a soul…you know that. But he's *Englisch*."

"I know that. Do you think I haven't thought of that a million times over?"

"Don't worry." Chelsea patted her hand, then yawned. "*Der Herr* will send you a good Amish man and you will forget your fancy for the *Englischer*. I thought I'd marry a half dozen men before John. But when I met him, I knew it was right. The same will happen for you, I know."

Sarah nodded, watching as her sister drifted off to sleep, but in her heart, she wasn't sure she liked the idea of a good Amish man. After all, did one have to be Amish to be good in God's eyes? The thought shook her and she rose just as *Mamm* entered the room.

"I'm going to stay tonight, Sarah, and Father and Luke will take you home. Make sure you get up extra early to do the breakfast before you go to the stand."

"Yes, *Mamm*."

"Chelsea got you a journal, eh? It'll be good for you to put down your thoughts. I've worried that something has been troubling you." *Mamm* caressed her cheek as she passed.

"I am fine, *Mamm*," Sarah responded, hurrying to get out of the room before anyone could make any other observations about her personal life.

She gained the door and had her hand on the knob when her mother whispered to her softly. "*Hallich gebottsdaag*... Happy birthday."

She smiled and nodded and left the room before Chelsea's next wakening.

Grant drew up before the Bilder farm and found it to be more ramshackle than its neighbors. Little boys, dressed so much like Amish men, ran about in small black hats playing kick the can, while a woman hummed and strung laundry haphazardly on a sagging line.

He grabbed his bag from the back, trying to pick out a dog from the parade of chickens, ducks, and geese that seemed to dot the place like confetti, and finally went over to Mrs. Bilder and her wash.

"Hello, ma'am. I had word that you have a sick dog?"

The woman spoke without removing the wooden clothespins from between her thin lips. "Dead already."

"Oh, I'm very sorry. I would have come sooner had I known…"

"Dog's been dead for two months."

"All right… I guess I'll move along then."

He turned to go, chagrined at wasting his time when the woman called out to him, "I do have a sick cow in the barn, though."

He turned back with a sigh. "How bad off is it?"

She pulled the last clothespin from her mouth and started walking to the barn, cutting across the array of children and animals like someone negotiating a New York City street at lunchtime. Grant followed reluctantly.

They entered the murky barn and Grant was surprised to see an Amish man with a thick beard, tilted backward in a chair, sound asleep against one of the stall doors.

"That's Mr. Bilder. He's got a sleep problem. Sleeps all day, is up all night. Always been that way."

The man suddenly let out a roar of a snore that sounded somewhere between a bobcat and a woman screaming. Grant shivered in spite of himself.

"Strange, ain't it?" Mrs. Bilder remarked. "I make him sleep out here 'cause he scares the young ones with his snoring."

"Have you tried seeing a physician?"

"Nah… What for? Ain't no way to change a man's snore; it's part of who he is."

Grant nodded, unable to keep from whispering in case he brought on the snore again. "Where's the cow?"

"Over there, far stall. She's cast her withers."

Grant nearly groaned in despair. "Cast her withers" was the polite Amish way for saying that a cow had expelled her uterus following a vigorous birth. It wasn't anything painful for the cow, but for the vet, it meant a lot of trouble getting things back inside.

"Leave you to it then," Mrs. Bilder announced, turning to exit the barn and slide the door closed behind her.

"Yaowwwwhmmmmmhrrrrrr!" Mr. Bilder snored again and Grant jumped. He'd just have to get used to it.

He walked over to the stall to find the cow eating at the trough while a giant, pink organ protruded from her backside. Her tail flicked with goodwill, though, and she didn't even seem to notice that she was missing half of her insides. Grant rolled up his sleeves, then, recalling numerous fretful battles with "cast withers" during his training, he stripped his shirt off entirely. He hung it on a convenient nail, then set about scrubbing up his hands and arms and chest with a bottle of antibacterial lotion from his bag. He washed away the apple butter and thought of his kiss with Sarah.

"Yaowwwwhmmmmm...hrrrrr...hmmmmm!" Grant jumped again and shook his head. He had a good notion to go over and squeeze Mr. Bilder's nose until he choked awake but decided that wouldn't quite be professional. So he finished lathering his arms and slipped into the stall.

"All right, old girl. Let's see how we get on, okay?" He began to soap the bulbous organ, which was covered with bits of hay and afterbirth. The cow continued to chew contentedly.

"Ya...wwwwaawaaaahmmmmmhhrrrrrr!"

"I hear him, old girl. Let's just think about us." He took a deep breath and grabbed hold of the giant organ, filling his arms and chest with it. It was heavy but relatively easy to position so long as the cow cooperated, and the cow was cooperating. He had things back in place in no time, relieved that it was an easy go, and moved back to a nearby bucket of water to soap down his arms and chest once more. He pulled his shirt back on and gathered his instruments back into his bag.

"Yaaaahmmm...yahmmmm...yahmmmhrrr!"

He'd had enough. Sleeping problem or no, somebody had to stop Mr. Bilder from terrorizing the animals in the barn, let alone his own children. Grant caught up his bag and stalked over to the sleeping man. In his best attempt at imitation, he leaned close to the sleeper's ear, drew a long breath, then hollered like a wild banshee. "Yaaaahmmhrrrwawawawahrrrrr!"

Mr. Bilder opened his eyes and let the feet of his chair fall forward so suddenly that Grant jumped back a step.

"What is wrong with you, Son?" the older man asked, staring at Grant with an injured frown.

"What's wrong with me? What's wrong with you? Get up, man! It's daylight! You're missing your children grow up; you're missing your wife. You snore like a...like a..."

The Amish man laughed. "*Ach*, you mean this— Yahmmmmmmhrrrrrhmmmmrrr!"

"Yes," Grant said, deflated. "That's what I mean."

"Well, that's just to get me some peace from the young'uns. Once they grow up, I'll go back to sleepin' regular and snorin' regular too."

"I'm going to tell your wife," Grant warned.

The older man rose and placed a placating hand on Grant's chest. "Doc, don't do that, please. Me and the wife get along just right like this. I'd hate to have anything interfere with our relationship."

Grant shook his head in disgust and started for the barn door, then paused. "All right, Mr. Bilder. Your secret's safe with me, but in *Englisch* terms—you owe me one."

The Amish man smiled and nodded, tilting back in his chair once more, his eyes drifting closed. "Anytime, Doc…anytime."

It was nearly dusk when Father turned the buggy out of the Kemps' lane and started the drive for home. Sarah and Luke crowded in the backseat and checked the LED batteries in the reflectors and turn signals to make sure that they were working properly. There'd been many an accident between Amish buggies and *Englisch* automobiles, and Father insisted that they be as careful as possible.

As they moved along and the first stars appeared, Father, enraptured with the new baby, began to sing in his rich, soothing baritone.

Schof, bubbeli, schloff,
Der dawdy hut die schof,
Die mommy hut die rote kuhn,
Un steht in dreck bis an die knie.

Sleep, baby, sleep,
Thy father keeps the sheep,
Thy mother shakes the dreamland tree.
To make the dreams fall down on thee.

Sarah and Luke joined in, singing the age-old lullaby, and Sarah felt a brief sense of peace and renewal wash over her. She knew that the Lord would work things out right between her and Grant Williams if she would be willing to trust like a child does. She clutched the journal Chelsea had given her in her arms and mentally composed the sights and sounds of the night—the silhouettes of the mountains, a passing buggy, the low hung stars, and the smell of fall. She had not written much since she'd finished school, but now she looked forward to having a secret place to share her thoughts and feelings.

As they drew within a mile of home, the distinct smell of smoke and something like burnt popcorn drifted eerily over the night, dissipating her reverie. Father clicked to Shadow to hurry him to the top of the hill, then he drew the horse to a stop. Below them, in the creek valley, the King farm stood with many beaconing lamps lit, while the yet-to-be harvested field near the house blazed with fire.

"Father!" Luke cried. *"Was in der welt?"*

"Crop fire, Son. Hold on! Come, Shadow!" He slapped the reins and Sarah clutched the side of the buggy as the dizzying scene came more into focus. Many neighboring buggies were pulled a good distance from the flames while men ran back and forth with buckets. She saw her brothers plowing fire breaks in the ground near the side of the house and around the boundaries of the field. She heard the fearful whinnies of the horses as they smelled the smoke, and, in the distance, the long whistle of an *Englisch* siren and then the clanging of a bell. She looked at Father and thought how old he seemed in the harsh contrasting light of flame and night. He pulled Shadow up as close as he dared and jumped down. Luke and Sarah scrambled after him while he called over his shoulder.

"Luke, take Shadow back a bit, then run and help your brothers. Sarah, stay near the horses; try to keep them calm."

Sarah shivered as the clanging of the *Englisch* fire truck grew louder and the long vehicle suddenly swung into their lane, followed by the whirling red light of an ambulance. Soon, *Englisch* firefighters were unrolling hoses and hooking them to the pump, sending streams of water into the cornfield. Her throat began to burn and her eyes watered as Shadow began to prance. She turned to soothe the animal when the doctor appeared behind her and took the reins, gentling the horse with a deep humming.

Sarah nearly sagged against Grant's tall, dependable form when a fireman hurried past with a radio in hand.

"Send the police too." The man's voice carried on the wind and smoke. "It looks like arson."

Chapter Twelve

In the dawn's first light, while Father and her brothers still slept, Sarah stood barefoot at the edge of the burnt field. *Mamm* had been alerted about the fire and that the damage was limited to the corn crop. She'd sent word that she would stay with Chelsea and the baby for one additional day, providing that Sarah could manage. Now fog rose from the charred ground, giving it an eerie, choked appearance. Sarah was praying, thinking about the loss but more about the anger and hatred that would drive someone to such an extent of destruction. She knew about hate crimes against her own faith, of course, everyone who was Amish did. But there was a reason that the Amish would not use force to retaliate, why Father did not want to pursue an investigation; it only provoked more violence, and it was not a reflection of Christ's way.

She heard steps behind her and turned to see the doctor picking his way to her over the plowed fire breaks that had done so much to contain the fierce blaze. He came and stood behind her while she turned back to the field.

"What do you think of, Sarah, when you see this?"

It was not a question that she had expected and her eyes welled with tears.

"Maybe what you did when you saw the sun bear," she replied. "Only the trapped person is the one who did this; the one who is held by all of this."

"'And her worth is far above rubies.'" He stepped closer, then placed his hands on her shoulders.

She swallowed and felt the tears fall at his compliment from the Bible.

"Why do you say those kinds of things to me?"

"Because they're true. I told you from the time we first met, I wanted truth between us. I don't know why or how or for what reason... I just wanted it. And still want it."

She drew a deep breath. "Last night, before this, I felt peace that the Lord would work this thing out between us, but now... It's all a mess when I'm with you. I forget who I am, what I believe."

He gently rubbed her shoulder blades with his thumbs. "No, you never forget. You remind me in a thousand ways that you are different...as unique as any jewel. Your faith is real and vibrant and alive."

They stood still for long moments.

"Tell me about the Fishers," he requested, breaking the silence.

She shook her head. "The Fishers? What is there to tell?"

"They have a story; everyone does. What happened?"

She gazed out over the broken land and thought hard. In truth, her understanding of the Fisher family was shadowed by childhood perceptions, vague references caught but not understood from her brothers. Only as she matured did she realize the extent of the distance that the family had drifted into the world's ways.

"There were only two sons and one daughter... small for an Amish family."

He squeezed her shoulders, acknowledging her words.

"Matthew was my age, and Ammon was three years older. Mary Ann was somewhere in between... I'm not sure how old exactly. Mr. Fisher had a quick temper; I remember hearing him yell at the boys outside of meeting once for not hitching up the buggy properly. Everyone was pretending not to stare out of the windows of the house, but we did. Actually, the horse was lame... Mr. Fisher began to beat it, but Father came out and spoke to him quietly and he stopped. His face was beet red, and he hustled his family into the wagon and then drove off. They didn't come to meeting again for the next month, sending word that Mrs. Fisher was ill. Mother went to call, but no one came to the door. This is unusual for an Amish family, to stay behind locked doors when visitors come to minister to the sick. When they did come to the next church meeting, Mrs. Fisher's face was scarred...burned actually, from inside her *kapp* on one cheek to the bottom of her chin. She said it had been an accident with the kerosene lamp…"

She shivered and he pulled her back into his chest.

"Go on, Sarah." He pressed his mouth against her temple and she struggled to concentrate.

"The bishop didn't believe it had been an accident. He and the elders confronted Mr. Fisher, who became enraged. He swore he would leave the community, and he did. But Mrs. Fisher took the children and left first, hiding somewhere in the *Englisch* world. Then Mr. Fisher sold the farm…to you. No one has seen or heard of him or the family, except that day at the stand with Matthew. Why do you ask about the Fishers?"

"I'm not sure exactly, but I think there's something going on here that has to do with that family and your own."

"Yes," she murmured. "Remember, I told you how Matthew accused my family of being part of why they left. He was so angry." She shuddered, and Grant dropped to his knees behind her.

"Where are your shoes? You're going to catch pneumonia." He caught up her left foot, forcing her to turn and balance with one hand on his shoulder as he set about rubbing her ankles, arch, and toes. Sarah gasped at the warmth of his touch and the intimacy of what he was doing, but he didn't look up and went briskly on to the other foot. She let him because it felt so good, but then she realized that they were within eyeshot of anyone from the farmhouse, and soon her father and brothers would be awake.

"I have to go," she told him, pulling away from his touch. "Good-bye."

She ran back across the damp earth without looking back and entered the house with her feet tingling. She proceeded to make breakfast for Father and the boys while she struggled to clear her thoughts. She felt torn within, part of her so alive and vibrant when she was with Grant and another part of her feeling dark with the secrecy that was beginning to consume her. So she tried to focus on the mundane doings of scrambling eggs and frying bacon.

After the griddle had been scraped clean and the last of the dishes washed, she decided to make corn-bread for the coming lunch hour. She lifted an egg and cracked it against the rim of the yellow mixing bowl. Her brothers had gone to the fields, and Luke was at the stand, while Father had stayed behind to wait for a neighbor who was interested in buying one of the Kings' cows.

Father put his coffee cup in the sink and sighed as he gazed out the small kitchen window to the fields beyond. Sarah turned toward him. "We were all so happy last night," she murmured.

He smiled at her. "And you are not happy with what comes from *Der Herr*'s hand today?"

"Not the loss of the crop, *nee*."

"You forget our new grandbaby, Sarah."

She bowed her head. "No, I am grateful for him."

"Then perhaps it is something else that discontents your soul, hmm?" Father laid his hand on her arm. "I saw the doctor walk from the field early this morning. Were you with him?"

Sarah was amazed at the desire that welled up in her to lie to her father. She remained silent instead.

"*Ach*, Sarah. Be careful of your ways. You may convince yourself of one thing, but it may be far from the will of *Der Herr*."

"I know that," she choked out, thinking of the heat the doctor's touch had inspired on her bare feet.

"I told you before, *Mamm* and I trust you. You're a good girl, Sarah—you will do what's right, what's honorable. I know this."

"*Jah*, Father, but I—"

A knock at the back door interrupted her.

"That'll be the buyer for the cow," Father announced, going to open the door. But it was Jacob who stood there instead, his hat in his hands.

"I came to see if all was well this morning, sir."

"*Jah*, come in, come in."

Sarah turned her back to him, facing the counter and staring blindly down at the wet cornmeal. Father trusted her, believed in her, yet she'd been betraying him and *Mamm* again and again. Her heart was wrung within her and she thought how much easier it would be if she could just return the affection of an Amish man instead of the complicated attraction she felt for an outsider.

She closed her eyes and prayed. Maybe it was as

easy as choosing how to feel, choosing to do the right thing, no matter how her emotions interfered. She opened her eyes and turned back to find Jacob alone in the kitchen.

"Your father went out to the barns to sell a cow. Are you all right?"

Sarah stared up at him, his familiar handsome face, his beautiful eyes. She knew that he was kind and competent. More than that, she liked him, even if it was nothing more than as a friend.

"What is it, Sarah? You look funny."

She stepped away from the counter and held her hands out to him. He took them and squeezed, an old, familiar greeting.

"Jacob," she murmured, and her eyes filled with tears at the word.

He shook his head. "Sarah, don't cry. I'm sorry about the fire. I'm going to try to find out who did it so we can stop any more of this from happening."

"*Nee*," she sniffed lightly. "It's not the fire—it's you—us. I just want to do what's right."

He frowned down at her. "What are you talking about?"

She swallowed hard. "I've been wrong lately, not walking with *Der Herr*. I—I've just been doing what I want, not what's right. I've thought since that day we went for a buggy ride; I've been a fool." She couldn't stop the tears that dripped down her cheeks, and she steeled herself when he cupped her chin and reached gentle hands to thumb away each damp drop.

He leaned close to her, and she lifted her head with determination, closing her eyes. When he didn't kiss her, she opened her eyes once more to find him watching her sadly.

"I'm the fool, Sarah, not you. It would be so easy for me right now, to hold you to a promise, to bind you to me—I want it so much I can taste it." He brushed his mouth across her cheek, then drew back. "But I won't have you like this, forcing yourself—not when I know you'd just be thinking of him."

He put her from him and stepped back. "You've got to wrestle with your own heart, Sarah. I can't help you in this. I—I've got to go." He grabbed his hat off the table and made for the back door, letting it close quietly behind him.

Sarah sank down on the floor by the table and sobbed. She couldn't get anything right, it seemed. And not even trying to choose mattered. She closed her eyes in despair and tried to pray.

As Grant was heading home, the early morning fog still curled across the highway, and his low beams barely picked out the bulky shape on the road before he braked. It was a deer, bloody, but still struggling. He stopped and pulled off, leaving his lights on and grabbing his bag from the back. He'd never treated a deer, and he thought it ironic that God should place him in this position considering the way his parents had died. It was a doe, from what he could tell, and it was flailing in misery. There was probably no helping it, he thought grimly, and threw his coat down on the ground as a makeshift slide to get it off the road. He looped the two slashing back hooves together with a rope from his bag, then eased his coat beneath the animal, inch by inch.

In the gleam of the headlights, he saw that its neck was broken. He reached for his bag to draw up a needle to euthanize the animal, but something made him take a second look. He knelt to run a hand along the abdomen to find it swollen in the latter stages of pregnancy. He drew out his stethoscope and listened; a rapid heartbeat filled his ears– too rapid. The fetus was in distress, but in the time it would take for the injection to kill the mother, he might well lose the baby. He looked down into the desperate eyes of the doe.

"I know, old girl. I know." He briefly wished he carried a gun like some rural vets he knew but had never come to terms with doing that, so he drew a lean scalpel from his bag and neatly cut the pulsing veins in the valiant neck of the animal. As soon as her head dropped, he did a hasty cesarean and slid his jacket from beneath the mother to wrap up the wet fetus. He wasn't completely sure of the gestation period of the whitetail deer, but the baby seemed to be fine and breathing on its own. He opened the car door with one hand, laid the little bundle in his backseat, then moved to drag the doe farther off the road into a field. He thought it to be a waste of good meat for some hungry family, but he didn't have room in his car and couldn't take the risk of leaving the fawn to chill. So he got back in, wiping his bloody hands on his jeans, and cranked up the heat, making time toward home.

Mrs. Bustle greeted him at the back door as he parceled the fawn inside.

"Sir…you're covered in blood! What happened?"

"A rather unhappy delivery; I lost the mother." He laid his coat on the kitchen table and opened its sticky folds to reveal the beautiful animal inside.

Mrs. Bustle's maternal instincts kicked in at once. "The poor thing! Will it be able to survive?"

"Yes, if we get her on fluids and then on a bottle quick enough. If you'll clean her up a bit and wrap her in flannel, I'll go back and Google some information on the whitetail." He left Mrs. Bustle to it, paused to wash his hands and explain to Mr. Bustle, then made his way to his recent Internet connection. He searched for the right site, but one part of his brain was occupied with Sarah, wondering if she felt all right after the fire. How strange that he should be brought to rescue the fawn on a morning when he worried so much for the one he loved.

The one he loved… He'd admitted it to himself before, of course, on some level, but today, seeing the fragility of life, he thought about the fact that he loved Sarah irrevocably. And that meant risk to him. Of course, there was nothing in life that was worth having that didn't call for risk. Risk in pregnancy, risk in relationships, risk in faith. There would be a huge risk in attempting to speak to Sarah's father about his feelings.

He stared at the computer screen for a long time before rising to go and help the innocent creature that was virtually cast into his arms and decided to name her, for the time being, Risk.

Chapter Thirteen

The harvest was in, and *Mamm* declared that Chelsea could do with an extra pair of hands with a new baby and said that it would be good for Sarah to go help her for a week while Luke ran the stand.

Sarah had reluctantly agreed, though her heart wasn't in it—and more than that, she had no chance to see Grant to tell him she was leaving. But she told herself that this was probably for the best and determinedly tried to be happy for the upcoming time with her sister.

"Be sure to get some fresh air each day while you're there," *Mamm* instructed, as Sarah climbed into the closed buggy with Luke. "You're far too pale."

"*Jah, Mamm*," Sarah replied.

They'd started off on the crystal bright day. The late October air was bitingly cold, and Sarah half closed her eyes over her scarf top as she watched the farms drift past. Housewives were gathering half-frozen Amish clothes from clotheslines to take indoors to iron dry, and Amish men were working on fences and rooftops, securing all for the coming season.

Everything looked the same to her, though, and she tried to push Grant's face from her mind for the thousandth time. She started when she realized Luke had spoken to her.

"What?"

"I've only been speaking to you for the past mile, Sarah King. What part haven't you heard?"

"I'm sorry; I was watching the scenery."

"*Nee*, you're heartsick, that's what, and over an *Englischer*. I never thought I'd live to see the day."

She was too weary to deny anything. "I'm just confused."

"*Jah*, you're confused all right."

"Well, he's your friend too."

"Friend, *jah*. Friend is okay. But for you, it's more. You need to get things straight, Sarah."

She nodded and blinked back tears as Chelsea's house came into sight. Luke was right. Perhaps a change of atmosphere would be good for her, though she felt she could go to the moon and find no solace for her restlessness.

Still, when John Kemp opened the front door to them and took Sarah's satchel, she felt a keen sense of welcome that did much to lift her spirits.

Chelsea looked fit and carried John Jr. around in the crook of her arm, having become adept at doing everything one-handed. When Aunt Sarah was asked if she'd like to hold the baby, she took the warm bundle with amazement and tenderness. She sat in a rocking chair near the woodstove and pulled back the quilt she'd made to reveal the baby's long blue dress, traditional garb for boy and girl infants, examined the tiny toes, and then felt her heart melt at the gentle coo the tiny one gave her when she smiled down at him.

Luke stayed to lunch, a happy, laughing affair of sweet creamed tomatoes, roast beef sandwiches, blueberry pie, and fresh cheese. John Kemp was known for making cheese, and his cheddar was considered some of the best in the community. Chelsea's mother-in-law joined them for lunch, coming over from the *doddy* house. She was old, but still her eyes sparkled with life. Sarah knew that she had lived through the loss of seven children and her husband, and her brown eyes were both wise and tempered by the grief she'd born and conquered with the Lord's help. Sarah thought she might find a kindred spirit in the woman and promised herself to visit the *doddy* house often during her stay.

After lunch, Luke drove off with the promise to return in a week's time. Chelsea took Sarah upstairs to a small, beautiful room that looked out onto the sloping snow of the back acres and the far-off rounded mountains, dotted here and there with pine and evergreen, and dusted with light snow on their tops.

The room had a small bed covered in a patchwork quilt made with a delicate mixture of purples, pinks, and white, which Sarah recognized as the Harrison Rose pattern. A small writing desk stood beneath the window, which was dressed in white lawn, and Sarah's satchel lay on the bed.

"Chelsea, the room is so pretty! I don't recall it from my first visit."

"I've done some rearranging in the house, but I especially wanted to have a pretty guest room. John's cheese buyers often come from miles away and end up talking on and then having to stay the night. I hope that you will be happy here, little sister, and that the shadows will disappear from beneath your eyes."

Sarah fingered the delicate quilt and shook her head. "I've just not been sleeping well. You know that I always miss the garden this time of year."

"And you're usually studying your seed catalogs for hours on end and have your garden sketched out."

Sarah thought of the last garden she'd sketched, the one for the doctor, and shook her head. "I've not had the time lately."

Chelsea put her free hand on her hip and snuggled John Jr. closer with the other. "Sarah King, don't be telling me that you haven't had time. Why, I've known you to—" She broke off when Sarah gave a sniff.

"Chelsea, I came here to get away, *ach*, and to visit with you, of course, but I just can't talk about… things."

Chelsea came close and wrapped her in a hug, including the baby, until Sarah laughed through her tears. "I won't say another word about it," Chelsea promised, and she was as good as her word. Instead, she kept Sarah busy reading the circle letter, a letter

that circulated among women of both near and far
Amish communities to keep each other abreast of
happenings and visitings, births and deaths. Each
woman who read the letter added on her own piece of
a few sentences or so, and the letter kept going until
it reached its original sender.

Chelsea was also involved in a quilting square
circle letter in which the women writers would also
include their hand-drawn pattern of their favorite quilt
square and the story behind it. Sarah volunteered to
copy each of the twenty-four patterns that had been
sketched on the pages of the letter thus far. She enjoyed the odd titles given to the squares, like *Browning Bread* and *Hen House Solace*. It was like she could
touch these women, from as far away as Ohio, and feel
their emotions on the day they sketched the pattern.
Some were sad, like *Lost Love* or *Buggy Accident*,
and Sarah found herself weeping as she matched each
piece of news in the letter with its corresponding quilt
square of choice. Chelsea caught her with the tears and
snatched the letter away.

"*Ach*, you're not going to just sit here being sad; go
and see *Mamm* Kemp. And don't be crying with her
over there either."

So Sarah pulled on her shawl and hurried to the
small *doddy* house, which was only a few steps away
from the main house. Mrs. Kemp came to her knock
and invited her in.

"Come in, child, and have some hot cocoa. I've just
got it fresh."

Sarah followed the aged woman, admiring the little house so crammed with quilts and crocheted items, as well as books and copies of the *Budget* and framed paintings of different birds filling up the walls. The miniature kitchen was just right for someone to feel independent if they did not wish to go to the main house, and the tiny icebox looked more like that of a doll's house. Sarah could smell the chocolate brewing and perched on a tiny chair near the woodstove while Mrs. Kemp rattled about in a crowded china cabinet, producing two cups and saucers with bright fuchsia flowers on them.

"Some spring flowers for an autumn day, eh, child?"

"They're lovely, and this cocoa is wonderful. Do I taste cinnamon?"

"*Jah*, and a hint of cloves. My eldest son, Seth, won those cups and saucers for me for a penny at a ball throw at the fair. *Ach*, but his father wanted to wail him good for it too, called it gambling. But I said they were beautiful, and that was that."

Sarah took another sip, thinking about the incredible amount of life the woman had lived and how she'd survived. "What happened to Seth?"

"A tractor accident. It was a rainy day; we'd had so much rain that year. The flowers were blooming when we laid him to rest. I picked them fresh myself for the grave."

Sarah stared into her cup. "And your other children?"

"My Sarah died with the influenza, so did David. Paul was in a buggy accident, and Anna caught the pneumonia deep one winter. Abel had childhood cancer, and Titus died as an infant—the midwife said his heart wasn't right."

"I am so sorry. I don't know why I asked you to remember all of that."

"*Ach*, now Sarah King, I know young people. It's only when they're sad themselves that they want to hear about others' sadness. So, you tell me, what is it that troubles your heart?"

Sarah answered; she felt safe to be truthful with her hostess. "An *Englischer*—the new vet, Dr. Williams."

"Ah, then it's true trouble, because no doubt your good father and *Mamm* have warned you against feelings for those on the outside?"

"*Jah*, and I've tried…so hard, but not really. I'm dishonoring them."

The old woman rocked for a few moments. "And what does your heart tell you?"

Sarah looked at her blankly, then gave a broken laugh. "My heart? My heart is to be trusted least of all."

"The heart is not just emotion; sometimes it's a very keen source of wisdom."

Sarah drew a shaky breath and stared into her teacup.

"You'll see, dear…it will all work out. Love finds its way with the help of *Der Herr*."

Sarah slipped into the gentle routine of the cheerful household and felt her soul begin to feel at peace.

Grant shifted gears and slid on the long, dirt drive for the second time and sighed. He had no desire to make a call like the one he had to today. He'd gotten word that the beloved cat of *Grossmudder* Stolis was dying, and would he come to help put it out of its misery?

He had a particular affection for cats and found them to be more companionable than even a good dog. He liked their savoir faire, their independence, and their predilection to survive in even the most remote possibilities. But a twenty-year-old cat had none of its nine lives left to call upon, and he took his bag with the usual euthanasia meds with reluctance and made his way around the back of the dry goods store to the *doddy* house.

He knocked on the door and had to bend his head to enter the lovely cottage. The woman who greeted him surely must have been ninety-if she was a day, but her wizened elfin frame was spry and her bright blue eyes shone up at him with clarity.

"Mrs. Stolis? I'm Dr. Williams… I got word about your cat. I've come to put it down as you asked."

Just then a fat, happy black cat strolled across the room and landed its considerable weight onto one of his wet boots.

Mrs. Stolis looked perplexed. "You say you want to put Tom down?"

The black cat rolled over, three paws in the air, one anchored for balance, expecting a belly rub, and Grant bent to comply.

"Yes, I'm afraid so. At his age, there's probably not much more that I can do."

The old woman dropped into a delicately carved chair covered with a crocheted throw; her lips began to tremble. Grant suppressed another sigh. He hated this part too and wished he could produce a kitten on the spot to cheer her, though he knew that each animal's life must be grieved for in its own time and worth.

"I'm sorry, ma'am." He looked down at the black cat that had fixed its clear, green eyes on his boot string and was having a fun go at getting it untied. He loosened the string a bit and waved it between the large batting paws.

"*Jah*…but I want to be here. It's the least that I can do for him." Mrs. Stolis straightened her already erect spine.

"Of course, I'll just get things ready." He stopped playing with the cat and reached into his bag for rubber gloves and the syringe. The black cat poked an inquisitive head into the opened space of the bag.

"*Ach*, he knows—he knows." The old woman suppressed a sob.

"He'll not know a thing, I promise," Grant soothed, rooting for a particular vial. "Now, if you'll just show me where Tom is, I'll do my best to make this easy for him."

Mrs. Stolis stared at him as if he'd taken leave of his

senses, and he stared back, waiting. Maybe she wasn't going to be able to bring herself to do it, he thought—which only made things worse.

"Ma'am?"

The black cat was back to belly rub position, and Grant used the toe of one boot.

"Where Tom is?" she asked.

"Yes, ma'am."

"Why, you're rubbing his belly, that's where!"

Grant stared down in amazement at the happy cat beneath his boot. There was no way that this was a twenty-year-old animal.

"I'm afraid that I don't understand."

"Why, that's Tom. He's been with me for going on twenty-one years now. I thought that you said you came to put him down."

"I got word—" Grant petted the cat, then pulled off his rubber gloves and dispatched the syringe into an empty vial. "I apologize, ma'am. Twenty-one years or not, he still is a healthy animal. There must have been some mistake in the message. I'll just go around front and check with them at the store."

Grant closed his bag, gave Tom a last rueful pat, and rose, nearly knocking his head on an overhead straw ornament. Mrs. Stolis saw him out onto the tiny porch, clearly thinking he was addled, and he had to agree at the moment.

He walked into the dry goods store. Mrs. Stolis left her few customers and greeted him. "Oh, Doctor, is it done?"

"Is what done? That cat's healthier than a horse."

Mrs. Stolis stared at him in surprise. "You do mean Tom, *jah*?"

"Tom...the big black cat who plays like a kitten."

"*Ach*, but he's near death."

Grant shook his head and tried to ignore the stares of interested customers. It would be fine grist for the gossip mill if the local *Englisch* vet couldn't tell a near death cat from a healthy one.

"I'm closing the store for a bit," Mrs. Stolis announced to his amazement, and the customers groaned. "Just for a few minutes; I'll be back. I must take the doctor to see the cat." She snatched up her shawl, and she and Grant followed the disgruntled customers out onto the porch.

Grant trailed after her determined form to the *doddy* house, wondering if the woman had a cruel streak and wanted the cat put down as a nuisance. When he reentered the house, *Grossmudder* Stolis sat in her chair, Tom on her lap, with the cat looking about as close to death as Grant had ever seen an animal. He stared perplexed at the cat, its tongue hanging out as it gasped for breath, its eyes rolled far back in its head. He dropped to his knees and reached for his bag. Grabbing his stethoscope, he listened for a heartbeat and found it so faint as to be negligible. He sank back on his knees and stared up at the women. "I don't get it—this cat was fine a few minutes ago. I tell you, he was playing with my boot string."

The younger Mrs. Stolis arched a disbelieving

brow as the cat gave a pathetic wheeze that sent Grant scrambling for his syringe again. He couldn't understand it, but he also couldn't let an animal suffer in such a manner. He gathered a fold of skin around the great neck and prepared to administer the injection.

"*Ach*, Tom does this often," *Grossmudder* Stolis muttered. "And there ain't no need to kill him over it."

Grant froze. "What did you say?"

The old woman leaned closer, as if he were hard of hearing. "I said, Tom does this often!"

The younger Mrs. Stolis appeared as perplexed as Grant. "What do you mean, *Mamm* Stolis?"

The old woman glared at them, then started to laugh. She laughed so hard, she wheezed, and when she did, Tom jumped up to rub his face against hers.

The young Mrs. Stolis screamed, and Grant felt a chill run down his spine.

Grossmudder Stolis stroked the now purring cat with a gnarled hand. "You've seen things, Doctor, but you ain't seen everything yet. Can't you tell when a cat's playin' possum?"

"What?"

"He plays dead. How do you think he's lasted in and out of all the nights of twenty-one years? If he looks dead, most things won't want to be eating him. I tell you he's got years left in him. Years. Just like me, ain't that right, Tom?" Tom blinked at Grant and seemed to agree.

Grant drove away, realizing the old woman and the old cat had taught him a valuable lesson. He did not know everything there was to know about life and about love, he thought. There were things of the heart that endured beyond time and medicine and expectation, and he wondered if he'd ever get the chance to really have that kind of a heart experience with Sarah. He sighed as he glanced in his rearview mirror and decided he should have asked the old cat for some advice.

He had just driven past the boundary of the King property when he noticed someone in a blue jacket moving through the starkness of the empty field. He pulled the car over and got out. His long legs made short work of the distance across the field, but the person in the blue coat must have caught sight of him because he took off, headed for the tree line of the woods at the back of the property.

Grant pressed on and, in a sudden burst of speed, was able to grab the tail end of the blue coat just as the man entered the woods. He pulled, realizing that he was much taller and outweighed the other runner, and felled the man against the cold earth.

"All right," Grant gasped, turning the struggling body over. "Who are—"

He broke off when he recognized the angry, dirty face of Matthew Fisher.

The boy had ceased to struggle and glared up at him, much as he had the day Grant had grabbed him by the nape of the neck at the stand.

"You're the Kings' arsonist, aren't you?" Grant asked, still taking deep breaths of cold air.

"I don't have to tell you nothing."

Grant eased up on his hold and leaned back on his knees, somehow feeling that the boy wasn't going to run again at that moment.

"Why Sarah? Why the Kings?"

"What difference does it make to you?"

"I lost my father when I was ten. I know you lost your father in a way—it changes you."

Matthew wrenched from him, his dark eyes filling with sudden tears. "Just shut up."

"No...not until I know that you're done with the fires."

"Ha. Do you think that's the only way to make somebody pay?"

"It's your way...like your father burned your mother's face. Do you want to be the same kind of man?"

"Shut up, you..."

Grant let him go. "Go on, run away; but you're going to have to face yourself sometime. Don't wait until it's too late."

The boy took off between the trees, and Grant rose slowly to his feet to pick his way back across the field. It had only been a suspicion really, about the arson, but the blue coat matched up. He'd have to let Mr. King know, though he doubted the police could catch the boy in the maze of the woods even at this time of year.

He sighed, chilled, as he got back in his car and

thought about old Mrs. Stolis. No, he didn't know everything, and he wished Matthew Fisher didn't know as much as he did about the evil of man.

Chapter Fourteen

The week at the Kemp farm seemed to take wings, and Sarah found herself feeling better as she spent time talking with John Kemp's *Mamm*, eating the tasty meals Chelsea prepared to tempt her, and holding her tiny nephew. When she returned home, there was color back in her cheeks and a renewed spirit within her, but when she went to greet Father, she found him pale and somewhat absentminded.

"Father," she asked with concern. "Are you ill?"

"*Nee.*" He smiled, patting her cheek. "I'm just growing old, that's all."

Sarah looked at *Mamm*, but she only shrugged with a worried frown and turned back to the stove.

So Sarah went back to the stand the next day and sat close to the kerosene heater Luke had brought that morning. She clutched her gloved hands together and tried to repress a shiver. She found it hard to believe that she'd ever thought, in the summers past, that it was too hot when the early November weather was as cold as it was.

The stubborn wind blew, shifting the light curtain of near-freezing rain into the deeper regions of the stand, and she moved to adjust some needlepoint pillows farther back on a shelf. She gazed over the baskets of pinecones, both natural and dipped in cinnamon wax, and the ten pumpkin and custard pies she'd made the previous night. In truth, she had fun arranging the various wreaths, dried mushrooms, and jars of canned items each day. And despite the cold, cars stopped. She learned to have an assortment of ribbon and brown paper for passersby who stopped on a whim, wanting a gift for the upcoming holiday season or some token to take home or to a party.

Mamm had also given her several quilts from the attics that she'd completed some years back. It amazed Sarah how fascinated the *Englisch* were with quilts and the act of quilting.

She glanced up at the thought, realizing that she was expecting Grant. She hadn't seen him since she'd returned, but a car pulled in, and a man got out who was not the doctor.

He was clad in one of the puffy coats the *Englisch* seemed to prefer in cold weather and wore sunglasses against the glare, as the light began to pierce through the thin rain, catching the dim corners of the leaden surroundings.

He took the glasses off as he mounted the steps to the stand.

"Mornin', honey. I'd like to see your quilts. Want to get one for my wife for Christmas."

Sarah rose, dreading the moment when she'd have to tell him the cost. *Mamm* had insisted that quilts in Lancaster and other places sold for as much as a thousand dollars and had also said she'd have the arthritis in her neck to prove her workmanship was just as fine.

"No lower than four hundred, Sarah. Don't forget what I say. Your heart is soft enough to give them away," *Mamm* had told her as she'd bundled the quilts into Sarah's outstretched arms.

"*Jah, Mamm*," Sarah had replied.

So she wriggled her cold fingers inside her gloves and unfolded the blue and white double wedding ring quilt first. She could see the pleasure in the man's eyes as he surveyed the stitchery.

"That's real pretty. You got anything with more purple and red in it?"

Sarah opened the Jacob's Ladder quilt, and the man smiled in satisfaction. "That'll be the one. I'll take it."

Sarah took a deep breath. "It's four hundred dollars, sir."

He looked surprised and she shifted nervously, hating this part of the stand. "Four hundred? Honey, you're selling yourself short. A quilt like this would go for nearly a thousand in some places."

He ran a rough hand over the colored fabric. "I'll give you five hundred and you learn a lesson from an older man. Don't sell for less."

Sarah swallowed. "Thank you so much. I hope your wife likes it."

His face took on a faint shadow, though he still smiled. "Well, me too. It'll be her last Christmas you know—if she can hang on that long. She's got the breast cancer real bad...gone through to the chest wall. The doctors don't give her much time." He was counting out the bills as he spoke and Sarah's eyes filled with quick tears.

He looked at her as he handed over the money and she took it reluctantly. "Don't feel bad, honey. We're believers in the Lord; I'll see her again one day."

"Please," Sarah choked. "Will you let me give you the bed pillows that will match the quilt? I—I'd like a chance to bless her."

The man smiled. "Why that'll be fine. Thank you."

"Can I wrap it for you? I have paper and ribbon."

"Sure."

Sarah was concentrated on fitting the paper around the quilt, thinking how much she had to be grateful for when others were suffering so. She wound ribbon around two of the needlepoint pillows, binding them together.

"Thank you, honey. You keep your chin up now!"

"*Ach*, you too and your wife!" Sarah called as he placed the items in his backseat, then got in and drove off with a wave.

Keep your chin up... Sarah pondered his words. He was telling her to be strong, when he had such a weight to bear himself. It made her bow her head in silent thanks to the Lord for sending someone to give her a message of hope that provided her a different perspective on life.

She returned home that evening, frustrated at not having seen Grant, only to encounter *Mamm*'s anxious face.

"Sarah, Father is much worse today than he has been. He doesn't want to leave his chair."

Sarah took one look at Father's ashen complexion and the indecisive faces of her brothers and spoke quickly.

"He needs to go to the hospital. I'll run to the telephone shack to call an ambulance; I'm faster." And she flew out into the freezing darkness.

Grant swung the car into the lane of the King farm, not even sure why he was doing it. He'd taken the fawn to the animal sanctuary that morning and had then been tied up with a difficult cesarean on a cow, followed by prolonged visits to several farms to complete herd vaccinations, which he'd been working on for nearly two weeks. He hadn't had the chance to see Sarah in forever, and he chafed at the darkened roadside stand as he passed it. His headlights suddenly picked up a woman crossing the road and he recognized the strands of light brown hair.

He ground the car to a halt and got out. "Sarah, what is it?"

She looked at him wild-eyed, and he caught her

shoulders. "It's Father. He's very ill. I need to telephone…"

"Get in." He sped a few yards down the lane, then muttered and stopped again. "Sarah, the battery's dead in my cell. Run to the telephone shack. Pick up the receiver and dial 9-1-1; someone who will help will answer. Run fast. I'll go to your father."

She was out of the car before he'd finished speaking and started back through the field, stumbling over the earthen clods. She was praying with each step, but she knew that the Lord had sent Grant at that moment. The Lord was in control. She kept repeating the thought over and over as she gained the small gray shack that housed the telephone. She flung the door wide and saw nothing but blank, rough walls and a black telephone and wires mounted on the wall opposite her. The fitful light of the moon allowed her to see the numbers. She lifted the handle with a shaking hand and put it to her ear. She'd never had to use a phone before. She heard a buzzing sound and recalled the number that Grant had spoken. She put her thin finger in the circle by the nine and turned it clockwise, then did the same for the two ones. She waited, her heart beating in her ears.

"9-1-1 emergency. How can I help you?" The woman's voice sounded calm and competent.

Sarah sagged against the wall in relief. "Father… my father…he's very ill. He needs an ambulance."

"Is he breathing?"

"*Jah*…yes… He's just very pale and sitting still."

"Can you take the phone and go to him while I ask you some questions?"

"No," she sobbed. "I'm Amish; I'm in a telephone house in the fields."

"All right, honey, hang on. Can you give me your address?"

Sarah carefully gave her address and directions to the farm from Lockport.

"All right, now I want you to go back to your father and wait for the ambulance. Do you know CPR?"

She thought desperately. "No...no... What is it?"

"It's all right, honey. Just go back to your father; try and make him comfortable. The ambulance is on its way... Should be there in ten minutes or less."

"I'll go," Sarah breathed. "*Danki.*"

She raced back toward the house, her feet beating a steady rhythm to the refrain in her heart. *Let him be well, Lord. Let him be well...*

Chapter Fifteen

Grant entered the farmhouse to an eerie quiet. The family was gathered around Mr. King's chair, and Mrs. King sobbed. They looked up at him as he crossed the kitchen and *Mamm* cried out, "*Der Herr sei gedankt*, Dr. Williams is here. Please help him!"

Grant hurried to the chair where Mr. King sagged, with his head on one side. He felt for a pulse, relieved to find it weak but present.

"When did this start?"

Mamm wrung her hands. "He hasn't been himself for a few days, but tonight he complained about a pain in his arm and then he just seemed to drift off. I couldn't wake him; I thought he was just tired."

"It's all right, Mrs. King, but I think it's his heart. Let's get him down on the floor and make him more comfortable. Get some blankets too." He took off his jacket and pillowed it on the hardwoods while the boys helped him ease their father down and cover him up.

Mr. King's eyelids fluttered, and Grant breathed a prayer of thanks.

"Mr. King, it's Grant Williams. You're going to be all right. The ambulance will be coming. Sarah ran to call them."

Grant kept up the flow of simple sentences, trying to make an anchor of his voice; Mr. King groaned.

"Get a damp cloth, will you, Luke?" he said low.

Sarah flew back into the kitchen as Grant began to wipe down her father's forehead. She dropped to the old man's side, next to her *mamm*, and began a rapid flood of Pennsylvania Dutch, in between hiccupping sobs.

"Here." Grant gave her the damp towel. "Wipe his face and calm down. You'll transfer your panic to him. Speak to him slowly. Did they say how long for the ambulance?"

"Ten minutes."

"Great… He's going to be all right, I think. He's breathing on his own and his pulse is okay."

"That's good," James said in a choked voice.

The whine of the ambulance siren hurtled to a stop outside. Grant went to open the door to the paramedics, then eased Sarah and her *mamm* to their feet and away from the patient.

He watched with both sadness and interest as the paramedics pulled on gloves and shot brief comments back and forth and then radioed vital signs back to Lockport Hospital. Medicine in all its forms interested

Grant, but he could not fully concentrate with Sarah's and her *mamm*'s faint sobbing.

The paramedics brought in a gurney and wrapped Mr. King in blankets; then they strapped him securely.

"Are you going to follow the ambulance?" One paramedic looked at Grant.

"We'll be right behind you."

He glanced at the boys. "I can take your *mamm* and Sarah and come back for you."

James shook his head. "*Nee*, go on. We need to get chores done; that's what Father would want."

"And we must let Chelsea and John Kemp know," Luke added.

Grant nodded and bundled Sarah and her *mamm* into his car as the ambulance sped away and he shifted the car into gear to follow. He wanted to soothe Sarah, hold her hand, but he kept up a reassuring conversation that demanded little reply instead.

They arrived at Lockport slightly behind the ambulance to find that Mr. King had been taken to the ER.

"Can we go back with him?" Grant asked, catching the eye of a kind nurse.

"Yes, you're family?" She looked at the obvious difference in dress between Grant and the two women.

Mamm spoke up. "He's from out of town."

Grant smothered a smile and felt flattered by the compliment. They followed the nurse through the massive swinging doors and entered the ordered chaos of the emergency room.

* * *

Sarah was assaulted by the unfamiliar sights, sounds, and smells of the place. Father looked small and frail on the hospital bed. He had tubes coming from his nose and arms and his clothing had been replaced by a blue gown and white blankets. Strange machines beeped and displayed ominous, blinking red numbers, while the nurses swinging the curtain back and forth along the steel rod grated against her nerves. *Mamm* was seated in the only chair while Sarah stood with Grant behind her.

"I know you're both scared," Grant said gently. "Would it help if I explained what they're doing?"

"*Jah*," *Mamm* sniffed, then pressed her lips together.

"All right, the tubes in his nose are for oxygen, to help him breathe more easily. The tube in his arm is called an IV. It goes into the vein to help deliver fluids and medicine directly into his system."

"Where are his clothes?" *Mamm* asked, desperate to hang on to something familiar.

The nurse looked up. "Mrs. King? I'm Erin, one of the nurses. Here are your husband's belongings." She handed *Mamm* a white plastic bag, and Sarah thought how strange it was that all of one's external life could be so easily confined by a mere slip of plastic.

"Will he go home soon?" *Mamm* asked.

"One of the doctors will be in to speak with you about that. Can I bring you some juice or water while you wait?"

Sarah and *Mamm* both shook their heads.

"No, thanks," Grant murmured.

The nurse flung the curtain open and closed once more, and *Mamm* reached her careworn hand to touch Father's. Sarah's lip quivered, and Grant massaged the back of her neck.

The curtain was reopened once again, and a white-coated young doctor entered. He glanced at the women and Grant, then he took a stethoscope, brushed aside Father's beard, and listened to the old man's chest. He slung the stethoscope back around his neck.

"He's going to need a heart cath—stat."

"What…what is that?" *Mamm* asked.

"You're Amish, right? My girlfriend loves your quilts; bet they go for a small fortune."

"The patient, if you please, Doctor." Grant's voice was level.

The young doctor grinned at Grant. "Did you forget to get dressed up this morning?"

"I'll speak to your superior, now," Grant said. "Tell him Dr. Williams requests the presence of his or her company."

Sarah felt Grant stiffen behind her. She couldn't see his face, but something must have made the other doctor change his mind about his attitude.

The young doctor glanced at the chart. "My apologies…Mrs. King. I…spoke without thinking. Your husband will be taken to a special room where we will use a very small camera to move through his vein and look at his heart to see what sort of damage there is, if any."

"Will he go home soon?" Sarah asked.

The doctor glanced at her, seeming to notice her beautiful face for the first time. "No...no, ma'am... A few days in the hospital or more. We have a hospitality suite where you can stay if you would like to be close by. I'll send one of the nurses in to talk about it with you."

He avoided Grant's eyes, nodded, and slipped out of the curtain.

"Eyes like flame, Dr. Williams," *Mamm* said, smiling. "You scared him off, I think."

Sarah felt Grant nod, then she stepped forward to embrace her mother, who hugged her back and muttered something in Pennsylvania Dutch.

"*Nee, Mamm.* That's not true."

"What did she say?" Grant asked curiously.

Sarah looked back at him. "She remembered an old superstition—that a new life must be paid for with an old. Chelsea's baby for Father, but she's just worried, *jah, Mamm*?"

Mrs. King nodded. "I know...*Der Herr* is in charge. All will be well."

A pair of nurses came then.

"Mrs. King, we're going to take your husband up to the cath lab to take some pictures of his heart. You can all follow us; there's a waiting room up there for you."

Sarah watched as tubes were unhooked and gathered, locks were turned on the wheels of the bed, and side rails were raised in quick precision. She held *Mamm*'s arm and followed the rolling bed with the doctor in the rear. They came to a large steel door, where the nurse pressed a black button and an arrow pointing upward lit up. Sarah swallowed in faint alarm. She knew it was called an elevator, but she'd never ridden in one and she didn't want to reveal her fear to *Mamm*.

She felt a large hand press into the small of her back as Grant leaned close to her ear. "First time?" he whispered, and she felt a peculiar chill down her spine as she nodded. He patted her back as a *bing* sounded and the steel door slid open. The bed was wheeled in first, then Sarah, *Mamm*, and Grant followed. Sarah felt a trapped tightness in her chest as the nurse pressed a button on the steel wall and was grateful for Grant's sturdy presence.

She felt as if her body was falling through her feet as the elevator climbed, and a wave of nausea swept through her. She looked at *Mamm*, who appeared equally pale, and was grateful when the thing stopped with a jolt and the doors reopened. Then it was following an endless piece of yellow tape on the floor until they came to double doors marked Heart Institute. The nurse smiled at them kindly and gestured to a bright room to their left.

"Please go and wait inside; we'll let you know as soon as possible how everything goes."

Mamm bent to kiss Father's still face, and Sarah did the same. Then the doors opened and closed on the gurney and Grant shepherded them into the waiting room.

Chapter Sixteen

The waiting room was cluttered with magazines, puzzles, and vinyl chairs. Despite the late hour, two other families, both with young children, were waiting and looked up as they entered. A television played CNN without sound and a cheerful old woman in a pink jacket, sitting at a desk with a telephone, greeted them.

"Come in, folks, and make yourselves comfortable. There's coffee and juices over there, and just let me know of anything that you might need."

The Kings murmured their thanks while Grant smiled and waited until the ladies had chosen seats on the far side of the room before asking if they wanted anything.

"No, thank you, Doctor," *Mamm* said.

Grant shook his head. "If you'll allow me to insist, you're going to have some orange juice. Both of you look rather pale after that elevator ride."

"*Jah*, it was my first time." *Mamm* laughed.

Grant went to the juice stand, noticing the covert

looks his two companions were receiving for their obvious difference in dress. It bothered him. What a person wore should not be a source for whispers and stares. He smiled to himself. Yet how many times had he categorized patients who seemed to resemble their pets? He grabbed three plastic bottles of juice from the ice and took them back.

Sarah and her mother stared at the plastic lids, and he showed them how to peel them back to reveal the juice inside. He was glad to note that a little color came back into Sarah's cheeks when she'd drunk deeply of the liquid.

"Okay," he said. "We're not going to sit here and torture ourselves with waiting. Believe me, I know what it's like. So, you two are going to give me a sampling of some good old home remedies that would probably put that doctor downstairs to shame, and I'm going to take notes." He withdrew a small notepad from his shirt pocket and a blue pen.

He clicked the pen. "All right...I'm ready."

Sarah stared at him in dismay. "But we need to pray now."

"Can't you pray and talk at the same time?" he asked innocently.

Again he'd managed to coax a smile from *Mamm*. "You're a good doctor, and yes, we will help you and pray at the same time. What remedies do you want?"

"Oh, anything, really. I find that many homeopathic cures work the same for both animals and people. And I'm also interested in the more curious cures—the ones that have been passed down for generations. Heirloom cures, you might call them." He shot a look at Sarah while *Mamm* nodded in affirmation.

"*Jah*, all right," *Mamm* began. "We'll start with the old cures. Some are superstitions, but they're fun to remember. But maybe these are not what you want?"

What he wanted was to keep the two women occupied while the time went by, and if he needed to listen to folklore, it made no difference to him. He also recalled how slowly time passed when he was ten and had to wait with the Bustles while word came about his father and mother. He had no desire to repeat that scene in his life, so he smiled broadly.

"I'll take the fun folklore first."

Mamm elbowed Sarah slightly. "*Kumme*, Sarah… we'll play and see who remembers the most. Father wouldn't want you to sit around with a long face."

"*Jah*, *Mamm*."

"Now, when you get warts on your hands, you know?"

Grant nodded, scribbling on the paper.

"You get the warts from handling toads."

"Even I've heard that one." He laughed. "What's something else?"

Mamm pursed her lips in thought. "Do not cut your hair in the dark of the moon; it will cause baldness."

Sarah sighed. "That's not true, *Mamm*."

"I know that; we're having the fun. Now play along, *boppli*, like a good girl."

Grant watched Sarah draw a deep breath. "The root

of rhubarb worn on a string around your neck will keep you from having a bellyache."

"Really?" He arched one golden brow at her.

"No…not really," she snapped. "The root of rhubarb is good for growing more rhubarb."

"Ah…I see."

"Now, for the more serious…" *Mamm* spoke. "When a baby gets the croup, you mix cinnamon, cloves, allspice, nutmeg, ginger, and mustard with some lard to make a paste. You put this on the baby's chest with a warm piece of flannel."

"That sounds like it would smell good," Grant offered as he wrote.

"*Jah*, and when your stomach needs cleansing because you've eaten too much, tell him what we do, Sarah."

"We jump up and down on the person until he throws up."

"Sarah!"

"All right," she sighed. "You mix lemon juice, cayenne powder, maple syrup, and water, and then you drink it fast."

"And then you throw up?" he asked.

"Only if you've a mind to, Doctor, and I think that if you must write something down, it should be useful."

"Such as?"

"If you want to keep bugs off your plants, make a mixture of water, dishwashing soap, and vegetable oil and spray the plants with it."

"So that's folklore?"

"No, it really works."

"Miss King, I do believe you're trying to take all the fun out of—"

He stopped as a surgeon entered the room. The man searched the waiting room with a quick glance.

"The King family?"

"*Jah.*" *Mamm* raised her hand.

The doctor approached and Grant rose in a defensive posture, not wanting a repeat of what had happened earlier with the younger doctor.

The surgeon offered a quick hand all around. "Mrs. King, your husband had another minor heart attack during the heart cath; we discovered that two of his main arteries are blocked to his heart. We're going to perform surgery to remove those blockages, with your permission."

Mamm had sunk back into her chair, and Sarah put an arm around her.

"This is fairly routine, though, Doctor, is it not?" Grant asked.

"Oh yes…extremely. He should be fine and home within the week." The surgeon paused. "Oh, and I need to ask—does he have a living will?"

"A living will?" Sarah asked in confusion.

The surgeon patiently explained, and *Mamm* shook her head. "*Ach*, no. He doesn't have this."

"Okay…well then, we'll proceed. It shouldn't take more than an hour or so. Why not go down to the cafeteria and have a bite to eat? And you can stop by the business office and get things squared away on that end. I'll call out to the phone here when he's out of surgery."

The surgeon left and Grant thought uneasily of the medical bills. He'd read that the Amish had no type of health insurance but was unsure if it was fact or fiction. He cleared his throat as they left the waiting room and entered the hall.

"Mrs. King, about the billing office…"

"*Jah*, we have no health insurance, as you call it."

"All right," Grant said, wondering how he could make it happen that the bill would mysteriously be paid by an anonymous donor.

"Our community will pay; they will help us," Sarah informed him.

Grant found it hard to grasp that a mostly agrarian community would be able to come up with the amount of money needed to cover the costs of open-heart surgery. Mrs. King patted his arm. "Now, I tell you not to worry, Dr. Williams. Perhaps you should tell us of some of your home remedies."

Grant smiled. "Saw through that, hmm? Well, if you say people will help, then I guess you know what you're talking about."

"*Jah*," Sarah said. "We have helped others many times; now they'll help us. It's the way the Bible says we should be."

"That's true enough, but sadly not always true of the world."

"In our world, it's true," Sarah said with finality

and Grant decided to let the matter drop. He felt at a loss when Sarah spoke so definitively about the differences between his world and hers, and he wondered how or if he could close that gap or even bridge it. And at the rate his heart was becoming involved with this Amish girl, it was something that required a lot of purposeful prayer.

Sarah felt like she was in another world—the *Englisch* world, in fact—and she longed for the solace and quiet of her garden. Instead, she followed *Mamm* and the doctor to the cafeteria and took the orange plastic tray he handed her, clutching it against her chest like a shield. The bewildering array of foods and crush of uniformed people made her stomach drop, and she didn't know how she could possibly eat a thing.

"You're biting your lip." Grant bent to whisper in her ear.

She stopped immediately and picked up an apple to put on her tray, only to find that it was made of plastic and part of a display. She hurriedly replaced it and frowned at Grant's laugh.

"You're not the first one who's tried to buy that, I bet. It looks remarkably real. Try this instead." He put a salad on her tray and added a pear. Sarah glanced at *Mamm*, who'd somehow navigated through the crowd with ease and was dishing up soup for herself from a large metal container.

Grant ordered pizza for himself while Sarah tried

to ignore the looks she was getting from a clutch of nurses. She knew her dress was supposed to be a symbol of her apartness from the world, but at the moment, she felt like she'd give anything to blend in. Then she decided that such thoughts were vain, and she immediately repented of them as the doctor led them to the cash register and paid for their meals.

He found them a small table in the crowded room and they all bowed for a silent grace before eating.

"The soup is good," *Mamm* pronounced. "But they use a bit too much salt."

"Hospital food has the reputation of being bad." Grant grinned.

"Not bad…just salty. *Ach*, I wonder how Father is doing?"

"Me too," Sarah murmured, poking listlessly at her dry salad.

"Eat something, Miss King. Then we'll go back up and see what news there is."

She was relieved when they'd finally eaten and Grant guided them back upstairs to the waiting room. The phone at the little desk was ringing as they entered, and the old woman answered it cheerfully.

"The King family?" she called out, and Grant stepped forward to take the receiver.

Sarah watched his solemn, handsome face and thought how grateful she was to have him with them during this time.

"Yes…I understand… Thank you."

Grant handed back the phone and turned to them

with a smile. "Mr. King is well. He came through the surgery with no problems. You can see him soon."

Mamm began to cry softly, and Sarah put her arm around her mother. The two women clung together for a moment, then *Mamm* quickly embraced Dr. Williams.

"We thank you, Doctor, for helping Father right from the beginning."

Grant smiled. "But it was Sarah who called for help."

Mrs. King nodded with a smile.

Sarah ducked her head shyly. "It was the first time I used the telephone…and hopefully, the last."

After the difficult visit to the intensive care unit, Sarah longed for a place where she might lay her head. The doctors and nurses seemed confident and happy about Father, but to Sarah, he looked devastatingly pale and ill. There were more tubes than ever and more machines than she could count that went off in alarming discord. *Mamm* had chosen to stay in what the nurse called the sleeper chair beside Father's bed, while Grant had gotten all of the necessary paperwork done so that Sarah might stay in the hospital's hospitality suite, which really was a converted floor of nurses' dormitories from when the place had been a teaching institution. It was a long walk from the ICU, and Sarah felt sure she'd never find her way back.

"Do you want me to write down the directions?

Hospitals are like mazes sometimes," Dr. Williams asked.

"No...I'll be fine."

They turned the corner and came to a pink-painted corridor with cheerful flowers stenciled on the walls. They found her room number, and Dr. Williams gestured down the hall. "There's a laundry there, bathrooms, and the women's showers. Are you sure you're going to be all right here alone?" He glanced dubiously down the quiet hallway.

"I'll lock the door."

"All right." He took the key from her and opened the door, flicking on the lights to reveal a spacious room with a flowered bedspread and television. Long curtains covered the windows and he went to draw them back for her, revealing a disheartening brick wall.

"Not much of a view," he commented. "I feel concerned about leaving you here alone."

Sarah shook her head and smoothed the polyester bedspread with one hand. She turned to face the full length mirror on one of the closet doors and was surprised to see herself in one piece since they had no large mirrors at home.

"I've gotten taller," she told him, staring into the mirror.

"Since this morning?" he asked, moving to stand behind her.

She blushed and shook her head and moved to step away, realizing she was behaving with vanity.

"Wait," he said, holding her still before the mirror. "Tell me what you see."

"What do you mean?" she asked, the quiet of the room at once seeming close and intimate.

"What do you see?"

"I see me."

He smiled. "Let me tell you what I see, if you can perch for just a moment, little hummingbird."

She stood still, her eyes meeting his in the length of the mirror.

"I see a beautiful girl, with a face like fine porcelain and gentle strands of light brown hair shot through with gold. I see soft lips that get bitten far too often. I see hazel, forest-green-brown eyes. And you may be taller, but just right, with straight shoulders and gentle hands. I see…"

She put her hands to her ears. "Stop, please. It's not right for you to speak to me so."

"Why not? Should I tell you instead what I see that's not in this mirror? Your fine mind, generous heart, kind soul…" He eased her hands down.

"*Nee*, you shouldn't tell me anything."

"That may be truth," he breathed, bending to press his mouth close to her ear. "But I can't help myself." He brushed his mouth against the fine line of her neck and she watched, mesmerized, in the mirror, as her irises grew darker green, and she shivered when his lips found a tender spot behind her ear. She closed her eyes against the wash of sensations and nearly fell when he pulled from her.

"My apologies, Sarah. You seem to bring out the best and, shall we say, the worst of my *Englisch* nature. I'll say good night…or good morning, but lock your door."

He slipped from the room while Sarah struggled to catch her breath. She locked the door behind him, then sagged to her knees against the wood and prayed once more for direction.

When she rose, she felt something lumpy in her apron pocket and discovered the journal Chelsea had given her for her birthday. She'd intended on writing in it that morning, and now she withdrew it and went to the small desk in the corner of the room. A pen and paper lay nearby for guests to use, so she took up the pen and opened the journal.

She'd used to love to write in school, especially poetry. It had always given her a sense of freedom or release to put down in words what she was feeling inside. She began to write.

There are two of me, it seems,
Wood with twice-toned grain
One, the straight and narrow
Like the gate to my garden
One, the wandering path
Like the deer trail through the forest.
But I am not fleet,
Cannot run on stag's feet
To escape the touch and sound
Of his breath blending round

I shudder then recall
That I am one and all
Still my father's daughter
Still like deep pond water
Where no one can tread.

She put her head down on the open journal and drew her breath in and out as if she ran through a forest glade, being pursued by herself, and him—she wrote his name slowly.

Grant.

And then, *Grant me grace.*

Chapter Seventeen

Sarah awoke feeling refreshed. She needed to have *Mamm* come and sleep downstairs because there was no way the sleeper chair could be as comfortable as the firm little bed with its starched white sheets. She unlocked her door, peered down the hallway, and then went along to discover the mysteries of the shower. Once she'd washed and redressed, she went back to the room to tidy her hair and reapply her *kapp*, trying not to think about the doctor standing behind her in the mirror. She pocketed her journal and left the room as neat as she'd found it and then began the complicated journey back to the intensive care unit. She took a wrong turn, though, and was standing, debating outside a gift and flower shop, when a woman called to her.

"Are you lost, *boppli*?"

Sarah entered the shop, amazed to hear her home language, and then she looked at the woman's face. A thin scar ran from behind her ear to her chin; it was Mrs. Fisher. But a Mrs. Fisher that was scarcely recognizable except for the scar. This woman wore a cheerful pink jacket and had a becoming shoulder-length hairstyle. Her face was made up and she smiled widely.

"Sarah King...do you know me?"

Sarah was so surprised that she hardly knew how to answer. If an Amish family left the community, they were not to be acknowledged by any of the community. Yet Sarah could not bring herself not to respond politely; the woman looked so radically different and happy.

"*Jah*...Mrs. Fisher."

"Yes...well, it's Ms. Fisher, actually. I divorced Mr. Fisher—he's moved out of the state—and I'm living here in Lockport now and have this job, which I greatly enjoy."

"*Ach*..." Sarah trailed off. One part of her wanted to rejoice that the woman had gotten away from the man who had so abused her, but the other part of her mind wrestled with the difficult concept of divorce and all of its implications.

"Who is ill from your family? That's why you're here, right?"

"Father...he had heart surgery yesterday. They say he'll be fine. I—I lost my way going to the ICU."

"Well, I can't leave the shop to take you, but I'll page someone. I sure hope your father and *Mamm* will stay well. They were kind to me, or tried to be at least, as much as Mr. Fisher would allow."

"*Danki*... I will tell—" She stopped short, wondering if she actually would tell *Mamm* that she had spoken with someone who'd left the community.

But Ms. Fisher laughed. "You will probably not tell them, little Sarah. But this is okay. I am well and happy now at last."

"And your children?" Sarah could not help but ask when she recalled the day at the stand and Matthew Fisher's roughness.

At once, the smile dimmed on the older woman's face. "My daughter, she is with me and goes to college, but the boys... I do not know. They went the way of their father."

"I'm sorry."

"Don't be. And you, Sarah, you've grown into a beautiful young woman; you may not always find it so easy to stay among the constraints of the community. Please remember to do this one thing—marry the one you love, but also marry the one who loves you. One who is cruel to you does not truly love you—whether he's Amish or *Englisch*."

Sarah nodded and blushed. It was almost as if the woman spoke to her heart. And how truant a heart she'd had! She nodded to Ms. Fisher when another woman came to lead her to the ICU, and she left the shop in deep thought. There had been an air of freeness about Ms. Fisher that had seemed refreshing, not worldly. It seemed as though the woman had truly found her place in life in God's will. Sarah followed the pink coat with tears swelling in her eyes. She was thinking treacherous thoughts this day, and with her own father lying so ill down the way. She swallowed hard and blinked back the tears, focusing instead on thanking God for answering her prayer and allowing Father to live.

When the pink-coated lady led Sarah through the intensive care unit to her father's bed from the night before, Sarah found, to her horror that it was empty and made up. She made a small sound of distress and the other woman turned to her with a smile, patting her hand.

"Don't worry, honey. They've probably just moved him to the CCU."

"The CCU?"

"Cardiac Care Unit. It means he's doing better. It's amazing what they can do with heart surgery these days, and the patient up and about and home before you know it." She walked as she talked and pushed through another set of interior doors, where there was a pervasive feeling of less urgency. She stopped at the nurses' station.

"What's your dad's name, honey?"

"Ephraim King," Sarah replied, conscious once again of the looks her dress was receiving from the brightly shirted nurses.

"I'm his nurse, Eileen." A girl who seemed no older than Sarah herself stretched out a slender hand over a stack of files. "I'll take you to him; he's doing wonderfully. And he is keeping everyone entertained with his stories."

"And my *mamm*…my mother?"

"Right in here… What was your name again?"

"I'm sorry. It's Sarah."

"All righty, Sarah…Mr. King, Mrs. King, your daughter is here." She flung open a cheerful yellow curtain and Sarah found Father sitting up in bed and *Mamm* in a chair drawn close by. There was a doctor there who was laughing over something Father had said.

"*Ach*, Sarah. Come in," *Mamm* encouraged. "This is Dr. Caulder, who's taken over Father's case. Doctor, this is our youngest daughter, Sarah."

Sarah shook the hand outstretched to her shyly. Dr. Caulder was an older *Englisch* man with glasses and blond hair, graying at his temples.

"A very beautiful youngest daughter, if I may." He inclined his head to Sarah, who began to bite her bottom lip.

Father smiled, looking better than the day before. "The doctor is telling *Mamm* that she has to change her cooking ways; you'd better listen too, little Sarah."

"Well." Dr. Caulder smiled. "I'd like all of you to cut down on using a few things—butter, salt, syrups, heavy sugars, breads…"

Sarah stared at him in dismay, considering he'd just rattled off about half their everyday diets, but Father laughed and so did *Mamm*.

"*Jah*, we'll try."

"I read a recent report about heart disease and the Amish; it seems that you are the exception to the rule, Mr. King. Heart disease is supposed to be lower among your communities than the average population because you do such hard, physical labor."

"Then why did this happen to Father?" Sarah burst out.

"As I said, your father is the exception to the rule. His cholesterol, the fatty substance that can build up in your arteries, is very high. His own father passed away from a heart attack, which leads me to suspect that his high cholesterol is hereditary, so it may be something that you and the rest of your family should be aware of."

Sarah nodded, turning the words over in her head.

"So, Mr. King, my thought is that you can go home… Let's see…today is Tuesday… Let's try for Thursday, but you have to take it easy for a while. No heavy lifting, no stress on the heart. We'll go over all of that with you, and I'll be back tonight to check on you and to hear another story."

"*Danki*—thanks, Doctor." Father nodded. "I'll be ready for you."

Dr. Caulder chuckled again, patted Sarah's arm, and slipped from the room. The nurse, Eileen, then took over, dispensing pills and listening to Father's lungs.

When she'd gone, Sarah looked at *Mamm* and recognized the deep lines of fatigue on her face, then she glanced at the so-called sleeping chair and had an idea.

"*Mamm*, please, why don't you let me sit with Father while you go down and sleep in my bed in the little room for a while? I could take you there. You need rest."

"*Jah*, Mama," Father spoke. "I don't like to see you sleep in that contraption. Go and rest and let Sarah entertain me here."

Mamm looked ready to protest, but a yawn stopped her and she nodded. "All right, I'll do as you ask, but only for an hour or so. You have to come and wake me up, though, Sarah."

"*Ach*, you know that I will; *kumme*, I'll take you now."

Mamm shook her head. "I'll just find my way."

Sarah thought of Ms. Fisher but decided that the chances of *Mamm* seeing her were unlikely, and she handed over the key to her room.

Mamm bent to kiss Father on the forehead, then squeezed past Sarah as Sarah took her place beside Father.

"*Mamm* is independent," Sarah remarked, pulling her chair closer to the bed.

Father nodded, his eyes half closing as if savoring some memory. "*Jah*, it's why I married her."

"Tell me," Sarah prompted.

"*Ach*, you have heard it before, little one."

"I feel like you leave something out though each time, so that the story will be fresh for retelling. So tell, please—it will make you a better storyteller tonight for Dr. Caulder," she added slyly.

Father laughed. "*Ach*, well then, when I was young

and my eyes still bright…I had to tell a story to win the hand of my love, Letty Rimm."

Sarah leaned forward, her chin pillowed dreamily on her upturned palm. "And what did Letty Rimm say once you'd told your story?"

Father laughed. "She said that she chose me, for understanding that the hand of a woman is both tame and wild, until true love changes all."

"I love you, Father."

"And I too, my daughter." Then he drifted off to sleep, while Sarah kept steady watch.

Chapter Eighteen

Grant entered the hospital in time for afternoon visiting hours, eager to see Sarah.

He found, upon inquiry, that Mr. King had been moved to the CCU, but when he went there to poke his head in, the old man was sound asleep and no sign of Mrs. King or Sarah was evident.

"They went to the cafeteria," a pretty nurse whispered to him, her face revealing an interest as to what connection he might have with the Amish family.

But he merely smiled his thanks and hurried away. He passed the flower shop on the way and, on a whim, decided that a bouquet or two might be nice for the King ladies. So he entered and was immediately struck by the woman who smiled at him from behind the counter. There was no mistaking the scar that Sarah had described, but he decided there were probably many scars in the world and he blinked and looked in the refrigerated case of flowers.

"Something for your wife?" the woman asked, and he looked at her again, for her English possessed that distinct melodic undertone so familiar to him from listening to Sarah.

"No." He smiled. "But two bouquets, please. The fall bouquet in the front and the smaller posy nosegay in the back."

The woman pulled the flowers from the case and started to wrap them in green tissue paper, wanting to chat as she asked him who he was visiting.

"Friends," he replied. "They're an Amish family who live on one of the outlying farms."

There was no mistaking her reaction; she quieted and then proceeded to add cellophane around the flowers.

"Forgive me, I'm Dr. Grant Williams, a local veterinarian. Are you, by any chance, Mrs. Fisher?"

She met his eyes, the fact that he was a doctor obviously soothing her somewhat, and she nodded.

"I bought your farm—from your husband. I'm sorry I've never had the pleasure of meeting you until now."

"It's a sad house you bought, then, Doctor—if the walls can remember."

"I understand."

"I used to wonder if anyone could, but now I've come to find good friends, true friends."

"I'm glad for that."

"So you know the Kings?"

"Yes, I've come to. Mr. King had a heart attack."

"I know—I've talked with his youngest girl, Sarah."

Now it was Grant's turn to look uncomfortable, and the woman smiled.

"*Ach*, I see how the wind blows."

"No wind blowing," he lied. "Just friends."

"Is the posy bouquet for her?"

"You're very astute."

"I've had to be," she replied and her pretty mouth drooped a little, emphasizing the scar.

"I'm sorry for that." He paid for the flowers and gathered them up.

"May I offer a word of advice?" she asked as he turned to leave.

"Certainly."

"They won't let her go. *Ach*, the Kings are good people, but the community matters to them. It is their life."

"I thought God was life," he returned.

"They won't let her go, and she is too young to choose to leave it behind. It would be better for you if you would forget."

"I know. I have a problem, don't I? It's not that easy sometimes…" He paused.

"To forget?" she asked gently.

"Yes, I'm sorry. That's what I was going to say."

"Then we do agree. I wish you the Lord's blessing in your choices."

"Thank you." He smiled at her and nodded, leaving the shop.

* * *

Sarah had grown used to the cafeteria in the day or so she'd been there, and now *Mamm* and she sat eating egg salad and something labeled "yogurt parfait."

It was interesting to watch the *Englischers* and to observe their hairstyles, dress, and chattiness. In many ways, Sarah found the women to be just like Amish women except for when she saw a pair of high heels or an upswept hairdo held in place by butterfly combs. She was studying a woman in sheer nylons when Dr. Williams came smiling to their table.

"Mrs. King, Miss King. I brought you a little something to cheer your day. How is Mr. King?"

Mamm took the flowers with reverence. "*Ach*, Doctor—I've not had a bouquet of fresh flowers since I'd pick them myself as a girl on the mountainside."

"Then I guess I need to give Mr. King some lessons in romance when he gets home, hadn't I?" He'd meant it as a simple joke, Sarah knew, but the implications struck home and she buried her face in her small posy of rosebuds and baby's breath. He cleared his throat.

"I wanted to give you a message from the boys at home; they'd like to come and visit. But the work of the farm and stand is a lot to keep going."

"*Jah*." *Mamm* nodded. "It's better that they stay at home. We can manage."

"Okay, I'll just go get some lunch." He wandered off, and *Mamm* took another appreciative breath of her fall arrangement.

"He's a good man."

"*Jah.*"

Mamm gave her a sharp look. "A good *Englisch* man, Sarah, and one I think you've grown to care for overmuch despite your father's and my own trust."

Sarah could not speak.

"And does he know, little Sarah, this good man, that there can be nothing between the two of you? I would hate to see him hurt."

"I would not hurt him."

"Perhaps not on purpose, but he could be hurt. He is of the world, and his world is not yours."

Sarah nodded, feeling disheartened as the doctor returned with a sandwich and soup.

"Did I miss something serious?" he asked. "You both look sad."

"*Nee.*" *Mamm* smiled. "We're just admiring our flowers. I must get them some water. I'll take yours, Sarah, and you bring the doctor up to Father when he's done eating."

She rose and bustled off, while Sarah cleared up the remnants of their meal onto the plastic tray.

"Now what was that about? Are Amish women not supposed to accept flowers from an *Englischer*?"

She smiled and shook her head. "Of course, they're very beautiful."

"Not going to tell me, are you?"

"There's nothing to tell."

"Truth, Sarah. Remember?" he asked, spooning up

vegetable soup. She looked away. For the very first time, there was nothing to say, nothing that wouldn't sound presumptuous.

"There isn't anything."

"Your first lie to me," he pronounced. "In the middle of the *Englisch* world. We must be having a bad effect on you."

"Everyone here has been so kind to Father, to all of us."

"Before we go and see him, I'd like to take you somewhere."

She gazed at him, *Mamm*'s words echoing in the back of her mind.

He laughed. "Nowhere unwholesome; I give my word." He drained the last of his soup and stood up. "Come on, Miss King."

She followed him through corridors and past office suites and then on another brief elevator ride. They emerged to a lighted world with a giant aquarium taking up nearly the whole of one wall. Sarah approached it, mesmerized.

"What is it?" she asked in wonder, tracing the darting movements of colorful fish among waving aquatic plants.

"A very large aquarium. This is the children's section of the hospital; I heard Lockport had it redone, and this is a good color and scheme to hold a sick child's interest for a while."

She pressed tentative fingers to the glass as if she

couldn't quite believe it was real. A child in a wheel-chair rolled up and did the same, and Sarah stepped back.

"It's cool, isn't it?" the little girl in the wheelchair inquired.

"Yes, very…cool."

Sarah stood next to Grant, torn between watching the calm face of the child and the movement of the water. There was something resolute in the little one's face that made her believe that she'd probably been sick for some time.

"Come on, there's something else." Grant took her elbow and steered her down the hall, its lights recessed into hubs of deep purple and blue.

They entered a cheerful room with a colored carpet that was covered in bright golden stars against a royal blue background. Shelves of books lined the walls, and a woman greeted them with a smile.

"What's this?" Sarah inquired, not wanting to appear ignorant.

"It's a library."

"A library." She stopped in surprise. "Our library back at the schoolhouse didn't look like this."

"I bet not. Tell me about it."

"It consisted of two shelves of books; one for the younger *kinner*, one for the older. I read them all—many times." She smiled at the memory.

"Well, you can borrow a book from here while your father's in the hospital. Do you like fiction?"

She stammered over an answer, not quite recollecting what fiction was. He must have noticed her discomfiture because he pulled her by the hand down a row and away from the eyes of the lady at the desk.

"I'm sorry, Sarah. Fiction is a type of writing... made up, if you will, to entertain readers."

"You must think I'm stupid," she sighed.

"Don't say that again." He pulled her close. "The world is full of educated derelicts, and you are one of the wisest people I know."

"Derelicts?"

"Never mind."

"Do they have a book on cooking desserts?"

"Sure, I bet they do, but you don't need any lessons in that area." He patted his lean stomach in appreciation. "You forget how many treats I've had at the stand."

"*Ach*...I know, but I'd like to learn to make fancier things, maybe some things for Christmas."

"All righty, cookbooks it is." He pulled her with him and inquired from the woman at the desk about the cookbook section.

"We've only got a few," she speculated.

"That's fine," he said. "Anything on desserts will do."

Soon Sarah held a book with delightful pictures of elegant desserts on its cover, but better than that, she was able to walk out of the library with it with the simple information she'd given and the pledge to return it.

"This is *wunderbar*." She pressed his hand. "*Danki*, Grant."

"You're quite welcome."

He couldn't help but be pleased at Sarah's reaction to the library. He knew compulsory education for the Amish typically ended at the eighth grade, but he'd meant what he said to her, that he'd seen far too many educated people fall by the wayside when it came to leading healthy, vibrant lives. From what he could tell as he observed Sarah's community, the Amish culture had a way of meeting an individual's needs without the bane of individualism obstructing the way. Talent could be expressed in many different skills, as he'd learned from some savvy Amish men who understood things not taught in school.

And in Sarah herself, he found a resolute spirit and common sense that many girls he'd known lacked. For example, her desire to expand her repertoire of cooking; a lot of women in his life clung to that one great recipe that they were known for and wowed others at parties with it. But life was too short for knowing only one thing well, he thought as he gazed down at the hint of light brown hair visible at the front of her *kapp*.

"You'll make a good father," she remarked and he almost tripped over his own feet.

"What? Why do you say that all of a sudden?"

"It's a good sign in a man to have him care about books and learning new things. It shows that he's always willing to grow like one must when children come along."

"Thank you."

"You're welcome." He realized that she was studying the *Englisch* people they passed and wondered what she was thinking.

"The girls are so free in their movements," she remarked as if she'd read his thoughts.

Grant studied a passing pair of teenage girls and found them to be awkward and gawky. "I guess." He shrugged.

"*Nee*—I mean their comfort within themselves. They walk outward, not inward. Do you know what I mean?"

"You mean self-confidence?"

"That and something more. They know their place in this huge world, or at least, they can find their place."

"And don't you know your place in the world?"

"Not always...not lately."

Her words pulled at him. "Explain that some more to me. Here—let's sit down for a minute." He eased her onto a geometric-shaped sofa and she sat upright until he gave her a yank and she relaxed back into the softness of the vinyl.

"I don't know," she murmured. "I used to be just Sarah...with her garden."

"And who are you now?"

"Well, I finally made a quilt, for Chelsea... That's something new. And I run the stand, use the phone, ride on elevators, kiss people over brewing apple butter..."

He laughed. "Lots of people, or just one in particular?"

"Only one. There's only one." Her voice was low, serious, and he felt his chest burn at her words.

"Listen." He lifted her small hand and squeezed. He tried to go on, and she looked at him. He leaned close to her ear and whispered what he wanted to shout. "There's only one."

Sarah entered the hospital room with the doctor to find that her father was now well enough to have a roommate, it seemed. Father introduced a jovial old *Englisch* man named Mr. Geise. Mr. Geise's wife and daughter were also crowded in the small room. Sarah couldn't move a step without bumping into the doctor behind her. She saw the flower arrangements Grant had brought them on the windowsill in some pretty vases, and she met *Mamm*'s eye.

"One of the nurses said they keep a supply of vases under the sink."

Sarah nodded, and Father hailed Dr. Williams with much of his strength back in his voice.

"*Ach*, it's the good doctor who brings my wife flowers and leaves me to a lecture on my own lack of flower bringing."

"Sorry, sir." Grant smiled. "But I thought the ladies would like them better than you yourself. I can go down for some roses, if you're feeling down in the heart…"

The room at large laughed at the quip, and Sarah was happy to see some more color back in her father's cheeks. Dr. Caulder, the heart surgeon she'd met earlier, stopped in then and laughed to see so many people in the room.

"Now, what's the ruckus in here? I can hear you all halfway down the hall. These men need their rest," he scolded, but his eyes twinkled. "Fifteen more minutes, all of you, and then I want this room cleared. Understood?" He smiled again and left, leaving everyone to make a general move toward the door.

"Come back soon, Letty; the hours seem much longer here than on the farm," Father observed. *Mamm* bent to kiss him and Sarah looked away, only to encounter the doctor's keen glance. She blushed and he squeezed her arm, then dropped his hand away. In a few minutes, Sarah and *Mamm* were walking toward the hospitality suite and Dr. Williams left with the promise to come back again soon.

"Did I make you sad, Sarah, today—when I spoke of the doctor as an *Englisch* man?" *Mamm* asked.

"Not at all."

"I see that you have a book; you were gone quite awhile with Dr. Williams."

"*Jah*, he showed me the library. I can return the book when Father leaves."

"Which will not be soon enough, eh?"

Sarah agreed and opened the door to their room, thinking about her brief visit into the world with the doctor that afternoon.

Later that night, as Grant passed the hospital on return from a call, he decided to follow a sudden impulse and go and speak with Mr. King about his feelings for Sarah. He was probably cutting his own throat, he thought, but something needed to be said. He didn't like the idea of skulking about. So he slipped into the dim hospital room and found Mr. King to be awake. The older man looked pale, but his eyes were steady, and the oxygen tubes were absent.

"Come in, Doctor. Please have a chair."

Grant took the high-backed sleeper chair near the bed and moved the bedside tray so he could scoot the chair forward.

"It's a bit late for visiting, Son. You must have something more than this old man on your mind. Don't forget I get out tomorrow, and I feel right as rain."

"Good—that's good." Grant stared into the wise old eyes and swallowed hard. "I guess I'm not sure how to begin."

"We Amish have a saying: *Dummel dich net*. Take your time; don't hurry."

"You're right... Sometimes it's the hard things that we have to say that we want to rush out the most; I don't want to rush."

"Go on, my friend."

Grant listened to the steady beat of the heart monitor and closed his eyes. *Please, God, give me the words to say here. Please make this right.*

He opened his eyes and looked at Mr. King. "I'm not sure when…maybe it was the first moment at the stand, or a thousand moments after that, but I have come to love your Sarah, sir."

"*Ach…*" Mr. King drew a deep, unsteady breath. "I see…now, I must take my time with my words, because I don't wish to hurt you."

Grant felt his stomach fall and exhaled. "I know I'm *Englisch*, and that must be an affront to you. I—I haven't spoken to Sarah, but I believe she knows. I just—"

Mr. King raised a gentle hand. "Please, Son. It is not all as you think. Yes, you are *Englisch*, but you're a good man—a good friend to our family. I trust you; I like you. But for Sarah to marry an *Englischer*, she would have to give up all that she knows. All. Her community, her family, her faith. If you truly love her, then you won't ask this from her; you will let her go in peace."

"I know that she'd have to give up so much, but why? Why would she have to? I live next door; I see you almost every day…"

"It's true what you say: you are with us, but you are not one of us."

"Then I could change; I could change for her, become part of your community."

The old man shook his head. "I've heard of it tried

in my lifetime—an *Englischer* falls for one of our daughters. A community votes and allows them in; they are baptized—they try. But it doesn't work, and our daughters are left broken and alone. It's too great a risk."

Grant nodded, trying to blink back tears. There was truth in what Mr. King said, a truth he'd wrestled with for a long time these past months himself. He bowed his head, then looked up in alarm when the heart monitor's sensors increased. He gazed at the blood pressure machine and rose to his feet. He had no desire to force Mr. King into another heart attack. He would get over the girl; he'd gotten over much worse.

"Mr. King, please excuse me—I'll get your nurse. Thank you for your friendship; I hope that it continues. I will speak no more about Sarah." He left before the old man could speak and strode out of the room, stopping at the nurses' station. When he walked out to his car, he felt a chill in the air that went deeper than his coat, and he recognized the familiar layer of ice take form on the vestiges of his heart.

Chapter Nineteen

Father was home and slowly taking up the reins about the farm again, doing more and more as the weeks passed. The family had a lovely Thanksgiving together and Sarah came back to the stand for the season of Christmas. She could not deny that the doctor had been more absent than she would have liked, but she tried to concentrate on her work and on her prayer life. Father told her that her last day at the stand would be December 23, until the following spring. This would give her extra time to help at home with the cooking and cleaning, for many family members came to visit at Christmas and at Second Christmas.

The weeks passed quickly and the snow-covered mountains with their confectionary sugar trees took away the bleakness of November, leaving a joyful expectancy in the air. Sarah found some glad time to clear out her garden one Sunday afternoon, hardly able to believe that she was so late in doing so. She was equally glad as the weeks ticked down at the stand, though she couldn't help but notice that Grant seemed absent from his regular visits. She decided that he must be busy at this time of year with animal illnesses and tried not to worry over not seeing him.

On her last day at the stand, she sold her final holly wreath, and one *Englisch* woman paid her extra for an arrangement of berries and pinecones she'd done in a mason jar. Luke came to pick her up and she was glad to leave the stand, at least for a few months. For now, Christmas was in two days, which meant extra visitors, extra family, and extra work.

But Sarah moved with a cheerful grace, appreciative of being able to help *Mamm* with the daily work. She was also happier in her prayer life, having come to a truce of sorts with her own thoughts about Grant. When she'd finally poured out her heart to her heavenly Father, He gave her His peace. She certainly wasn't to the point of understanding everything about why Grant had been allowed into her life, but instead of worrying and fretting over it, God's Word made her feel as though things were clearer, and more stable, although she had to admit that thoughts of Grant permeated her day.

On Christmas Eve, Uncle Zebediah and Aunt Anna, Father's older brother and wife, came the fifteen miles to stay through Second Christmas, which was on January 6. This was an extended visit, but not uncommon for those whose children had grown and married or moved away. Other cousins and aunts and uncles would also be coming from the surrounding area, and *Mamm* cleaned right up until the first buggy arrived.

Sarah had worked too, in a flurry of dusting, re-arranging furniture, and prettying things up. She cut holly and ivy by the armful to fill vases here and about, and *Mamm* even allowed pine boughs to be laid across the many mantels of the fireplaces. The Amish of their community did not have Christmas trees, but they had a specially decorated round table that stood empty and waiting for presents to be laid upon it on Christmas Day. The family drew names from Father's hat to select who they would get a gift for, and Sarah drew Luke, for the second year in a row.

Luke had made no secret of the fact that he wanted a new saddle for Shadow so that in the spring he could race the boys. Sarah had no idea how she might purchase such a gift, even with all of her earnings from the stand, and she was also torn with indecision about getting a gift for Grant. It would be easy to fix a basket of preserves and canned goods for the Bustles to enjoy, but the doctor was another story. She pondered over it as she swept, washed the china that was used only for holidays, and prepared guest rooms on the mostly unused wing of the second floor.

She also took time each day to be outdoors or in the barn with the animals. It was her job, in the winter months, to tend the small flock of sheep that Father kept as a concession to *Mamm*, who liked to spin yarn the old-fashioned way for decorative threads in her quilts and rugs. Sarah had discovered in Novem-

ber that one of the older ewes was pregnant and had
shared this surprise with the family.

"*Ach*," Father had laughed. "A Christmas lambing
means a blessed spring."

Sarah hoped that he was right.

Grant struggled to stay away from the King farm
as much as possible. No one had seen or heard from
Matthew Fisher, and there were no more fires. Grant
busied himself with calls and checking up on past
patient animals and accepted more *Englisch* invitations as the holidays approached. He went with Bustle
to pick out a large tree that they cut at a traditional
Christmas tree farm, and he wrestled it inside and
drank Mrs. Bustle's secret-recipe hot chocolate afterward. But his heart wasn't in it, wasn't in much of
anything if truth be told, and he wrestled hard with
images of Sarah.

On the day before Christmas, he'd just settled the
last of the boxes of ornaments at the base of the tree
and prepared for Mrs. Bustle to offer placement sug-
gestions when a knock sounded at the front door. He
dragged himself to get it, and he recognized Sarah
through the glass, bundled up in a head shawl and
holding a festive basket. He ran his hand through his
hair and then opened the door with a smile.

"You're just in time. Mrs. Bustle's least favorite
thing to do is decorate the tree, so I do it for her. Now
you can help." He rushed the words out, half-scared

that she'd disappear from sight if he stopped talking or said the wrong thing.

"I brought you and the Bustles a few gifts." She shifted her feet under the weight of the basket, and he took it from her.

"Did you walk over here with this? It weighs a ton."

"Exercise is good for me."

He placed the basket on a side table and reached to help her unwind her shawl.

"Will you help with the tree?" he asked, like a small boy begging for a sweet, and she smiled.

"*Jah*—I never have before, though." She untied her bonnet and adjusted her *kapp*, and he had to resist the urge to brush a loose tendril behind her ear. He hung up her shawl instead.

"Mrs. Bustle? Miss King is here and has offered to help with the tree." He led the way into the parlor, and Mrs. Bustle immediately got to her feet.

"Good, I'm glad you're here, honey. I've got pecan tarts to finish baking and the tree is not my favorite thing to do. You two go on and have fun." Mrs. Bustle started out of the room when Sarah remembered the basket. She ran and got it and then gave the older woman a hug.

"It's just some simple things I thought you and Mr. Bustle might enjoy."

"Why, thank you, sweetheart! I'll take a look right now in the kitchen." She left with the hefty basket, and Sarah turned to Grant.

"I wasn't sure I should come. You...seem to be busy."

He looked at the tree. "Yeah, really busy. Come anytime, if you're permitted."

She seemed surprised. "Why shouldn't I be permitted?"

"I don't know. Do you believe in garland first or baubles?" He bent to the stack of boxes and withdrew a blown-glass ball that mirrored a snowflake falling deep inside.

She smiled. "Whatever you like best."

I like you best, he thought, but shook his head. "It's all the same to me."

"*Ach*, then the baubles please. I've never seen anything so beautiful."

"As the lady wishes." He knelt and with a flourish pulled the lids off the boxes of straw-nested ornaments. "Do the Amish have a Christmas tree?"

She knelt beside him and stroked an iridescent pink ball. "No, we have a present table. And no Santa Claus. We draw names for gifts; I got Luke."

"And what does that good fellow want?"

"A saddle for Shadow, to race him in the spring."

Grant rolled his eyes. "It's either race cars or horses with boys, isn't it?"

"I suppose they've got to have some fun...even grown-up boys and their red cars."

He put a hand out to touch her arm, then dropped it. "I've missed you, sassy girl."

"Me too."

He wanted to kiss her right then but knew he could not, not without starting the whole process of weaning his heart from her again, so he just smiled instead.

She reached into the folds of her apron pocket and withdrew a small, brown-paper-wrapped gift, tied with a single strand of green ribbon, and handed it to him.

"It's just a little thing…for you. For Christmas." She blushed and he took the gift with a tightness in his throat. He hadn't been able to bring himself to get her something. He'd wandered around Lockport, staring at hundreds of beautiful things, but he thought she'd find them vain and he hadn't planned on seeing her, not wanting to upset her father.

He opened the paper and marveled at the craftsmanship of the pocketknife.

"Mr. Stolis… He carves them and puts them together. I thought you might use it for work or around the farm."

He didn't speak and she rustled among the ornament boxes.

"Do you like it? Perhaps you have another…"

"Dozens," he admitted. "But none like this. I'll cherish it." He cleared his throat. "I…didn't have time—no, that's not true. I couldn't decide what to get you because I wasn't sure. Will you tell me what you want, please? Anything at all?"

She smiled and his heart melted. "Just this. Just this time with the tree; I'm happy."

He drew a deep breath and nodded in agreement.

Chapter Twenty

"Father, the ewe is having trouble with the birth. Shall I call for Dr. Williams?" Sarah whispered the words so as not to distract the fun. It was Christmas Eve and everyone was gathered around the fire listening to jokes and familiar family tales.

Father nodded, involved with Uncle Zebediah's storytelling.

Indeed, all of the family was engaged in the tale, holding their sides or wiping their eyes with laughter.

Sarah pulled on her wraps and *Mamm*'s coat and went out into the brisk cold of the starry night. Christmas Eve. She smiled as she blew out a stream of frosty breath and gazed at the lights in the Fisher farm across the way. She decided that a quick run across the half mile of frozen field would be the best way to reach the doctor. She'd only gone a few feet when she realized that her feet were freezing and that she had to break through the icy top layer of snow with each step, but she persevered with thoughts of the straining ewe forcing her to plunge onward, despite the fact that it had begun to snow.

When she mounted the steps of the doctor's house, she could hear the strains of Christmas music playing from inside. It seemed as though the doctor had guests, given the blur of color and movement that she could observe through the glass-paned door, and she bit her lip, not having thought of this. Still, she knocked and Mr. Bustle opened the door.

"Miss King…whatever are you doing out in this cold? Please come in."

Sarah stepped inside, only too aware now of her oversized clothing and soaking feet. The shawl she'd wrapped around her bonnet also dripped with snow and she stared at the puddle she was making on the floor.

"Why, look what the cat dragged in." An *Englisch* woman in a startling red dress stopped in front of her. Sarah glanced at the crystal glass the woman held filled with some mysterious bubbling drink. "Grant, come and see, one of those Amish girls, I think."

Dr. Williams came through the slight crush of guests, dressed in a magnificent dark suit, white shirt, and wine-colored tie.

"Sarah…what is it?" he asked, accepting the blanket Bustle produced and enveloping her in it.

"I shouldn't have come; I'm sorry," she whispered. "It's just that a ewe is having trouble delivering. If you could just tell me what to do…"

The woman in the red dress laughed. "Mary had a little lamb…"

Grant turned. "Bustle, would you mind serving Miranda some coffee…black, if you please. And I'll get my bag."

"A case, sir?"

"Yes, at the Kings'. I should be back shortly. Please keep the party going."

Sarah shivered when they went back out to the car, aware of her sopping feet, but also feeling distinctly angry and curious about the woman in the red dress. Grant turned the heater on full blast. "I'm sorry about Miranda. She's not always aware of the impact of what she says."

Sarah said nothing, her teeth chattering, her temper churning.

"Why didn't one of the boys come?"

"They're having fun with my uncle," she explained with a frown. "The sheep are mine to tend in the winter anyhow, but I certainly did not mean to interrupt your party."

"You didn't interrupt, but a winter lambing?" He shifted gears as the car began to slip on the icy road. "How did that happen?"

"I don't think I need to be explaining that to a doctor, do I?" she shot back, and he laughed.

"There's that sassy mouth of yours. All right, Miss King, you've got me, but do tell me how it is that this event is not in the spring. Are you trying alternate breeding techniques?" His voice was serious, but all she could think of was the woman in the vile red dress. She tried to chide herself into extending a spirit of goodwill toward the woman but couldn't quite do it.

"Are you listening?"

"Of course," she replied icily.

She felt him glance at her. "Okay, well then, I actually can't think of anything more symbolically wonderful than a lamb on Christmas Eve, can you?"

She shook her head, realizing the importance of his observance. She prayed to herself then that the lamb would survive as a celebration of the Lamb of God's birth and tried to dismiss the other woman from her mind.

They pulled past the gathered buggies and horses, and Sarah clambered out and headed toward the barn. The doctor looped his bag over one arm and caught her close with the other when she slipped on an icy patch.

When they entered the barn, the warm, mellow light of the kerosene lanterns and the warmth of the animals' bodies greeted them. Sarah led him to the stall where the ewe labored and was disappointed to see that she'd made no progress.

Grant took off his coat and suit coat, and he loosened his tie. He rolled up his sleeves and started to scrub up.

"Do you think it's breech?" he asked, approaching the animal.

"No, but it's got one foot back and I can't bring it forward. I'm afraid of hurting her."

"Well, you're right," he said after a brief examination. "The secret is hooking a finger around the front foreleg and then wiggling it bit by bit into place. Do you want to try?"

"*Ach*, no. She's been laboring too long."

"The heartbeat's strong, and there's no twin there. Come here and have a go."

Sarah sighed and did as he asked, not wanting to be near him when she knew that he had his party and guests…or *guest*…to return to. She rolled up her sleeves and disinfected her hands and arms, applying the proper lubricant in abundance.

She knelt down, smelling his familiar soaping, and swallowed back tears. She'd missed him so, even in such a short time as it had been since that afternoon, but he must not feel the same.

"Okay, now picture things inside there in your head. Think about the positioning of the leg; forget about what you're feeling and try to ease it back around." Sarah did as she was told, trying to concentrate, and felt the delicate limb begin to slide forward into place. In less than two minutes, the lamb was born and the mother was licking it clean. Sarah laughed aloud for the joy of the moment as they both plunged their hands into the bucket of fast cooling, soapy water that she had brought out from the house.

The doctor began to roll down his sleeves, his blond

head bent and his thick lashes catching on the light of the lamp.

"What's wrong, Sarah?"

"I don't know what you're talking about."

"Lies, and on Christmas Eve too... What has become of your virtue, Miss King?" His tone was teasing and she wanted to smack him a good one.

"My virtue? My virtue... Why, who are you to talk about virtues when you're attached to that...that... woman!" She rose to her feet and glared at him.

He got up too, one sleeve hanging loose, and stared at her like she'd lost her wits. "Woman? What woman?"

"*Ach*," she snapped. "You're impossible."

He caught her by the arm and she jerked away so hard that she would have fallen backward if he hadn't caught her. "What woman?" he asked again seriously, and she sneaked a glance at him.

"The one in the red dress."

"Red dress? You mean Miranda?" He threw back his handsome head and laughed and she longed to kick him in the shin.

She was just taking aim when he looked down at her. "Sarah?" He stroked her arms. "Miranda is my cousin."

She opened, then closed her mouth.

He looked into her eyes. "There is no other woman, none but you."

She caught her breath at his words as his hands encircled her waist. "I'm sorry. I was—"

"Jealous?" he supplied gently.

"Very. I'm sorry."

"You're forgiven." He leaned down to press his lips to the delicate line of her throat and she arched her neck.

"Oh, Grant..." she whispered.

He seemed to shake himself then and let her go, stepping away to concentrate on the wrist buttons of his hanging sleeve while Sarah grappled with her emotions. She watched him struggle with the button and had a sudden urge to do it for him. Though the Amish in her community did not use buttons on men's sleeves, she saw herself buttoning his sleeve, not only now, but for a thousand times to come. She understood with blinding clarity in the idea of that simple act of service that she loved him. Her heart began to pound, and her mind raced as she tried to trace time through seconds to discover when she had first started loving him and decided that she had all along.

She stepped next to him and gently brushed his hands away, then worked the button into its place. She looked up into his eyes, sliding her hands up his arms, her lips poised to speak the words of love that thrilled her soul.

A look of deep pain passed over his handsome face, and he set his mouth in a grim line.

"Don't, Sarah...please..."

"I don't understand," she whispered, her heart bursting like a glowing star within her. She'd felt the realization wash over her like a cresting wave—she loved him. She loved his dear face, and his kind hands, and his quick mind. She'd been so foolish to not admit it to herself and to him before. But now he stood tense beside her, as if the words would burn his skin if she uttered them aloud. Perhaps she had misread his intentions; perhaps he regretted the things he'd said to her, a simple Amish girl. She slowly moved back, letting her hands slip from his arms.

He looked at her, a quick glance that made her flush in its intensity when she caught his gaze. She still didn't understand, but something about his reaction was making her angry. Didn't he feel free enough to say anything that he liked, whenever he liked, no matter how it might cause her to feel?

"You're a puzzle, Grant Williams. How do you even know what I was going to say?" She spread her hands before her in frustration, and he moved then, caught her wrists, and pulled her up close to his face.

"Because I have wanted to say the same thing for months—say it, scream it... Do you think that I don't want—that I honestly don't..." He broke off and kissed her once, hard, then thrust himself from her. He stuffed his instruments into his bag and slung his coats from atop a stall door.

"Keep the lamb warm—you know that. And go in the house before you catch a chill yourself. Oh, I forgot..." He slammed the barn door and stomped outside. He came back just as heavy-footed and tossed a new saddle atop a bale of hay. "Give Luke my best wishes, and Merry Christmas, Miss King." He left, sliding the barn door open so hard that it rattled on its hinges and closing it with just as much ferocity.

Sarah began to sob. She couldn't understand what had just happened, only that he had not wanted to hear words of love from her.

Chapter Twenty-One

January set in with ruthless cold, but it didn't keep Sarah from a two-hour-long tramp round and round her snowy garden. She entered the kitchen and stripped off her wet outer things, intent on going upstairs to get dry socks. *Mamm* called after her. "*Ach*, Sarah, I forgot. There's a letter for you on your bed."

And if *Mamm*'s voice trembled a bit, Sarah was too hurried to notice.

Sarah opened the thin envelope that had been left for her and pulled out a single sheet of writing paper and a key. She began to read, sinking to her bed as the words telegraphed their meanings across the page.

My Dearest Sarah,
I must tell you that I regret having had to be so cold to you that night in the barn, but I had to steel my heart against the feelings that I have for you. I love you. There, it's said. I didn't choose

this love or you; God did. He also chose how much I love your people, their community and closeness and grace. But I am Englisch. Because of this, I must go away. I cannot explain why or where I'm going; I can't even promise that I'll come back. I don't want to write things like "please wait for me." I want the Lord to be in charge, not me.

Someone told me once that if I truly loved you, that I would set you free—so I do. You are free to love and choose to love as you see fit. I have asked the Bustles to take care of the farmhouse, and I do take the liberty to ask you if you would mind watching over the greenhouse for a few months. I received permission from your father for this, and he agreed. If you do not wish to watch over the plants, please ask Luke.

I wish that I could write more or explain more, but I cannot. Our differences stand between us, as you have often reminded me, but please know that my heart sees or feels no difference—just love. I love you, Sarah.

Good-bye, Grant X. Williams

She read the letter, then read it again, hoping to find a greater answer in the strong loops and curls of his handwriting, but nothing came. It was a farewell letter. She clutched the key until it left an impression in her hand; she didn't understand. She felt that she must have driven him away somehow, and she lay facedown in her pillow and sobbed until a gentle knock sounded at her door.

She sniffed and lifted her head. "*Jah*? *Kumme*."

Father entered, and she swiped hard at her face to try and hide her crying.

"*Ach*, Sarah. Please don't cry."

"I'm not any longer," she said, though stray tears dripped from the corners of her hazel eyes.

"May I sit down?" Father asked, indicating a rocking chair in the corner of the room.

She nodded, brushing away tears.

"He is gone?" Father asked.

"*Jah*… How do you know it?"

Father gazed at the ceiling and then nodded his head. "I told him to go."

"What?"

"He came to me when I was still in the hospital one night; I told him it was too great a risk to see an *Englischer* marry an Amish girl."

Sarah stared at her quilt, a white-hot fury burning in her chest. She had never felt such anger against Father, and she was both ashamed and taunted by the feeling.

"I love him, Father, and you, of all people, who told a story to win *Mamm*'s love, you should believe in true love," she cried.

"*Jah*, I know. I have also come to know that I was wrong to speak to him like I did. There might have been a way…to make things all right."

"But he's gone now," she sobbed. "Maybe we can ask the Bustles; they might know where he is."

"Sarah, do you hold the letter of a man who wants to be found? Or one of a man who wants the Lord to lead his path?"

She bent her head, fresh tears dampening the paper she held.

Father sighed. "As we get older, it seems that life is full of more difficult choices, but it is the simple faith of a child that leads the best. Ask the child in your heart what to do, Sarah, and then wait upon the Lord. He will help you. And we will all help you, my daughter. A broken heart"—he tapped his chest—"takes time to mend."

"*Jah*, Father," she whispered and understood what the doctor had meant about ice forming on the heart.

Grant admitted his midnight-hour guest and pressed his finger to his mouth to indicate the need for silence. The two men walked quietly down the hall to the doctor's office, where he closed and locked the door and then switched on the small desk lamp.

The doctor rested a lean hip against the edge of the desk while his guest took a chair.

"So, it's done then?" Grant asked.

"All is arranged… It's just up to you to finish."

"I know; I will."

"I'm counting on it." The other man grinned in the shadows of the light.

"So am I."

Chapter Twenty-Two

Sarah's dreams became more vivid, haunted by the presence of a handsome lean face, and the golden blue eyes that seemed to burn through her with all the intensity of the sun. She dreamed that he called for her, through a flurry of rose petals, and that she ran to him, unabashed. He caught her in his long arms and pressed his lips close to her own, breathing soft words of love into her mouth, causing her to labor to breathe. And when she woke, there was that breathless abandon shaking her to her very core, until she clutched her quilt about her and hunted the shadowed corners of her room with restless eyes as if he might be there.

One night she awoke from a deep sleep and sat straight up in bed. Turning up the kerosene lamp, she leaned over and lugged the wooden box of quilt squares onto her mattress, laying her shaking hands on top of the lid. It seemed important that she remember the quilt squares, and it felt like an eternity since Grant had given them to her. She felt so different inside now—turned over, exposed, like fresh soil waiting for the sun. She lifted the lid and stared at the wealth of fabrics and colors. Then she began to lay each square out on her quilt, side by side.

When she came to the iridescent fabric, she remembered everything he'd said to her, and she recalled how he'd reacted to her garden. "A patch of heaven," he'd called it. Her slender fingers felt the shining fabric and thought about how its brightness was like God's light in her life—always coming after the more dull or difficult colors of time to brighten and anchor her thoughts and her soul.

She turned the kerosene up a bit more and got on her knees with purpose. She hadn't pieced a quilt alone since the very small one that she did for Chelsea, but now it felt like there was a garden of a quilt calling to her from the box, a garden illuminated with bits of God's brightness and the potential for hope—for heaven.

She began to hum softly, feeling her heart lift as she thought of the words to the melody. "Oh, who will give me wings of a dove? So that I can at any time fly over mountain and hill and seek where my Jesus is." She reached for her mending basket beneath the bedside table and began working the squares until the light of dawn replaced the oil in the lamp.

She was amazed to hear *Mamm* call for her and realized that her neck ached from the many hours bent over her bed with thread and needle in hand. A brisk knock at her door sounded, and *Mamm* poked her head in.

"Sarah, *kumme*… What are you doing this…" Her words stopped as she entered the room and stared at the basted quilt top that covered and overran the sides of the bed like a waterfall of color. "Sarah, child, it's beautiful!"

Sarah smiled up at her mother, who reached a tender hand to touch the beauty of the pattern and the fabric.

"*Danki, Mamm.*"

"I've never known you to quilt like this; usually you cannot stand to be still for so long. I've always thought your garden was your quilt."

Sarah swallowed hard as she remembered Grant's similar words.

"I stayed up the whole night working on it, *Mamm*."

"*Ach*…but it was well worth it. What do you call it?"

Sarah gazed down at the rich pattern that seemed unique out of all those she'd ever seen quilted. Her eyes caught on the iridescent pieces of fabric, and she smiled. "A Patch of Heaven."

Mamm swallowed and reached her hand to cup Sarah's cheek. "*Jah*, that name is just right. It honors the Lord and His work in our lives." She sniffed, then withdrew a hankie from her sleeve and blew. "We must have a quilting, of course, to finish it."

"*Jah, Mamm*. I'd like that very much."

* * *

Though a quilting frame was a permanent fixture in the front room of the King household and many Amish households, it was a special pleasure to call for a quilting time when the weather was wearing thin on the nerves and made it more difficult to gather together for visiting. On a large frame, such as the Kings', twelve women could fit easily and *Mamm* and Sarah sat together after the breakfast dishes had been put away to decide who should be given a letter of invitation.

Sarah knew of peers who would only invite the best quilters to a quilting, because they wanted their skill and not to see their faces, and she was determined to have no such invitations to her quilting.

"I want it quilted with love, *Mamm*. That's what makes the best quilt or garden or anything worth doing."

Mamm eyed her askance but did not disagree. If she knew of the doctor's letter, she did not speak of it, and Sarah was grateful for this.

"Well, there's you and me." Sarah listed names on a yellow tablet. "And Chelsea. *Ach*, and I'd like to invite Mrs. Kemp, John Kemp's *Mamm*. That leaves eight more."

Mamm chewed her fingertip. "You don't want to offend anyone by leaving them out."

"*Nee*, but I do not want to invite just to invite. Suppose I ask the bishop's wife? Is that a good idea? Or will it offend the wives of the other deacons?"

Mamm continued to ponder, sighing. "I think it makes good sense to have the bishop's wife; I don't think the deacons' wives will mind that much."

"Good," Sarah continued to write. "And *Grossmudder* King, of course."

"Of course," *Mamm* agreed drily. *Mamm* was not fond of her mother-in-law's often critical observations about life and limb any more than Sarah was, but the old woman could not be overlooked.

"You're a model daughter-in-law, *Mamm*," Sarah encouraged.

"*Danki*... Now, I know—Mary Wyse."

"Of course," Sarah agreed, bending her head to write. She hadn't spoken to Jacob since that day in her kitchen, but that was no excuse to exclude his gentle mother.

Sarah finally chose a former schoolmate who was yet unmarried, added Aunt Ruth, then wrote down Mrs. Bustle's name, wondering what *Mamm* would say.

Mamm nodded. "Mrs. Bustle is a good friend and neighbor; I've no doubt she'll bring a lot of love to the frame, if not plenty of skill."

"Good." Sarah finished the last invitation in her copperplate handwriting. "Three weeks should be enough notice."

"And time enough for you to do any last-minute stitching on the top quilt, though I declare, it's as fine a piece of workmanship as I've seen." *Mamm* rose from the table and patted Sarah's shoulder, going into the kitchen to start supper.

* * *

On the day of the quilting, the boys double-checked to make sure everything was secure with the frame, and then *Mamm* and Sarah stretched the material taut while everyone worked to baste a heavy twine around the edges of the quilt and then to wrap it around the frame to hold it in place. The frame was secured on chairs, a hand-hewn pine frame passed down from *Mamm*'s mother as a wedding gift long years ago. Sarah had already sewn together the top and bottom pieces of the quilt and stuffed it neatly full of cotton batting before closing it off. To see the fabric squares ready to be quilted was a true pleasure, for they looked all the more attractive in the winter morning light that streamed in from two large windows nearby.

Once everything was settled, Father took the boys in the wagon and said he'd "make himself scarce" since a quilting was women's work and no place for men to be found. Sarah and *Mamm* waved them off, then returned to check on the food preparations, which had been going on since a week before. Waiting to be enjoyed were delicate chicken and egg salad sandwiches, pear jelly, grape sunshine, rhubarb pie, bread and butter pickles, and mint tea.

The guests began to arrive, some driving their own buggies while others were dropped off by sons or brothers or husbands who were immediately absorbed into the King men's plans and drove off to some predetermined rendezvous. Father even made sure to wait around for Mr. Bustle, whisking him away before his wife could murmur so much as a word.

Sarah was excited and had made a new pink blouse for the occasion. It matched the faint pink in her cheeks as she greeted each one in turn. The women arrived carrying various needles wrapped in sewing kits or carrying quilting baskets, which held all of the necessary items for a good sewing. Mrs. Bustle, just as *Mamm* expected, came with all equipment ready to go. She greeted Sarah with a smile and a hug.

"Thank you, sweetheart, for having me. Things have been a bit lonely…except for the bats."

Sarah nodded in understanding and pressed the older woman's hand before leading her to a seat.

Grossmudder King arrived next, leaning on her cane but moving as spryly as ever. She poked her cane at *Mamm*'s skirts.

"Letty, I swear that you get wider by the season. I remember when Ephraim said he could span your waist with his two hands."

Mamm smiled serenely as Sarah steered the old woman to the quilting frame.

"Please take your choice of seats, *Grossmudder*."

"Sarah King, of course I'll sit where I like. How old will you be this year? You'd think that this would be a wedding quilting, but maybe you're particular. Has anyone asked you yet?" Sarah's smile matched her mother's as she deposited the old woman into a chair near the bottom of the frame and drifted off without replying.

On the other hand, old Mrs. Kemp entered like the least of all, and Sarah was glad to seat her in what she privately considered the greatest seat in winter, near the woodstove. The others found places, and general comments were expressed over the beauty of the quilt and Sarah's cleverness of design. Only *Grossmudder* King sniffed at the fancy fabrics.

"In my day, an Amish quilt was known for its simple colors and bold designs. I can't make here nor there of all of this waterfall nonsense…'A Patch of Heaven'? Humph. Looks more like a 'Patch of—'"

"Who would like tea?" *Mamm* interrupted.

"Why, Letty." *Grossmudder* laughed. "What did you expect I was going to say?"

"I have learned that it's best to expect anything from anyone," *Mamm* returned.

Grossmudder King laughed and the quilting began.

Sharing news about pregnancies and childbirths progressed to the older women reminiscing about quilting lore and days gone by. Aunt Ruth laughed out loud as she thought of something, and Sarah begged to know the reason.

"*Ach*, it's an old story."

"Those are the best," Chelsea chimed in.

"All right," Aunt Ruth agreed, watching her stitches as she spoke. "Have you heard of the Undertaker's Quilt?"

Sarah's old school chum giggled and Sarah laughed. "It sounds scary."

"Ah. It was. It was. For you see, this was a quilt made from the clothes of the dead."

Grossmudder King clicked her tongue but still looked interested. "Well, tell it, if you've a mind to already, Ruthie," she snapped.

Aunt Ruth smiled and leaned forward. "Once, long ago, in an *Englisch* town"—here she paused to smile at Mrs. Bustle, who smiled back. "Over two mountains away, it was a common thing for the furniture makers to also be the undertakers, since they were the ones who had the wood to build the coffins. In any case, there was a particular undertaker named Mr. Bones who had a nagging wife. She nagged for this from the stores and she nagged for that. But an undertaker does not make much money, and neither does a furniture maker, if times are hard. Finally, Mrs. Bones began to nag about the fact that she wanted to have fabric squares to make a quilt. She nagged and she whined and she cried, until one day, Mr. Bones had an idea. As the dead came through his shop to be prepared for burial, they were normally dressed in their very best, and since Mr. Bones was the one who laid them in their coffins, and no one but the Lord was going to take them out again, Mr. Bones decided to cut fabric squares from the back ends of their outfits."

A shocked titter ran around the frame as the ladies leaned closer to listen. Sarah smiled to see Aunt Ruth, so like Father, in her element of storytelling.

"It was Mr. Bones's habit, in any case, to simply half-dress the dead who came his way, meaning he'd cut a line down the back of the dress or suit or what-ever, to make it easier to fit on the body. So Mr. Bones began to bring home, just at first, small squares of fabric…a blue-patterned organza here, a bit of tweed there, until Mrs. Bones ceased to nag and began making a quilt. If there was a lull between deaths in the town, Mr. Bones learned to fix the problem by just cutting a bit more cloth from the outfit to make more squares. So by the following spring, Mrs. Bones had created a truly beautiful quilt that held all of the best from every worthy contributor. Mr. Bones was happy because his wife no longer nagged him, and Mrs. Bones was happy because, unbeknownst to her husband, she decided to enter her quilt in the town's spring fair."

Here, a collective groan echoed round the frame as needles worked ten stitches per inch in time with the story. Aunt Ruth went on.

"There were many fine quilters among the *Englisch* of this town, who'd spent many long hours at the frame, but none could compare to the quilt of Mrs. Bones, which she'd innocently titled 'A Walk among the Lilies.' It won the blue ribbon and, as was the custom, was displayed for all to see in the exhibition hall of blue ribbon winners, hanging proudly where all who entered could not help but notice it.

"Mr. Bones, being one of the interested passersby that day, did indeed notice the quilt. He'd not seen it in its entirety, but it was as if each scrap of cloth from the quilt was an accusing face staring at him from above. He hastily tried to lose himself among the jellies while Mrs. Bones preened near her creation with delight. Around about noontime, though, something odd began to happen to certain people as they passed the quilt. They'd stop, stare, then pass on by, shaking their heads, only to return for a second look. Women pushing prams with hot, discontented toddlers would stand in the crowd at the quilt for long minutes, and men, eating popcorn or hot dogs, would also stop, arrested in their movements as they passed the winner for the second or third time. Finally, a tall *Englischer* with a broad moustache pointed an accusing finger at the quilt and bawled out in a loud voice, 'Hey, that's my mama's burying dress color, it is!' Suddenly, the crowd was electrified as the thing that had eluded them about the quilt's fascination took shape before their eyes.

"'And that's my daddy's burying tweed suit cloth! We got it sent in special to fit him!' one hysterical woman cried.

"'And that's my aunt's organdy pink rose that she wanted to meet Jesus in!'

"By now, the crowd was in an uproar, and Mrs. Bones shrank into the background to go and find her husband hiding behind a stack of canned peaches.

"'Albert Bones, what on earth possessed you?' she hissed.

"Mr. Bones was speechless. Soon, the tall man with the moustache swept a keen gaze around the exhibition hall and pointed an unerring finger in the direction of Mr. and Mrs. Bones.

"'There they be!' The crowd swarmed after him, and Mr. Bones quivered in his boots.

"'Well, Bones? What's the idea? Stealing clothes from the innocent dead? Why I ought to...' Mr. Bones's collar was in the death grip of the mustached man when suddenly he had the only moment of intelligent inspiration in his life. He swallowed and choked out the words.

"He was dropped to the floor and rose shakily. 'What did you say?' the greater man growled.

"Mr. Bones spoke for his life. 'Why, I wanted to have a way for you all to remember them, like. Together—and, living, like in a town of a quilt—the way they once did here.'

"The mustached man pursed his broad lip and he gazed back over at the quilt.

"'Bones.' The broad lip quivered. 'If that don't beat all. Why it's like they're still here at the fair with us.' He drew a great sniff and pulled out a bright red handkerchief and blew his nose loud and long. The rest of the crowd was weeping as well, ladies dabbing delicately at their eyes and men wiping their noses on their shirtsleeves. The undertaker and his wife were embraced by the entire community, and Mrs. Bones discovered a calling in making memory quilts. The townspeople now found it a distinct privilege to have Mr. Bones cut a square of fabric from the clothes of their beloved dead. And every year the townspeople who died and were buried were remembered in the memory quilt at the spring fair, living together in a town of a quilt, just like the undertaker said."

Aunt Ruth finished in triumph and the ladies applauded, even *Grossmudder* King, who begrudged, "*Ach*, Ruthie, you always could tell a good tale, even if it's the oddest thing I've ever heard."

"Well, I loved it," Sarah declared. "And now it's time for lunch."

The ladies took their plates to the large kitchen table and shared tidbits about recipes, seed ordering, their husbands and children. John Kemp Jr., the only baby there, was passed about and admired until he found a tender place to nap against *Mamm*'s comfortable shoulder. Sarah moved about refilling teacups and offering more sandwiches and had a good time until *Grossmudder* King spoke up once more.

"Sarah, I may be back in the woods, but the news still gets to me just the same. What's this I've heard about you and that *Englisch* vet taking up together?"

Sarah set the pitcher on the table and ignored the sudden, uncomfortable silence around the table. She glanced at *Mamm* and Chelsea, who both looked ready to do battle on her behalf and then at Mrs. Bustle, who wore the look of a mother lion.

"You misheard, *Grossmudder*. It was just idle talk; nothing more."

"I'm glad to hear it just the same; no granddaughter of mine will ever marry an *Englischer*, and that's for certain."

Mrs. Bustle shifted ominously in her seat, but Sarah gave her a pleading glance, then spoke.

"Really? I would have thought by your interest in marriage that marrying an *Englischer* would be better than not marrying at all."

Sarah felt as surprised at herself as the other women looked, but *Mamm* had gotten up from the table with the excuse of changing the baby's *windel* while *Grossmudder* King gasped for air and voice.

"Have some more tea, *Grossmudder*," Sarah offered. "Although it is an *Englisch* blend."

"You are a sassy girl," *Grossmudder* King snapped, when she found her voice.

Sarah smiled. "So I've been told."

Sarah curled in her bed that night with a pencil and her journal. She wanted to recapture the day's events with a poem but wasn't sure she could make it all fit. She especially thought of Aunt Ruth's story about the undertaker's quilt and thought how much truth was woven into the humorous tale. A quilt was indeed like a community, and one that endured, like the promise of renewed life. She thought of the faces of the women sewing, even her grandmother's, and dear Mrs. Bustle holding back her temper. Sarah knew that God must quilt their lives, blending and matching each piece, each hope and problem, until the pattern was as He desired. She chewed on the pencil tip, then began to write.

> ### "To Keep and Not Forsake"
> Quilting as one,
> But one by one.
> Together we seem a united front
> Able to face an army past
> But each woman carries her own needle
> Stitches in her own time.
> Do we unite?
> Each silver point a sword tip?
> I can edge it toward my sister,
> If I'm not careful.
> I want no blood
> On my quilting.

She took a deep breath when she was done and realized that *Grossmudder* King's sharp words had wounded her today and must be haunting the back of her mind. It seemed that there were many ways to age, she thought as she closed her journal—like *Grossmudder* King, full of tartness, or like John Kemp's mother, full of gentleness. She snuggled beneath her quilt and decided to choose in advance which she would be, if the Lord so blessed her with long life.

Chapter Twenty-Three

The cold days of late January and February length-ened with relentless weather and even the extra minute or so of sunshine each afternoon did little to cheer her once the joy of the quilting was done. Though, when Easter came, Sarah found great pleasure in collect-ing extra eggs and sitting with *Mamm* to paint them in the afternoons.

They used colors made from vegetable dyes and decorated the eggs in the traditional fashion, spend-ing painstaking hours painting flowers and miniature scenes on each of the eggshells, once they'd used a pin to blow out the yolks and the whites.

Sarah thought for a long time about what to paint as she looked at eggs from the past, which the boys had brought down from the attics in crates of hay. The eggs were painted and then lacquered to protect them, and she could study eggs made by *Mamm* when she was young as well as those of other relatives from throughout the years.

Sarah chose a small flat brush and began to put a blue and crimson wash over the entire egg as her base coat. It looked like the morning sky, as she had hoped. She then added greenery, a rose of Sharon bush, and the gray of a rock-hewn tomb. She painted the rolled-away stone, lying on its side, and a rich light radiating from within the cave of a tomb. She added tiny dabs of birds and then the silhouettes of three women as they approached the tomb. She showed *Mamm*.

"*Ach*, Sarah, you've had a creative spirit lately. First the quilt, and now the egg; it's beautiful."

"*Danki, Mamm*. I think I've just discovered that there are many ways to have beauty with a purpose, not just my garden."

"One day your own daughter will study your handiwork and you can tell her about today."

Sarah didn't respond as the image of a blonde-haired child with blue-gold eyes wavered in the back of her imagination. She pushed the thought aside and chose another pale white shell to paint, this time doing a rosebush in full bloom. By then, the spring sunshine had stretched to later afternoon, and Sarah ignored the constant pang of pain in her heart and listened with only half an ear as *Mamm* spoke as they sat at tea in the kitchen. Though, when she heard the words "Jacob Wyse" and "sledding outing," she sat up straighter and took abrupt notice.

"What was that, *Mamm*?"

"I said, I told Mary Wyse that it would be fine if Jacob came over this afternoon to take you out to go

sledding. You need the fresh air, and he's been working on a new cutter sled, so I hear."

"*Mamm*!" Sarah raised her voice, which she never
did with *Mamm*.

"There—now what is it that you're shouting about?
You need to get out. It's only to the doctor's greenhouse and chores that you're in the air for. Normally I
can't keep you from your garden, not even in winter.
Now it is spring, and here you just sit..."

Sarah groaned aloud. "*Mamm*, I don't want to go
sledding with Jacob Wyse or anyone else for that
matter."

Mamm shrugged her shoulders. "I thought I was
doing a good thing to arrange some fun for you, Sarah.
That's all."

Sarah ground her teeth at *Mamm*'s downtrodden expression, but she knew that she would not disrespect
her by cancelling the outing.

"One time. One time, *Mamm*, I'll go sledding with
Jacob Wyse, and then please let me to make my own
outings."

Mamm beamed. Sarah knew she'd been got at, but
it didn't matter. She'd just be firm with Jacob, and that
would be the end of that.

At 2 p.m., a knock sounded on the kitchen door and
Father opened it. Sarah stood, shifting her weight near
the stove, bundled in her most unbecoming wraps, and
gave a careless glance at the guest.

"Mr. King. Mrs. King. Miss King. Thank you for
this afternoon. I hope it will be a pleasure." The fa-

miliar deep voice was laced with a faint humor that caused Sarah's ire to rise.

She nodded to Jacob and then spoke to *Mamm*. "We won't be gone long. I'll be back in time to help with supper."

"*Ach*." Father smiled. "Then young Jacob will join us perhaps?"

"It would be a pleasure, sir."

"It seems that much would be a pleasure to you, Jacob, but I'm sure that you have other things to attend to than to have supper with us."

"Sarah!" *Mamm* threw up her hands, but Jacob only laughed his normal laugh, a natural, happy sound that seemed to come from somewhere deep inside. He inclined his head to the Kings and followed Sarah out onto the cold porch. She was pulling on her mittens and barely glanced at the sleek cutter sled and fine horse that stood waiting. The horse tossed its bridle merrily but did nothing to improve her mood. He offered his arm to her as they descended the steps, but she declined with a toss of her head, then had to flail for support when she lost her footing on a patch of ice. He caught her and marched her to the passenger side of the sleigh, only to leave her to clamber in alone.

He spoke to the horse and they were flying down the lane before Sarah settled. She had to clutch at the side of the cutter or else balance herself against him in order not to fall over.

"A little slower, please," she gasped when they went

up and down a slight hill, which sent her stomach into her throat.

He spoke again to the horse and it dropped its gait.

"If it makes you feel any better, Sarah King, it was only to please *Mamm* that I came today. Believe me, the thought of taking a girl who's in love with someone else out for a ride is not my idea of fun."

"He's gone," she said blankly.

"So I've heard, but I doubt that's dimmed the fire in your heart any. You've got the loyalty of a Labrador."

"Thank you. I've never quite been compared to a dog before."

"When the coat fits…"

She glanced at him, furious that he managed to irritate her.

He grinned, a flash of white teeth and something quick like lightning, and she recognized his teasing. A reluctant smile tugged at the corners of her mouth.

"I think you're a nasty boy, Jacob Wyse, just like you've always been."

"And I think you're beautiful, Sarah King, just like you've always been."

She could not hide the pain that crossed her face, and he was quick to notice. "Sarah—I know you miss him. I know he ripped your heart out. I'd like to put my hands on him just for that alone. I can tell how badly you're hurt."

"*Nee*…" she denied, her thoughts far away.

"I know what it's like to lose someone," Jacob spoke quietly, and she turned back to him.

"I haven't lost—" Then she stopped. Why bother to lie to him? Or to anyone for that matter? "That's not true."

He nodded. "For me, there was this girl… I watched her grow up, from a skinny, dirt-loving shrew to my best friend. It broke my heart when I finally accepted that she was gone."

Sarah felt a rush of pity at his tone and stared at the dancing mane of the horse.

"You were too good for her. Will you please forget her?" she asked, laying a hand on his sleeve.

He smiled again. "Will you let me have dinner at your house tonight?"

They both laughed and the ride held a hint of fun for Sarah.

Sarah eyed Jacob covertly when he'd taken off his hat and scarf to wash at the basin before dinner. His rich chestnut hair with its faint hints of dark blond was attractive, she had to admit. But of course, she'd always known that he was attractive, charming, and strong—and Amish. Her mouth twisted at the last thought, but it made him right in so many ways. He glanced up and caught her studying him, and she gave him a sour look to which he replied with a smile.

"Look all you want," he whispered as he passed her to play a game of checkers with Father while she went to help *Mamm* prepare the meal.

She felt irritated with herself that she even cared what he looked like, but they'd had a good outing that afternoon, and she was so lonesome of late for someone to talk to. Or maybe not, she thought, considering how *Mamm* was beaming at her.

"Was the ride *gut*, Sarah?" *Mamm* asked under cover of the soup kettle lid.

Sarah sighed as she diced fresh herbs from the window box to add to the rich potato soup. "The weather was nice, *Mamm*."

"*Ach*, you know that's not what I mean."

Sarah concentrated on stirring the herbs into the soup, giving an ear to the conversation Father and Jacob were having.

"How goes your way with horses, Son? Has business been good?"

"*Jah*, sir. I've just had two buyers up from Philadelphia and one who flew down from Boston."

"Still, a difficult occupation—the breeding and all," Father remarked, losing his checkers fast.

"*Ach*, but I've grown into a patient man, sir," Jacob returned, then looked directly at Sarah, who once again was caught observing him.

She wasn't so much interested in Jacob as a man, she considered while they ate, but in the fact that she compared him in every way to the doctor. Was Grant then to be the full measure of a man as far as she was concerned? It seemed a futile pursuit considering his likely permanent absence from her life. She flicked the tea towel as she finished the dishes after they'd eaten, then folded it. She did not want to be held by a memory, but there was something within her that refused to believe Grant was gone forever. Yet could she live on the whim of something that she might just be creating out of her own wants? She sighed and moved to watch the resumed checkers game.

Father lost, which meant that he favored Jacob, since he only lost on purpose after years of playing. Jacob looked pleased, and Sarah felt restless. She rose when the last king was crowned. "I'm going out for a bit," she announced. "Thank you for this afternoon, Jacob."

Mamm and Father stared at her as she bundled on her wraps.

"It's dark, my daughter," Father spoke the obvious. "Where are you going at this hour?"

"*Ach*, to my gardening. I didn't have time today." She glanced at Jacob.

"I'll come along," he declared. "I wouldn't want you to have a fall trying to dig up an iced turnip or something."

"I'd rather be alone."

"Sarah!" *Mamm* exclaimed.

"Fine then…come along." Sarah stomped to the front door and went out onto the porch, trying to ignore the murmur of voices from inside. Jacob stepped out a few seconds later, his black coat half on, his scarf hanging past his waist.

"You'll catch your death of cold," she informed him and made for the kitchen garden gate, which was visible only by the fitful light of the winter moon.

"Then all your problems would be over, it seems." He returned genially, following her along in the half dark.

She marched up and down the dead rows of plants, loving to imagine them full and blossoming once more. She'd read somewhere that "a garden was God's promise that winter would end," and she took this to heart. She was halfway to the naked apple trees when she turned back to find him behind her. He ran into her, setting her straight on her feet when she slipped from the impact of his solid form.

"If I didn't know that you can see every future tomato and leek in that pretty little head of yours, I'd say that you were mad to be out here. But it does something for your soul, doesn't it, Sarah King? To see things as they will be, as they might be, instead of the way they truly are?"

He blew on his ungloved hands and rocked back and forth, waiting for her response.

"The heart sees what it likes," she said, her pale face lifted in profile to the light of the moon.

"*Ach*, and that's the truth, isn't it?"

He reached out a hand to tug the shawl from her head, and she gasped at the sudden blast of cold air in her ears.

"What are you doing?" she gasped, trying to adjust her wrap.

"Letting you feel the cold. It might do you some good to feel the moment, because that's all we truly have. All you truly have is a dead garden at this moment, not sleeping, not waiting, dead."

She turned her back on him and crunched through the snow to the nearest apple tree. "Where is your faith, then, Jacob Wyse?"

She heard him step up behind her. "Stop looking at the tree. Look at me."

She whirled then, angrier than she could ever remember feeling, and not exactly sure of the reason.

"Why? *Jah*, because you're more alive right now to me than he is? Well, you're wrong. You have no idea what it's like to be in love, to love—you're selfish and arrogant and mean! That's what... And I don't have to spend any more time with you to know that to be true! You deserve to be alone... I deserve..." She broke off, sobbing, her breath coming in gusty puffs as she realized what she'd said to her friend.

She sank to her knees in the snow and laid her face in her hands, crying deeply. "I'm sorry—I'm so sorry, Jacob! I don't know what to say... I don't know anything anymore." She sobbed, and he dropped to his knees in front of her and enfolded her in his warm arms.

"Shh...Sarah...'tis all right. You didn't hurt me; it's you who's hurt. Shh..." He rocked her from side to side, then drew her to her feet next to him. "Come, you're all worked up. You need to go back inside. I was wrong to push you so; I don't know why I did it."

"Because I deserved it," she said in a muffled voice.

He caught her by the shoulders and shook her then.

"Listen. Listen to me. You asked me where my faith was—well, here it is. In what I can feel, what I can know, what's now. And God knows from His throne in heaven that people were made to love one another, that love is something active and alive and now...not later. You deserve love, Sarah King. That's what you deserve—and never, ever forget it."

He helped her onto the porch and knocked on the door. *Mamm* came.

"What's wrong with her? Her skirts are soaked!"

"She had a bit of a spill in the snow. I believe she needs a good night's rest. Thank you for the day, Mrs. King, Miss King."

Sarah watched him leave and jump into the cutter. With a word to the horse, he was off, bells ringing in the night air. She started to sob again and fell against *Mamm*'s neck. *Mamm* held her worriedly in the doorway.

"Ephraim?" Sarah heard her call. "I think Sarah's ill. Help me take her up the stairs."

Sarah gave in to the idea that maybe she was ill and spent the next week in bed. She did indeed catch a bad cold, and the midwife had to come by to give her a poultice and some medicine. When she had fever dreams, they were all of Grant, but riddled somehow by Jacob's mocking words and the idea that "love is now." Finally, on the seventh day, *Mamm* sat beside her bed far into the night and read from the Psalms, and Sarah found the first true rest that she'd had in months.

* * *

When she was well enough to be up and about, she asked Luke to drive her to the greenhouse. She could only imagine the state of affairs since the plants had gone without watering for well over a week and a half.

"Well, you're wrong there," Luke said with a smile. "I've kept up with them every day."

She felt for the key around her neck and he handed it to her. "*Mamm* gave it to me; I hope it was okay."

She gave him a quick hug, and he shied away. "All right, all right. Let's take a ride over there; you look too pale."

Mamm didn't want her to go, of course. "Rest a few more days, child. Those plants will be fine."

"No," Sarah pleaded. "It will make me feel better faster, please, *Mamm*."

Mamm sighed and threw up her hands. "Go on then, but wear my coat."

Sarah obeyed, lost in the ample folds but feeling so much happier to have the sunshine on her face and the bitingly fresh air in her lungs. She had a faint cough and pulled her scarf close.

"Jacob's been by most days to ask after you," Luke told her as he drove the buggy down the high road.

"I don't know why."

Luke barked out a laugh. "*Nee*, you've no idea."

She gave him a swat on the arm. "I haven't encouraged him." Then she bit her lip, wondering if that was exactly the truth.

"It seems he needs little to encourage him, then."

"You don't like him?"

"Me? Jacob is a good man. I haven't really given it a thought…"

"Yes, you have."

Luke replied slowly. "He's not the doctor."

"That's the truth."

She glanced out onto the fields, glazed with white light and the occasional stray stalk poking through with bleak brown. They pulled into the doctor's lane, and she wondered if the Bustles were home. She concentrated on the ample greenhouse at the back of the house, though, as they drove past the sturdy farmhouse. Luke helped her down, and she felt for the key in the folds at her neck. They entered to the humid warmth and began undoing layers of clothing.

Sarah inspected the plants. The ones on the raised beds were doing well, and the added pots on the tables were growing like wild. The catnip, in particular, stood up straight as wet hair could, and she snipped a bit to take home to Grimes, the barn cat.

Luke called to her, bent to the ground and studying something.

"Sarah, *kumme*, look at this."

She came around the table of paste tomatoes and bent to the ground. "What is it?"

"Cigarette ashes and several halves of cigarettes. Someone's been here."

She thought of Grant but could not imagine him smoking.

"I think we should change the lock on the door," Luke declared.

"*Nee*… It's probably nothing. A teenager having some fun…"

"Don't forget the arsons, Sarah. I want you to be safe…the Bustles too."

"There haven't been any more arsons, and Matthew Fisher is probably long gone from here. I'll be fine, but I will sweep this up."

She went to fetch a broom and came back to find Luke still kneeling. "Move over, Luke King, and don't be such an old woman."

"You're my sister," he said, rising to his feet, and Sarah was surprised for the first time to see how much he towered over her.

"You've grown since I've been sick."

"Thanks."

She swatted the broom at the ashes until they disintegrated, then scraped up the butts.

"There, no worries now."

"No, but I'll be bringing you over here in the future, just the same."

"Luke King, you're growing into a fine gentleman."

He burped, pounding his chest, and they both laughed, forgetting the mysterious sweepings.

Chapter Twenty-Four

"Sarah! Sarah King? Are you here?"

Sarah was startled by the deep, masculine voice calling her name from somewhere in the vast reaches of the attics. She scrambled from her desk and entered the main room, amazed to see Jacob standing in her private sanctuary.

He grinned at her irritated expression. "Your *mamm* sent me up—she thought that it might be good for you to have a visitor. What could I say?"

She groaned and turned her back on him, wending her way to her desk, where she plopped down and began parceling away the seeds she'd been dividing. He followed, of course, and she glanced around to see him duck his head to enter the smaller offshoot room, then to whistle in appreciation as he ran a hand over the top of the desk.

"There's not many of these around anymore."

"No."

"It's a man's desk, meant for hard thoughts, not for piddling about with seeds and stuff."

She swiveled around in the chair to open her mouth in a tirade, and he bent to place a long finger against her lips.

"Shh… I'm sorry; I'm just teasing. You bring it out in me. Here, proof of my goodwill." He laid his hat on the desk and dropped a stack of the latest seed catalogs in front of her. She forgot all about him as she lifted the top edition.

"*Ach*… I've been waiting for these." She studied the pages like a visual feast and started scribbling notes on a pad and murmuring aloud. "*Catskill Brussel Sprouts, Schoon's Hardshell American Melon, Purple Podded Pea…*"

"Is it English you're speaking?"

She looked up to find him studying her with amusement, his hip leaned against the edge of the great desk. She bit her lip.

"Sarah King, it's a shame to treat lips like yours in such a manner." He leaned closer, his eyes more green now than brown.

She scrambled backward and out of the chair like a scalded cat, hugging the seed catalog to her chest.

"What? Haven't you been kissed before?" He hadn't moved but arched a dark eyebrow in disbelief.

"Of course."

"*Ach*, that's the problem then," he said drily. "Still holding out for the first kisser, aren't you?"

She turned her back on him to face the window. "No… At least, I'm trying not to."

He moved to stand behind her. "Then let me help." He laid warm hands on her shoulders and she closed her eyes, allowing it. She felt him bend to press his mouth against the nape of her neck and then trailed gentle kisses up to her ear. She tried to feel the same passion she had with Grant, but it just wasn't there, only an empty ache that left her feeling adrift and lonelier than ever. She turned in his arms and stared up at him. His dark lashes lay heavy on his flushed cheeks and he lowered his head to find her mouth.

"Jacob, please. Stop."

He opened his eyes and took a deep breath. "I'm sorry, Sarah. I went too fast." He stepped away and leaned back against the desk, his fingers clenched white against the wood.

"No… It's just…me," she whispered miserably.

"No, it's not you. Look, I felt awful when you got sick; it was my fault for taking off your shawl."

She shook her head. "No, it was my fault. I think I was sick for a long time, just heartsick."

"Can we agree, then, that you're wounded right now, and just—just try to be the friends we've always been?"

She took a long time to respond. "I'll try."

"Fair enough. I'll come by later to take you sledding if your health permits?"

"Fine."

"Fine."

She listened to his steps echo as they receded and stared out the window to the muddy ground below as she whispered aloud, "*Ach*, Grant Williams…where are you? Where are you, my love?"

Grant Williams was less than two miles away studying Pennsylvania Dutch grammar at the home of the bishop. He bent his powerful mind to a differentiation in tenses between the spoken language and the High German used at church meetings and then flung himself back on his narrow bed with disgust. He should have taken a language in school besides Latin, he thought, gazing out the small window to the mackerel sky above. He missed Sarah so much that he hurt, but he had no choice but to finish the course he'd laid out for himself—no, the one that the Lord had laid out.

A brief knock on his door broke him from his reverie.

"*Kumme*," he called.

The bishop, Ezekiel Loftus, entered, and Grant contained a groan. The little man had been gracious enough to talk in private to all of the deacons, and they had all, including Mr. King, agreed that Grant might study to become part of the community through baptism. However, Mr. King had requested that the studying and preparation might be done confidentially so that Grant would discover if baptism was of a man's heart or *Der Herr*'s desire.

Ezekiel had latched onto the secrecy idea like an old dog with a bone but still loved to bring Grant bits of community gossip, mostly about Sarah, in an attempt to do Grant was never quite sure what. Sometimes he believed that the man cared for the relationship between him and Sarah, and sometimes he just thought he liked to tease. In either case, any news of her was welcomed as he felt like he was half starving for want of her company.

He pillowed his arms behind his head and looked at his friend, teacher, and jailer. "What is it today?"

For once, Ezekiel looked hesitant and Grant sat up.

"What's wrong?"

"*Nee*—there's not really much wrong."

"Not much?"

The old man produced a satchel from behind his back. "I've brought you a disguise."

"What? What for?"

"*Ach*, you just have to go…"

"What's wrong?" Grant asked again, beginning to be alarmed. Perhaps Sarah was ill or worse.

Ezekiel raised a placating hand. "There's nothing wrong with your Sarah, just a bad cold. There's nothing else wrong, not yet, anyway."

"Bishop…my patience is about out."

"All right. You know Jacob Wyse?"

"Yes, so?"

"Word has it that he took Sarah King for a sled ride last week."

"What?" Grant looked as though he'd been struck a physical blow.

"Now, now, here's just what Ephraim King was

speaking of. Are you here studying for the girl or for the community?"

Grant frowned at him and thought hard.

"I want to be Amish, to be part of the community, and I feel closer to the Lord."

"Fair enough. But I say there's no reason that you can't take a look at the competition, so to speak. And word is they're supposed to be out for a ride again today."

"I can't go out and about. You know how people talk!"

"Which is why I've brought you your own Amish man disguise."

"Amish man… I sound like a bad superhero. What do you mean 'again today'? And how bad is the cold? Does she need a doctor?"

"Just a cold, nearly passed now. The midwife saw her. And just for a little bit of a drive—not like the *Englisch* do it, sliding down hills on their backsides. A sled ride, in a cutter."

Grant was emptying the disguise satchel. "A cutter?"

"A hand-tooled sled—Jacob's got a way with horses, you know."

"Yeah, well, he can just dream on when it comes to having a chance with Sarah. Why, I'll—"

"Remember, restraint, governance of the self, yielding of the will." Ezekiel ticked off the virtues on stubby fingers.

"Right. You're right." *I'll knock Jacob Wyse flat,*

Grant thought while he tried to appear submissive. The Amish thing was a lot harder than it looked.

"Now put on your disguise. I brought airplane model glue to put the beard on, and the wig should stay with a couple of Ellie's hairpins."

"Where did you get this?" Grant asked, holding up the too large pants and suspenders in one hand and the black fake beard in the other.

"Lockport—last Halloween. I used it in a sermon to illustrate the falseness of 'putting on' Amish when the man inside is not right with the community."

Grant looked impressed as he crawled into the clothes. He peered into the small mirror and squirted on the small tube of glue. The beard stuck. He added the wig and the hat and stepped back. "Well, how do I look?"

"Like you, in a bad Amish costume."

"That's great."

"*Nee...nee...* I have a good idea. You'll rub yourself down with some manure, then no one will get within ten feet of ya."

Grant snorted. "I don't think so."

"I guess it all depends on how bad you want to see Sarah and Jacob."

Grant growled something beneath his breath, and the bishop looked satisfied. "Come on, we'll go out to the barn and then we'll try it out on Ellie first. She always gives an honest opinion."

"Fine...let's get it over with."

They went downstairs to the side door and headed outside to the manure pile.

"Whooeee…you stink!" The bishop rubbed his hands together. "One more thing—put on these dark sunglasses to hide those blue eyes of yours."

"But the Amish have blue eyes," Grant protested.

"Not like fire and ice, they don't. No—one look at your eyes and Sarah would know you for sure."

"All right." Grant put on the round sunglasses and didn't feel like himself. "Let's go and scare your wife."

The bishop laughed; Ellie screamed.

"Ezekiel," she yelled from where she'd shooed Grant off the porch. "I know the good Lord wants you to bring home the poor and the homeless, but this one needs to stay in the barn! The barn, I tell you! Why, when I think of my kitchen floor—"

Grant removed the glasses and smiled at her. She screamed again.

"Dr. Williams! What are you doing out of this house? Do you know how many womenfolk I've had to drive off because they come sniffing the air like there's a secret just wafting about? You go take a bath and get right back upstairs!"

"I'm sorry, Mrs. Loftus. I promise no one will find out."

"Ezekiel, if this is about that sleigh ride, just let the poor man here alone. It was only a two-hour ride in an open cutter—it meant nothing."

"Two hours?" Grant repeated.

"*Ach*, Ellie, you let him alone. We're just going out for a little while; we'll be back before supper."

"And you'll both bathe...in the barn!"

"Let's go," Grant pressed.

"We'll use the wagon, Doctor, if you don't mind. You're a foul-smelling man."

"At least my soul and conscience are clean."

"That will be determined one day, but for now, not even the good Lord Himself would step near enough for you to have your judgment."

"Then I should be able to look at Sarah all I want, if she won't come near enough to recognize me." And that thought sent a chill down his spine.

"We'll see, Doctor. We'll see."

Jacob was as good as his word. Later that afternoon, Sarah watched from the window as the cutter came down the lane. She put on her wraps, wanting to avoid any interaction or comment from *Mamm*, but that good lady already had the door open and chattered merrily away.

"*Mamm*, we'll be back shortly." Sarah sidled past her parent.

"*Jah*, take all the time you like, child. And stay out of the snow in your skirts."

"I'll keep a watchful eye," Jacob promised. Sarah sighed and waited for him to escort her to the sled.

"You do love to tease," she scolded when he'd seated her and spoken to the horse.

"Guilty as charged."

"What's your horse's name? I've never asked."

"Thunder. He's a good boy but was a bit hard to handle at first. He'd been badly broke by some Amish man down in Lancaster. I had to talk to him for quite a while to build his confidence back up."

"I remember you telling me when we were young about how you talk to the horses."

"*Jah*…and I've told no one since."

"Well, it's a gift anyway."

"I suppose." He shrugged, and Sarah knew he'd rather not talk about it, that he didn't like to be the center of attention. They were so much alike, she thought. If only she could have just fallen in love with Jacob, things would have been so much easier. But, then again, she didn't expect that love on any course was easy.

"Your *mamm* did beautiful work at my quilting," she praised, changing the subject.

He smiled at her. "*Danki*, Sarah. She loved your quilt. Talked about it 'til I was tired of listening actually."

She smiled back at him. "Men don't really have much to do with quilting."

"Oh, but I'm a good hand with the needle."

She gazed at him in wonder, finding it strange that he'd admit such a thing.

He laughed. "You forget that I do leatherwork, saddles and satchels and stuff."

"So do my brothers; they're getting ready for the spring fair in Lockport."

"I need to do that one year—"

A stray piece of ice flew up and nicked his strong-boned cheek. Sarah gazed at the trickle of blood and used the end of her scarf to wipe it away as he spoke to Thunder and slowed the horse for a passing wagon.

"Why, there they are," Ezekiel hissed to Grant, then drew back from the smell. "And in case you're wondering why I'm so dead-set on showing you Sarah and her life without you, it's because I want you to be sure…very sure…that it's Amish that you want to be, not just Mr. 'I Married an Amish Girl.'"

"Thanks." Grant's voice was dry, but his eyes behind the strange dark glasses welled with pain. Sarah was so achingly beautiful in the clear light of day that she surpassed all of his remembrances of her, but she was also gently wiping her scarf against the face of the handsome, dark-haired Amish man.

Jacob Wyse, Grant thought, a feeling of anger coming over him. How could he be furious with someone he barely knew? Then again, it was easy when he watched the other man clearly enjoy Sarah's attention.

The bishop pulled the wagon up against the cutter, nearly startling Thunder off the road. Jacob Wyse leaned forward and spoke to the animal, and Grant was quick to see that the horse responded and calmed.

"Hiya," Ezekiel began in a jovial manner. "Sarah King and Jacob Wyse…it's a pleasure to see you out and about. Sarah, are you feeling better?"

"Yes, *danki*," came her soft answer, and Grant longed to speak to her so much that his throat ached.

"And you, young man, Jacob. I see it's true that you have a way with horses."

"Yes, sir. Thank you, sir. Who's your passenger?"

Grant's handsome mouth thinned atop the fake bushy beard. He didn't like the other man's attitude or knowing grin.

"*Ach*, just a wayward soul I happened to pick up along the way."

"When the wind drifts wayward then, it's a smell to offend a lady I think. Perhaps we should drive on."

Ezekiel looked at Grant as if grasping for the next piece of conversation.

"*Ach*, sure, sure, but I—uh—I'm havin' a bit of trouble with one of my wagon wheels. Perhaps we could take a look—"

Jacob handed the reins to Sarah and jumped down with a grin. "I don't mind, but your stranger looks hearty enough to help you if he cared to."

Grant wanted to growl, and he didn't like the way the horse was beginning to prance in absence of his master at the reins. Sarah looked nervous.

"Perhaps you've a mind to see to your horse before you've got a runaway," Grant said roughly. Sarah looked up then, seeming to study him. Grant could sense Ezekiel holding his breath, then she looked away as the wind carried the smell of manure thick through the air.

Jacob grasped the bridle of the dark horse and

spoke to it. Then he looked up to Ezekiel. "Your wheels look fine, Bishop. It must have been the road; we'll be moving on to enjoy the afternoon." He was back in the cutter, the reins in his hands, and the last Grant saw of Sarah's beautiful face was a passing profile, for he could not turn around to look without arousing more suspicion.

"Well, there we go. And here's your lesson question for today. Could you live in this community and see Sarah married, perhaps to another?" Ezekiel sounded grim, and Grant swallowed.

"I know how the Lord has been calling my heart these many months to ask to become Amish. I lost my parents and have never felt that secure sense of belonging in life since, not until I came here and felt like I was observing it from afar. It's a way of life that brings peace to my soul—with or without Sarah."

The old man glanced at him through squinting eyes. "Then you've answered well."

Grant nodded. "It was a pleasure, though, to see her face."

"*Ach*, you've got it bad."

"Thanks—that's helpful."

"Don't be touchy; it's not my fault you smell like manure."

Grant resisted the urge to wring the good bishop's neck and concentrated on breathing the air, free and clean. He'd become too used to taking his exercise late at night, when no one was about, and he longed to pull off the beard, which was beginning to itch.

"If you don't like the airplane glue, just wait until it's your own hair growing in. Marry a girl, and it's a beard you'll have as your wedding ring."

"I know that."

"Good, that means you're studying to some purpose, then."

Grant repressed the urge to show him how much he'd been studying by uttering a few good oaths in Pennsylvania Dutch and instead flapped his coat in the wind. The bishop nearly gagged.

"What are you tryin' to do, boy? Kill the driver?"

"*Jah*," Grant answered with some return of his good humor. "I think I am."

Chapter Twenty-Five

The land was wide-awake following a hard spring. The last weeks of April were the best time to plant pumpkins, and Sarah added each seed to the earth in the predawn light. She then went inside to wash her hands, surprised not to find *Mamm* awake. Instead, by the light of a single lamp, Father was sitting at the table with his Bible.

"Father, where's *Mamm*?"

"*Ach*, she spent a restless night, so I convinced her to have a lie in for once."

He turned to her, looking tired and wan himself, and Sarah feared for his heart once more. She knew that she had been distant from him ever since he'd told her the truth about his telling Grant that he did not favor a relationship between them. She felt ashamed and went to lay her hand on his aged shoulder.

"Father, I've been like a foolish child, crying for the moon—ever since you told me of what you spoke of with the doctor. I owe you an apology and much more. Please forgive me." She bent to kiss the work-worn hand that had always treated her with love, and Father stroked her hair with his other hand.

"*Ach*, Sarah, my little woman, now. There's nothing to forgive, and you must keep your faith in what *Der Herr* can do, even when we least expect it. He is in control, not me. He is in control in your life as well, though you may not always see Him working."

"I know, Father. I will try to know better."

"*Gut…gut.* Now, how can I help you with the food?"

Sarah smiled at him. "I can do the food, Father. Please just relax a few minutes."

She hurried to scramble the eggs and grill the toast, then set tomatoes to grill as well and added mushrooms and slices of cheddar cheese to the bread. She'd just set the last plate, and Father was in his place when the boys came trooping down, asking about *Mamm*.

"I'll take a tray up to *Mamm*," Sarah announced. "And make it a true holiday of a morning for her."

Sarah knocked on her parents' door and entered, offering her *mamm* the treat of food she hadn't needed to prepare herself.

Her mother patted the edge of the oversized feather bed. "Come and sit for a minute, Sarah."

"You are okay, right?"

Mamm smiled. "Yes, I was just having a bit of extra prayer time. I want you to know, because it was for you."

Sarah smiled and leaned forward to lay her head on her *mamm*'s shoulder, breathing in that familiar and timeless scent of mother and comforter. "*Ach, Mamm,* thank you so much. I've needed extra prayer, extra wisdom these past weeks."

"I know." *Mamm* stroked her hair. "I've got eyes to see."

Sarah pulled back and looked at her.

"I'm sorry that I've been moping around so much."

"Now," *Mamm* interrupted. "None of that. You just tend to your garden like you always do and things will turn out all right. You'll see."

Sarah kissed her aging cheek, which was still rose-petal soft, and thanked the Lord that she had the parents He'd seen fit to give her.

"Well, your time's nearly up, Son. Do you still want to go through with the baptism?" The bishop forked down his eggs while he talked. The deacons had all agreed that, providing his studies of the *Ordnung* and the language went suitably well, Grant might "coincidentally" be free to go out among the community dressed as a young Amish man on the day that Sarah opened the roadside stand. It seemed appropriate, being a year out from when he had first moved to the community. His baptism would then take place on the following Sunday.

"I'm surer of going through it now than I've ever been. It'll also be good to be able to practice again without skulking about. I shudder to think of the animals that have met with bad ends because of the drive to Lockport."

"There now, enough of that. You can't save the world; you're doing something to serve *Der Herr*. Now which is more important?"

"I know." He munched his toast with a sigh. He had to study the translation of the baptismal questions and ceremony today. "Listen, may I go out to the barn loft to study today? It's a bit stuffy up in that room."

"Ha! You're spoiled! Missing your air-conditioning?"

"*Jah*, I guess I am. Although I've enjoyed thinking up ways to use alternative power to perform surgery and the like."

The bishop laughed. "So, becoming Amish means you've had to exercise your brain a bit more?"

"To some extent, yes. You're right." He didn't say more because he didn't feel like sparring today; he felt exhausted, like he'd run a long race and now, seeing the finish, didn't have the energy to end. He also knew part of him did fear the depth of relationship that Sarah might have developed with Jacob Wyse in his absence. He couldn't blame her; he'd left so abruptly. And that note he'd written... He'd gone over it a thousand times in his mind, wondering if he might have been more forthcoming, but he'd done the best he could.

"What's wrong, Son?" Ezekiel burst into his thoughts.

"I'm just tired."

"Listen to me, then." The bishop straightened in his chair and Grant looked at him, catching a glimpse of the great leader he had to be in order to keep the community at peace and in line. "You're tired because it's normal. Don't give in to despair. Have faith in what *Der Herr* can do, even if you feel that you have done all you can. That's where He gets His space to work, when it's at the end of what you are."

Grant looked at his plate and considered. His faith was being tested in more ways than one, but there was a lot of sense in what the old man said. "I'll try to give *Der Herr* His room to work, then."

"*Gut*, and go to the barn loft, by all means."

Grant rose to scrape his plate, and the bishop laid a hand on his arm and cleared his throat. "I—I will miss you, Son, when you're gone."

Grant put his plate down and enfolded the old man in a tight embrace. He hadn't hugged another man, except Bustle, since his father had died.

"There, there." The bishop patted his arms and cleared his throat. "I'm just glad you finally got the manure smell off."

Sarah found that her *mamm* was right, and focusing on her garden proved a balm to her spirit and soul. She also took to walking with Jacob in the afternoons for an hour each day, mainly because he persisted and because she sensed he was deeply lonely despite his banter and teasing front. It was when he tried to kiss her again, though, and she turned aside, that she knew she had to speak seriously with him. It was not fair to let him think there was hope for them. So now she skirted a mud puddle and cleared her throat.

"Jacob," she began. "There's something that I have to talk to you about…"

He looked at her from his keen eyes and smiled. "Definitely sure you're not interested in spending your life with this Amish man?"

She blushed. He always had her words two steps ahead. "No… I mean, yes. That sounds awful. I wanted to say it differently."

"No harm done, Sarah. I assure you, my heart will survive." He pounded himself stoutly on the chest, but she caught the slight edge in his voice. She'd hurt him.

"Jacob, don't joke. I was wrong to let you think. I mean, I didn't mean to…"

"Ask yourself, though, Sarah—will you stay in love with the past, with a dream that doesn't exist anymore? Can a dream give you your own home? Children? A life?"

She considered, knowing she'd asked herself the same questions. "No, but neither can I choose a life that would be…second-best."

"Thanks, you're really letting me down easy."

She laughed; she had to. He was good at that, at making her smile against her will, but she could not build a life upon it. She knew that even if Grant never returned, it would always be him that haunted her days and her nights and her heart.

"I'm sorry," she said again.

"Don't be… I suppose this should be our last walk together, then?" He sounded wistful, but she knew she had to be firm.

"*Jah*, you will find someone better, Jacob."

He laughed ruefully. "Will I, Sarah King? I think not when she'd have to match eyes like a forest glen and a heart like a breathing garden."

"You will," she said again with finality and was glad when he gave her a cheerful wave to show he had no hard feelings toward her. She went onto the porch and back inside, feeling much lighter in spirit.

Chapter Twenty-Six

The spring weather continued, and many of the plants in the doctor's greenhouse began to take on even more palpable signs of growth in the form of new buds and shoots, blossoms and sprouts. Sarah made it a point to slip across the fields and use the key that she wore on a ribbon around her neck at least once a day to water and check on the plants. This late afternoon, the Bustles had gone to Philadelphia for a few days and Sarah had promised to keep an eye on things. She felt a thrilling sensation when she realized that the door to the greenhouse stood ajar. Her first thought was that Grant had come back at last, and the idea of seeing him sent her heart racing. She pushed open the door, searching the corners of the building, but saw no one.

"Grant?" she called, beginning to walk among the rows of plants. When the door squeaked shut behind her, she turned with a smile to come face-to-face with Matthew Fisher. He looked bad, she thought. He was thin, his hair scraggly, his smell rank. He wore a blue jacket, and Sarah thought of the fire. Then, somewhere inside her, she began to pray, because she knew that she was in great danger. A hundred Bible verses swam in her mind, but especially she recalled the story of angels encamping around those who thought the odds were far too great against them. *Please, God, send Your angels to me now. Give me words to say to this man. Calm his troubled soul.*

"Calling for the doctor, Sarah King? I think I owe him one."

"Well, he's gone," she said, surprised at the steadiness of her voice.

"He should be," he said, reaching to give her *kapp* string a pull and dropping it to the floor. "Messing around with a good Amish girl like you—the *Englisch* dog."

Sarah stood her ground, resting one hand on a plot of tomatoes and feeling the fuzzy comfort of the vine.

"I saw your *mamm*. Father was in the hospital; she works there."

He froze at her words, then seemed to shrug them aside, reaching out to cup her chin. "You're beautiful, Sarah King," he growled, moving as if to kiss her.

"It's *Der Herr* that you see in me that is beautiful, nothing more."

Again her words arrested his movements, and he stopped, as if listening to something far off, but then he moved, his mouth coming toward hers. She turned her head, and his lips found her cheek. "I've prayed for you," she told him.

"That was a waste of time." He put his hands on her shoulders.

"Matthew, I saw the scar on your mother's cheek; I can only imagine the scars on your heart." Her voice was still steady as images of a younger Matthew came to mind, sitting forlorn in a buggy while his father blustered.

He shook her, but without much heart. "You think you'll turn my head with your gentleness, but I'll not have it."

She nodded as if in agreement. "Just talk to me; not everything has to be anger." She took a deep breath. "Then, if you wish to kiss me, I will let you."

"You will kiss me when I desire it," he stated, but there was a spark of interest in his eyes and she was quick to see it.

"Maybe I should tell you a secret about me," she said. "It's unfair to just hear everything from one person."

He scoffed and pushed her away. "What secret does a good Amish girl have? That you're in love with an *Englischer*?" He looked away. "You might be better off."

"No...that's not a secret. I love him, but he left me. That's my secret. He wrote me a letter and cut me off. I should have admitted it to myself sooner. I've hurt other people all because of wanting something that can't be—just like your father can never be the one you want."

Matthew took out a cigarette, then dropped it,

grinding it beneath his grubby sneaker. "I have no father."

"You will only get angrier if I say it, but you have *Der Herr*."

He barked out a laugh. "Yeah, what a great Father—to give me this life."

"We all want things to be different sometimes. But you have a choice. You can be a good father yourself. You can give a normal, healthy life to your wife and children someday."

He stared down at her hand. Tears welled in his eyes and fell down the hollows of his thin cheeks.

"Normal?" he rasped. "There's nothing left that's normal about me. You want me to talk to you? I cannot even bring myself to say the things my father did to me. You wouldn't understand half of them if you heard them. There's nothing left of me... I'm an animal, or worse."

"Matthew Fisher, I've seen your *mamm* outrun it, outlive it...somehow, someway...with the Lord's help. Do you think that she can do this and you can't? I tell you, you can."

"How?" he asked bleakly. "I don't have your faith. I can't regrow your father's crop; it's too late. If they catch me, I'll go to prison."

"I don't know if you would; I don't think Father would press charges. You can have a different life if you choose it."

There was a prolonged stillness, an uncanny sense

of breath being held, and worlds swinging in pendulum, while she prayed.

"I have an uncle in Ohio; he's *Englisch*," he said finally, and she almost sobbed aloud with joy. "I could go to him, maybe. If he'd have me… He knew what my father was like."

"Then let's go inside and use the doctor's phone to call him!" Sarah cried, her beautiful eyes wide and excited.

Matthew stared at her. "You would break the rules and call on the telephone?"

"*Jah*. Most certainly. I've used a phone before, so I know how to do it."

He shook his head. "I don't know his number."

"Do you know how to work a computer and the Internet? I have a key to the doctor's house. You could look up the number."

He was looking at her in amazement. "Why would you help me?"

She took a deep breath. "Because you're worth it. And you can take a bath while you're in there and find some of the doctor's clothes to wear."

"You're crazy, girl."

"Maybe I am," she said with a lift of her chin, as she walked to retrieve her *kapp*. "But I am going to help you."

Sarah unlocked the back door and walked into the kitchen she'd helped to paint in what seemed like an eternity ago.

Matthew followed her, looking hunted when she glanced at him.

"Let's switch on as few lights as possible," she said. "I don't want my family to notice and think something's wrong."

"You would make a *gut* criminal mind maybe."

"No, I'm just practical."

He was staring around the kitchen and peering into the shadow-filled living room. "It seems so different here now. I...can't seem to recognize it."

She went to him and patted his arm. "I forgot, Matthew, that this was your home."

"It was no home ever, no matter how much *Mamm* tried."

"But she is well now and happy. She worries about you."

He nodded but didn't speak.

"I'll show you the computer. Can you work it?"

"*Jah*...I learned a little here and there."

She watched as he dealt with the mysteries of the machine and then somehow found his uncle's phone number. "I'll go out while you call."

"Sarah?" He called to her from the desk, the telephone in his hand.

"*Jah*?"

"Are you going to leave?"

"No," she promised. "I won't leave you here alone."

He nodded and then started pressing buttons on the phone.

She paced the distance from the foyer to the parlor

and back again many times before he came out. He
looked exhilarated. "My uncle…he's leaving tonight,
to come and get me. I'll hide in the woods in a place
he remembers, and he will pick me up."

She clasped her hands together with joy. "I'm so
happy, Matthew."

He ran a hand ruefully through his long, greasy
hair. "I do wish that I looked better to greet him."

"Go upstairs and bathe. I'll cut your hair after and
find you some clothes."

"Not the Amish bowl cut?" he asked, half-seriously.

"*Nee…* I can do it differently."

And she did, layering his now-clean hair over the
too-large collar of one of the doctor's shirts; she cut
his hair into some semblance of the outside world.

"I have to go back now, or the folks will be wondering," she told him at last, after she'd fixed him some
canned goods and made him a cup of tea.

"I don't know how to say thanks, Sarah. I can't believe how you helped me, and I have to tell you something. The doctor…the one you love…he, well—he
helped me too, one day, though I didn't know it at the
time. He talked to me."

"It was the Lord," she said, thrilled to hear of good
that Grant had done, but noting that Matthew's mouth
turned down at the words. "Please, Matthew, don't
forget *Der Herr*'s love… Even if you've never believed
much in it before. You can be different; you can make
a difference. One day, you can be whole again."

He couldn't look her in the face, so she leaned near

to him. "I promised a kiss if you would talk with me. I freely give it." He glanced up, and she kissed him on his cheek. His eyes welled with tears.

"*Danki*, Sarah. You make me feel—human again."

They went about cleaning up and shutting things off and then went out into the oncoming evening. She pressed his hand as she began the run across the fields and turned over her shoulder only once to see him loping off into the woods to wait at his rendezvous point. "Dear Lord." She laughed, praying aloud. "Dear Lord, You are amazing. You turn the darkness into light and set the captives free! Amen. Amen."

"Well, she's up to something good, she is." The bishop rubbed his hands together as he perched on the edge of Grant's bed.

Grant was still half asleep in the predawn hour. "What's that?"

"Sarah helped Matthew Fisher escape to Ohio last night, used your house to do it too. Edith, at the post office, gets all the gossip. They say Matthew has an *Englisch* uncle who's going to help him, and it was all Sarah's doing."

Grant rubbed his eyes blearily and ran a hand through his hair. "Am I dreaming?"

"*Nee*." The bishop laughed. "But she's becoming a woman of her own, she is. I always wanted to help that boy but could never get around the father. Guess it took a woman's touch, after all."

Grant shouldered the light blanket. "I'm going back

to sleep until chore time. You can tell me later that this was a dream."

The bishop slapped his back. "You've got three minutes to sleep, Son. The cows are waiting."

"*Gut*...three minutes. I'll take it."

Chapter Twenty-Seven

The King family decided to make their annual trek to the farmers' market in Lockport on a beautiful sunny day of the last week of April, when the bees had come back to life to flit about in the fresh air. Each family member had something to sell; the boys had leather tooling; Father, fishing lures; *Mamm*, crochet work; and Sarah had her Patch of Heaven quilt. She had thought long and hard as to what to do with the quilt, but as the months had passed and no word had come from Grant, she decided that holding on to it would only serve to remind her of a brief time of happiness that now caused her great pain. It would be better to let the quilt bless someone else with its warmth. So the family set off in the wagon and stopped by the Kemp farm, where John, Chelsea, and the baby joined them in their own wagon full of various cheese wheels.

They sang snatches of cheery songs as they rode along or called back and forth to each other with jokes or riddles. Even Sarah joined in, feeling some of the fun spirit of the day. She could remember being a very little girl and going to the farmers' market for the first time. She'd been so excited that she could not sleep the night before as she worried and wondered whether anyone would buy her tied rug made from *Mamm*'s scrap bag. Sure enough, the rug had sold early, and Sarah had spent the day sitting on a pile of potatoes and watching as Father and *Mamm* did business with both *Englisch* and Amish. She smiled at the memory; life had seemed so much simpler when she was a child.

They arrived early in Lockport, and Father paid the fee for the stalls where they could set up their wares. Sarah helped arrange everything attractively, then draped her quilt over a couple of piled baskets in the background of all the different canned goods. There were other quilts across the way. She could see the patterns of Jacob's Ladder and Solomon's Rose and the more traditional, Sunshine and Shadow. Embroidery work and crocheted pillows were also in abundance.

"*Ach*, Mama," Father urged. "We'll have to stroll around later and see everything."

"*Jah*, we will," *Mamm* assured him.

The boys had drifted off to meet with friends and to see the harnesses and stock, and Chelsea and John were involved in slicing cheeses for passersby to sample and purchase. Sarah perched on a crate and spoke to her parents. "*Mamm* and Father, please go for a walk around. I will watch things for a while. It won't get busy until later."

Father looked so pleased that Sarah knew *Mamm* couldn't help but go. As they walked off, Sarah considered how strange it was that she should be willing to offer to watch everything. Last year, at this time, she would have probably been hesitant to even suggest such a thing, but her months at the stand had taught her much, in more ways than one.

An *Englisch* woman and her husband stopped in front of the stand. "Bob, look at that quilt. I've never seen one like it!" She looked at Sarah. "What do you call it?"

Sarah hesitated for only the briefest of seconds. "A Patch of Heaven."

"Oh, Bob. You know I love quilts—what do you say?"

"How much is it?" Bob asked.

Sarah considered, remembering the man who had bought a quilt from her that winter at the stand for his ill wife. "Five hundred dollars."

The woman clapped her manicured hands. "Bob, that is a steal!"

Another *Englisch* couple had strolled over and heard the woman. The man studied the quilt and then looked at Sarah. "I'll give you eight hundred."

Sarah opened her mouth, beginning to feel flustered. A small crowd was gathering with each person admiring the workmanship and beauty of the quilt. John Kemp came over and threaded his way to where Sarah stood.

"Is everything okay, Sarah?" He asked above the now-growing cries of prices being shouted out.

She spread her hands helplessly as someone called out for a thousand dollars.

"Sarah," John Kemp questioned. "Do you want to sell the quilt? Pay no attention to anyone else."

Sarah let her gaze wander to the iridescent patches of fabric and felt like she was somehow defaming what she had meant the quilt to be, a symbol of the Lord's light in her life, and the acknowledgment of all that a quilt stood for in community and creativity and spirit. She flushed and had the horrid sensation that perhaps she was like the temple money changers whom Jesus was so angry with so long ago.

She shook her head. "No. No—I'm sorry, but it's not for sale."

John ignored the angry babble of voices and calmly took down the quilt, folded it, and handed it back to Sarah.

"No sale," he announced, and one by one, the customers drifted away, clearly annoyed.

After that, the day seemed to be overshadowed with gloom for Sarah, though she did her best to hide it. John Kemp explained to *Mamm* and Father, and Sarah tucked the quilt away under some blankets in the back of the wagon.

"I'm glad, Sarah," *Mamm* said, patting her arm. "That is a quilt for you to treasure."

"*Jah, Mamm.*"

Sarah felt embarrassed by the encounter and concentrated on selling and wrapping various items. She was grateful when Luke brought her back a ham-and-coleslaw sandwich and cold lemonade. She ate in the back of the wagon and felt her headache of the morning begin to ease a bit. She had just thrown out her paper plate when she glanced up and saw Ms. Fisher moving happily through the crowds.

The woman's hair was shiny and bouncy, and she wore a jean jacket and pretty collared shirt and denims. She seemed to be walking with friends, and in the bright sunlight of the day, her scar was all the more apparent. Sarah had a sudden inspiration.

Scrambling from the back of the wagon, she pushed through the crowds and called out, "Ms. Fisher! Ms. Fisher?"

The woman turned.

"Why, Sarah! How lovely to see you! How is your father?"

"*Gut*—he's good. Listen, please, I—I want you to have something. I made it this winter. I call it 'A Patch of Heaven.'" Sarah thrust the quilt into the woman's arms and felt a keen sense of being in the Lord's will when Ms. Fisher's eyes welled with tears.

"But, Sarah, it's beautiful! I've never seen anything like it. I can't take this."

The crowds were milling around them, and Sarah nodded.

"Yes, you can…as a blessing from *Der Herr*. He told me to give it to you, to warm you."

"Thank you." Ms. Fisher smiled, and Sarah embraced her before scampering back to the stall. She didn't look back; she didn't need to. She knew the quilt had come full circle and found its proper home as a symbol of love and light.

Chapter Twenty-Eight

On the first Monday in May, Sarah squirted the hose on a handful of radishes, washing away the mud to reveal the rich cherry red and white globes. She added them to the basket with the cleaned carrots and then set about rinsing the lettuces and dabbing them dry with a cotton towel. Luke had pulled the wagon back for her and was lugging the baskets of potatoes into place.

"Well, Sarah, it's been one year since you began the stand, and now it's a new year. It'll be easier this time, *jah*?"

"*Jah*," she replied because it was the expected answer.

She couldn't say what she really felt, that her heart was a torn song within her—that she tried but couldn't sleep, didn't seem to take full heart in her garden, and wouldn't want to go to the stand at all, except that it was her responsibility and duty.

She recalled taking Grimes the barn cat with her

last year for company, but even his sleek form failed to comfort her this day, and she climbed into the wagon and tried to remember how much the Lord had been willing to teach her this past year.

"Maybe you'll find your husband this year," Luke joked as he slapped the reins.

Sarah turned to stare at him. "Do you even know what you say sometimes?"

Luke returned her gaze and flushed. "I'm sorry, Sarah."

She gave a brief nod and sighed.

"If it means anything to you, little sister—I miss him too. Dr. Williams was my friend. He…didn't treat me like the young fool that I am sometimes."

Sarah's eyes welled with tears, and she bent her head into her hand. "*Danki*, Luke—it's good to speak of it with someone."

"Have you talked to Chelsea?"

"*Jah*. She says that I will forget, but I will not. Not ever."

Luke's voice was soft. "Have you talked to *Der Herr*?"

She caught her breath at this, knowing that she had not poured out her heart to the Lord in the way she might have in times past. She prayed for Grant to come back, prayed for acceptance and peace, but she had not confessed that she harbored a great amount of anger inside and that it ate at her like a vicious blight on an otherwise healthy plant. She clutched Luke's arm.

"Luke, please…stop the wagon. There's something that I must do. Please, will you watch the stand for just a little while? I'll run there when I'm through."

Luke stopped the wagon in bewilderment as Sarah slipped from her seat and began to run back toward the farm.

Sobbing, she rounded the house and entered the shelter of her garden. She raced through the plants until she found her favorite prayer spot beneath the wild rosebush and dropped to the ground, turning her face to the earth.

Her heart burning within her, she began to pray aloud. "Oh God, my Father, my everlasting Father, I confess to You now that I've been so angry these past months, angry with You, my Savior. I was angry with my earthly father, and I'm angry with Grant. Dear Lord, please accept me with mercy; make my heart anew. Let me grow forgiveness and grace in spirit and not brokenness, though I know this brokenness brings me closer to You if I allow it. Help me, God. Please. I want to live again with things right. In Christ's name, I pray. Amen."

For long moments she lay thus, until she felt the relief and peace of old begin to cover her heart and her mind. She sobbed with the release of it, with the knowledge that she was loved by the Lord of heaven and earth, and that she had been the one who'd held herself off from Him, not the other way around.

She rose with the grace of a young deer and gaily started the mile back to the stand, only to be met by

Mrs. Bustle, barreling down the dirt lane in the driver's seat of the red sports car, with a trapped looking Mr. Bustle beside her. They drew abreast of Sarah with a loud gunning of the engine, and Mrs. Bustle had to struggle to contain her mirth as the vehicle popped dramatically in a cloud of dust.

"Mr. and Mrs. Bustle, what's wrong?" Sarah cried, waving away the dust and bending to peer in one of the lowered side windows on the passenger side.

"She's got her license, that's what," Mr. Bustle muttered.

"What was that, my dear?" Mrs. Bustle asked, then smiled over at Sarah. "Our cat…er, the cat you gave us last year, just had a kitten," she announced proudly, indicating a pet carrier in the backseat. "We were just in to Lockport to see the vet…" She trailed off, but Sarah kept a fixed smile on her face. She just had a time of communion with the God who loved and made her; she was not going to let anything interfere with that.

"Of course, if the doctor were here…" Mr. Bustle began, but he soon stopped too.

Sarah reached her hand inside the window to squeeze Mr. Bustle's arm. "We all feel the same, but we need to go on…to go forward into God's grace."

"You're right, my dear," Mrs. Bustle sniffed, gunning the engine. "And we're going to move forward to show your mother the kitten. We named her Thimble… I've become quite the quilter since your quilting party, Sarah."

"Oh, I'm glad."

"Good-bye, my dear." Mr. Bustle patted her arm and she watched them tear off toward the farm. She turned and walked determinedly. Her simple quilt, made from squares she was sure she would never be able to use, had borne fruit in more ways than one. Grant had given her a lasting gift and lasting memories.

She arrived at the stand to find Luke pacing and eating an apple.

"I'm sorry... I ran into the Bustles."

He grinned. "I saw them. At least they didn't run into you."

Sarah smiled. "Have a good day in the fields."

"You too here. I'll be back tonight as usual."

She watched him drive off and then looked around to take stock of the stand. Father and the boys had been out to secure any loose boards, set the tables aright, and put the tubs of flowers in their usual place on either side of the steps. Everything was the same, yet so different. She turned to arrange some early salad greens into attractive miniature bundles when she saw an Amish man walking down the high road out of the corner of her eye.

She went back to finishing the greens, then moved to take her place in the small chair next to the checkout table. A paper wrapper, carelessly thrown, lay in the grass within her line of vision and she frowned at the litter. The Amish man had his head down, so she had a quick moment. She rose and darted down the steps, snatched up the paper, and had gained the top step again when she tripped and fell flat on her face.

She instinctively covered her head as a heavy rain of onions fell from the table above and rolled around her. She knew she'd made enough noise to attract the attention of the Amish man, so she decided that she might as well get up and see who it was when she was suddenly lifted and set on her feet with strong hands.

"Didn't you drop an onion the first time we met?"

Sarah turned at the warm voice and stared up into the blue-gold eyes that she knew and loved so well. "Grant...*jah*...but what...?" She ran her hands in wonder down the light blue sleeves of his Amish shirt.

He put an onion in her hand. "Kiss me, Sarah King."

She lifted her mouth to his, moving as if in a dream. Her heart pounded and the morning sunshine warmed her lowered eyelids until she felt that she was drowning in sensation, stars twirling in bursts throughout her body until she had to stop to breathe. She opened her eyes and gazed at him, half afraid he might disappear.

"I just can't believe it," she whispered. "*Der Herr* is so good."

He grinned at her. "I've come to know that more and more over this year. And I've found a community, Sarah, a belonging that I'd never thought possible." He was belatedly dusting down her skirt. "Are you hurt?" She shook her head, her eyes filling with tears.

"No…not anymore." And she wasn't, she realized. She'd felt whole since this morning when she'd poured her heart out to her Savior.

He stilled, then stood tall at her words. "I'm sorry, my love, my heart…I had to go away. I had to study. To become Amish was something I had to be sure that I wanted, that the Lord wanted."

She stood on tiptoe and kissed him again. "I understand. I've just missed you so."

"And I've missed you too, Sarah. You say how good the Lord is…oh, but how good. And here I've felt half-scared to death that you might have fallen in love with Jacob Wyse." He searched her eyes at the confession, but she shook her head.

"*Nee*… It's only you. It's always been you." *You*, she thought. *Englisch or Amish. Your hand twined in the earth with mine like the root of a single plant, your fingers touching the iridescent fabric square with mine until it became part of something alive and flowing and healing. Always you.*

A passing car tooted as they embraced again, and Grant smiled. "I also want you to know, my love, that I talked with your father before I began to study, and he gave his approval."

Sarah nodded, too happy to speak as he went on. "Before we go tell the Bustles, I have a surprise for you… The bishop helped me, and I hoped that you wouldn't notice."

"What is it?"

"Let me lead you and keep your eyes closed."

She felt him take the onion from her, then carefully guide her down the steps. The dew-drenched grass caressed her ankles above her shoe tops as they made their way onto the rocky path that led behind the long back of the stand. He stopped briefly, lifting her eager mouth to his in a lingering fashion and then walking on a few steps. He steered her close to a plant; she could feel the small leaves on her arms like touches in a hundred places, and she shivered.

"An engagement present?" he asked tenderly.

"Oh, Grant, yes." *I'll marry you. I'll marry you and love you forever.*

"*Danki*, Sarah." His voice was hoarse. "Now, please, open your eyes."

She did so with excitement.

"*Ach*, Grant...I can't believe it."

"Hothouse grown, I'm afraid."

"I love them."

He held out his hand and she took it, and then he pulled them both into the shelter of greenery. An abundance of tall, new rosebushes were trellised against the back of the stand wall and she moved to press her lips to his, feeling a welter of petals fall down and around them, landing on her *kapp* and on the shoulders of his light blue shirt.

"I love you, Grant Williams."

He half closed his eyes in pleasure at the words, enjoying the feel of her against him.

"I love you, Sarah."

And the tendrils of the rosebuds seemed to reach to encircle them, a marriage of new green and shy pink, until she pulled on a vine and rained down more petals to fall in time with the rapid beating of their hearts.

* * * * *

Acknowledgments

First and always, for Scott, my rose and the one true love of my life—you're my best friend.

For Scott II and Dutch Wolfe, Grant, Gracie, Grace, and Joy—I love you all.

For Sara, who gave up home and hearth and exercise to give me peace and security and a safe place to write. I look forward to spending eternity with you.

For Dad and Mom, who believed in me and actively worked to make this book a possibility.

For my mother-in-law and father-in-law, who are always praying.

For Ruth and Faith, who were here from the start and who gave up their vacation to help.

For Noelle and her wonderful photography skills—you're walking sunshine!

For Gramp and Grambo who pray.

For Tamela Hancock Murray, my agent, who makes me feel like I'm her only client.

For Mrs. Ring and Marti—thanks for the day in the pool and on the farm.

For Anna, my friend.

For Donna and Mobile Masterpieces, who made the kids happy while I wrote.

For Dr. Kelly, vet to the Amish and the source of all veterinarian knowledge herein.

For Dan Miller, who told the truth.

For Julie, who believed and cheered.

For Berkley, who gave good feedback.

Especially for Gaye Orsini, who edited, gave me stories of love, and who knows how to quilt.

For Natalie Hanemann, my editor and "internal cheerleader."

For Dottie at the Bookmark and Mr. and Mrs. Massey, who prayed.

For the Amish people of North Central Pennsylvania, of Rote and Beech Creek—thank you.

For all of you, friends, family, and anyone I've neglected to mention—thank you for helping me on this wonderful journey of faith.

Reading Group Guide

1. In what ways does Sarah know that God is speaking to her and helping her make decisions in her life? How does God guide you in your own life?

2. John 5:16–18a says: "So, because Jesus was doing these things on the Sabbath, the Jews persecuted him. Jesus said to them, 'My Father is always at his work to this very day, and I, too, am working.' For this reason the Jews tried all the harder to kill him;" Do you think Sarah broke the law of not working on the Sabbath when she helped Grant learn to set up his own garden? Was it perhaps an act of service?

3. What vulnerabilities does Grant experience due to the loss of his parents at a young age? How can personal loss ultimately produce strength in an individual?

4. How do cultural differences, like those between Sarah and Grant, make it difficult at times to form relationships or friendships?

5. How is Sarah's quilting cathartic for her during this uncertain period in her life? Do you

think being creative can help you solve difficult problems?

6. What keeps the Bustles "young at heart" despite their age? What are their secrets for living a happy and abundant life?

7. What is the meaning of community in this story? How does community extend beyond the boundaries of where people live or what they believe?

8. Why does Grant become Amish? Why does his conversion have to depend on more than just his love for Sarah?

9. How are the seasons of the gardens in the story reflective of the character's lives? Why are the gardens, both Sarah's and Grant's, symbolic of their love?

10. What are the hidden meanings of the various deer in the story—the one at the creek, the one on the road, and the one in Grant's past?

11. Why does *Grossmuder* King get away with her attitude? How would you respond to someone like her?

12. Describe the relationship between Sarah and Luke. How do they function as both siblings and friends?

13. How does Sarah grow up and change throughout the story? How do these changes reflect in what she says and does?